DATE DUE			
JUL 07 1997	SEP 07 2010		
FEB 03 2000			
AUG 05 2009			

The
Tale
Maker

The Tale Maker

Mark Harris

DONALD I. FINE, INC.
New York

Library of Congress Catalogue Card Number: 93-074483
ISBN: 1-55611-397-8

Manufactured in the United States of America

10 9 8 7 6 5 4 3 2 1

Designed by Irving Perkins Associates, Inc.

For Josephine

1

HIS loving, affectionate father drove him one hundred miles from Zygmont to University City to settle him in. Three years later, beginning to make fiction of the milestones of his life, Rimrose wrote a story called "His Father's Fingers Clawing at His Back," based on his memory of this first day.

On the road his father said, "I hope you see the day coming when you're going to start driving a car. Maybe you'll meet a nice girl down here she'll teach you driving. Every Rimrose as far as I know jumped right from the cradle into the driver's seat except you. You've never tried it or wanted to try it."

"I get everywhere," Rimrose said.

"We're all too scattered anyhow," his father said. His sons and daughters lived in five states of the Union. This boy beside him was his youngest. "That's not right," he said. "I'm glad you're staying close to home. A hundred miles, that's just the right distance. I know it's going to pay off for you."

They arrived at the campus in University City. Somewhere inside himself, on his cynical side, the father thought this university thing was a racket. He had paid unspeakable tuition as the price of admission to this playground of drunken children and Communist apologists. He was editor of the Zygmont *Herald,* "a newspaper," he liked to say, "notice my tongue in my cheek." He was cynical about almost every project organized by man. But his *Herald* was a sterling newspaper, affectionate and straight-talking like the editor himself.

Where had mother been on this day? Rimrose could never

1

remember if she had driven down with them from Zygmont. In his story "His Father's Fingers Clawing at His Back" no mention is made of the mother of the boy. Maybe she had been there in actuality, only to be omitted by invention. In a learned article years later a scholar of literature maddened by numbers undertook to statisticalize "The Phenomenon of Absent Mothers in Selected Stories by Rimrose." What did the scholar mean by "Selected"? Selected how or why? Many Rimrose stories have mothers in them, many of them have no mothers in them, grandmothers, stepmothers, foster mothers, unwed mothers, anybody can make a case for anything.

Father bought Rimrose his required freshman textbooks at the University Book Store. Mother loved books and never stopped reading. Father seldom read a book. "I'm glad to see they've got a few books on the premises," said father, "since this is supposed to be a university, but I'm going to tell you what worries me. As I look around I see all these sweatshirts with the name of the university on front, and all these mechanical practical-joke gadgets and all these little cutesy-pie artsy-craftsy drinking cups with the name of the university on them. I'm betting dollars to doughnuts most of your students as you begin encountering them are going to be more interested in wearing the sweatshirts than reading the books. Their life ambition is to plaster their cars with university stickers. They want to identify with the institution, not with the *purpose* of the institution."

"Dad, I can tell you it's the *purpose* of the institution I want to identify with, I don't care for the sweatshirts." Rimrose knew it was the tuition money that pained his father.

"I worry about you. I worry about what you're getting into. Look at all these books you're supposed to buy. I don't believe these students necessarily want to read all this literature."

"They might read it in spite of themselves," said the boy. "They want the grades. That's how the grading system works. It forces them to read the literature in spite of themselves."

His father tried out that idea. "Cramming it down their little

throats. That's a good idea. You may be right. That's a damn
alert thought," father said. "You're so damn alert I don't know
why you're going to this university. I'll tell you what your
mother already told you. You're already a great writer. You're
probably a genius, no doubt about it. Your mother thinks so.
From the time you were six years old you wrote stories about
spiders and deep-sea divers and those moon stories. You'll
never make a living writing moon stories, but it's a start. What
other kids in Zygmont ever wrote anything like the stories
you wrote? Half the kids in Zygmont can barely write their
own names. You don't need a university education. You already got one."

"I'll make you a promise, dad. If I'm too smart to be here,
I'll come home."

Rimrose had arrived with a big battered green war-surplus
footlocker purchased for four dollars. He seized a strap handle
at one end and his father seized the other and they carried the
footlocker from the car to the residence hall called Westby.

His room was in Westby Second East. His roommate was
Delbert Herndon from the town of Ferdinand, who had arrived an hour before Rimrose, chosen the bed he preferred,
and was asleep in it when the Rimroses entered. Herndon
would live in that room for four years, two of them awake and
two of them asleep. In an interview with Herndon in *Sentinel*
Rimrose was yet to write, "Herndon says the first rule of
health is to get your sleep and if you start running short get
several other people's sleep at the same time."

Herndon was bound to become a distinguished varsity athlete. He would win letters—the joke in Westby Hall was that
he couldn't read them. But that wasn't a joke Rimrose would
make, for Rimrose found Herndon to be as worthy a person as
ever he would know, living proof of the advantage of acquaintance over hearsay.

The two young men had never met. They had been "scien-
tifically" selected as roommates on the grounds of their proba-
ble compatibility. Science knew its stuff. In their four years

together they never argued about anything. They understood each other perfectly well. One of Rimrose's journalistic crusades as editor of *Sentinel* would be his exposure of the scandal of the paid athlete—"the exploited professional masquerading as amateur, the human being converted to waste." The boy wrote fiery stuff. His lucky phrases perfectly described Herndon, who with never a breath of self-interest applauded his roommate for his powerful attack on the athletic program which rewarded him so well.

Rimrose was not an athlete but he was athletic. He had not come to college to play sports. He had come to educate himself to become a great journalist. He intended to write for the New York *Times* and the London *Times* and Time and Atlantic and Harper's and the New Yorker and Commonweal and the New Republic and Esquire and Playboy and Penthouse and the Christian Science Monitor and the *Wall Street Journal* among others. Rimrose was a boy of tremendous energy. He worked and he played to his limits. He was acute and he was sensitive. He was tall and strong.

At the moment, in his new room, the virgin boy was eager for his father to get back into his car and go home, for he wanted to get off to a fast start doing all the things his father feared he would do once he had been granted the gift of this university. He intended to explore all the vices, drink beer, run around all night chasing girls (in his fantasy he rather chased them than achieved them), infatuate himself with foreign socio-economic-political notions from behind the Iron Curtain. But the odds were much against him. He was already the unshatterable image of the union of his sober, well-disciplined parents.

When at last Rimrose and his father left the room, Herndon had not yet awakened. They walked to his father's car. "I know you won't make me sorry," father said.

"Dad, you won't be sorry. I promise you," and he and his father embraced and almost kissed. Rimrose's father dug his fingers hard into the boy's back, as if he might yet prevent their separation by dragging the boy home with him and setting him to work on the *Herald*. He had dreamed of himself and his talented son side by side getting the damn sheet out on the street every day.

All his life Rimrose would carry the affectionate memory of his father's fingers clawing his back, dragging him home if he could. But he couldn't. The boy desired to attend the university. That was all, and nothing could stop him. If his father hadn't made him a gift of this education, the boy would have figured out how to give the gift to himself. He had refused to remain in Zygmont writing for his father's paper.

When Rimrose glimpsed long shelves of books through Kakapick's open doorway down the corridor in Westby Second East he was eager to introduce himself to the occupant. Rimrose was an open, friendly, gregarious boy or young man, he held out his hand to everybody, and almost everybody held out his hand to him. But the occupant did not offer his own hand. How strange!

Kakapick admitted people ambiguously, to make them promptly understand that he did not really need them or want them or like them or welcome them. Almost nobody knocked on his door except the athletes, who amused themselves by abusing him. As for Rimrose, he was usually fascinated by these odd fellows of the world. Many of the great men of literature and science had been the oddest boys!

Kakapick was surly, and his teeth were black. Rimrose was amazed to see such teeth. He thought he must be looking at dental history. Kakapick lived alone. In the process of the scientific selection of roommates, none could be found compatible with him. Science knew its stuff. Although he was himself a State Subsidy Student, he declared he would withdraw from school before sharing his room with another State

Subsidy Student. On his housing application he boasted, "I'm afraid of no man," but he was afraid of everybody.

Rimrose said through Kakapick's ajar door, "I'm Rimrose."

Kakapick produced a business card. This was funny, but Rimrose kept from laughing. He had never heard of a student with a business card. Kakapick pronounced his own name. "The accent's on the second syllable," he said. "Say it *cap* like baseball cap or thinking cap. Ka-*kap*-ick."

"Gotcha," Rimrose said. "I think it's important to pronounce a person's name the way the person prefers it. I just noticed all these books you've got and I thought I'd stick my head in and introduce myself."

"I don't lend titles to anybody," Kakapick said.

Wasn't that a strange way to say it? Titles! A book is a book, not a title. The book is the thing. The title is only the name of it. But Rimrose did not argue the matter. "I wasn't thinking about borrowing any. I just like to look at people's books and see what they have. I read a lot myself. I read everything."

"I don't read everything," Kakapick said. "I only read literature."

Rimrose gave this some consideration, and soon he said, "That raises an interesting question in my mind. Just exactly how do you know what's literature?"

For Rimrose's question Kakapick had both a long and a short answer. For the long answer mankind must wait. He was in the process of drawing a list of several score or several hundred (soon he would decide how many) of the best titles of the world for everyone to read. People could stop there and never worry that they had missed anything. He imagined this plan as a wonderful convenience to mankind, one which would unify the world and make its creator rich. On this day of their first meeting, however, Kakapick gave Rimrose only the short answer. "Literature is what's established in the university," he said. "You don't have to read anything else. Nothing else is worth reading."

*   *   *

Rimrose "tried out," as they say, for the student newspaper, *Sentinel*—"Champion of Justice," the masthead boasted. The editor said, "Do you think you can work for a woman editor?" and he replied that he didn't *think* he could—he *knew* he could. She said, "I like that, but it's a hard thing for a squirty-ass young man to do." "It won't be a problem," he stated.

She asked him if he could type and he said he could. He wiggled his fingers to show her. She asked him if he knew the difference between a news story and an editorial, and he replied, "My father is the editor of the Zygmont *Herald.*" She said, "Where is Zygmont?"

Her name was Polly Anne Cathcart. Her public was fifty thousand people affiliated at all levels from—she wrote—"university janitor down to president." Her public read her *Sentinel* Monday through Friday, September through June.

Rimrose the freshman fell in love with Polly Anne, although she was a junior. It was a class distinction. Could it work? He wondered if he would ever kiss her. Only last year he had spied a female reporter named Valerie Eischberg, of the numerous family of Zygmont Eischbergs, kiss his father beside the teletypes. Here at *Sentinel* the clattering of the UPI teletype machines gave him the comfortable feeling of familiarity.

For Rimrose's trial assignment for *Sentinel* he was to write an editorial governed by the title, "What's Wrong With the University?" At a desk in the *Sentinel* office he sat at an old battered wobbling standard Underwood, turned his back to the editor he hoped to please and banged out his editorial in fifteen minutes almost without pause.

For the voice of the editorialist he adopted the role of Rimrose Roving, in imitation of his father's clever gambit in many editorials over the years—Rimrose Roving, Rimrose Reflecting, Rimrose Reacting, Rimrose Rejoicing and so forth.

Rimrose regretted even as he sat there banging out his editorial his dependence upon his father's method. He felt himself expending the capital of memory, traveling on the experience of his father. He vowed to break away and become himself, leave far behind him the techniques of his father and the accents of Zygmont and speak in his own voice without delay. But first he must win this job on *Sentinel*. His copy contained not a single false stroke nor typographical error nor lapse of spelling or punctuation. He handed his page to the editor. She said, "What took you so long?"

She read his editorial to find out who he was by what he said. What was he all about, this boy from Zygmont whose father ran the paper there? When she had read his editorial she said, "You're not only fast, you're good."

Fast and good he was. He'd get better but never faster. The editorial he wrote for his tryout typified in important respects the spirit of his vision of the perfection of the world. Characteristically he had drawn for his assignment upon a recent experience, his moments with his father only yesterday in the University Book Store.

Here in this editorial Rimrose employed the technique which would characterize his later storywriting, converting the "real" moment, the "truth," to a tale, borrowing from a "real" speaker (in this case his father) language and thought bestowed upon the invented hero (in this case Rimrose Roving), to the end of a rearranged truth.

What's wrong with this university is its students, whose being here every keen observer might sincerely question. Rimrose Roving through the University Book Store one fine recent day came upon these thoughts he passes along to the reader now.

Think of the Book Store as a palace of books. Here on all the shelves is anything anyone might want to enhance their understanding, but as Rimrose Roved the bookstore, where did he see the students? Were they at the books? He saw that they were not. He was glad to see a few books on the premises, but he was worried to see the students not standing or perusing the books but buying little trinkets, gadgets and sweatshirts imprinted with the name of our university.

Students do not care to identify with the noble principles of our university, ideas of truth, learning, science and justice. They don't even know we have them. Students want gadgets, postcards and triangular banners to hang on their walls to prove that they (the students) belong to the university.

But to what do they belong? Not to our educational ideals but to the university in name only, the big-shot place where students go if their fathers can afford it, to prove that they are of that upper-crust environment where dwells the football team. Students can tell you when our football team last went to the Bowl. But can our students tell you how Socrates fared in the Hemlock Bowl?

Rimrose Roving was betting dollars to doughnuts most of your students as you encounter them are going to be more interested in wearing the sweatshirts than reading the books. The institution is big and powerful with resources in the millions and its fame spread 'round the globe. Students want to identify with the institution, not with the *purpose* of the institution.

On campus stood a graceful classroom structure in imitation of Victorian public buildings known for seventy-five years as the Chapel of God. Compulsory morning chapel had once been conducted there. But now, in the spirit of the Constitutional separation of state from church, pressing the issue day in day out on their old battered Underwoods, Polly Anne and Rimrose and the combined forces of *Sentinel* and campus activism forced or persuaded the university to change the name of the building to Chapel Arts.

Was it much? In the history of the world probably not much. But it was much in the moment for Rimrose. It was the victory of writing over establishment. With his writing he might change the world.

It was the first of the *Sentinel* campaigns Rimrose and Polly Anne fought together, one of a succession of victories and defeats Rimrose would associate with thousands of half-sheets of copypaper, hundreds of leaden fast-food meals gobbled out of waxpaper bags, oceans of coffee and the eternal burning cigarette. He and Polly Anne lingered at the press five nights a week putting *Sentinel* to bed.

Twenty other students hired by her assisted *Sentinel,* but it was she who ran the shop and Rimrose who was her loyal critical undisputed second-in-command. When she was indisposed he served as editor—made his father proud by telephone, "got the damn sheet out on the street."

He was often impatient of Polly Anne's carelessness of herself. Robust as she appeared, she was often a little bit ill, or thought she was. She sneezed, she coughed and she cried a lot. Her dependence upon medicines appalled Rimrose. Almost every day of her life she popped aspirin for a headache that never quite arrived and never quite went away. She forgot to eat, and under pressure as *Sentinel* editor she lost the knack of sleep.

Rimrose worried, too, about her safety on the road. She sometimes drove her nifty Karmann Ghia convertible while intoxicated, and from time to time lost her license. Thus reduced to walking, she endured her only exercise.

In Polly Anne's constant company Rimrose learned to drink beer, as his father had expected he would, and soon enough whiskey, as his father had feared. After Rimrose and Polly Anne had several times been drunker than they cared to be, they vowed together to stop, but she never could. For one long weekend during the first year of their acquaintance she checked into the infirmary for rest and recuperation. The thing she adored about the university was its Health Plan.

One evening in Westby Second East when Rimrose was studying and Herndon was sleeping, an Olympic sprinter, a sarcastic basketball player, a record-breaking hurdler and a religious swimmer arrived at their room with the intention of rousing Herndon for a night of running about.

However, they fell to lounging and never left. They sprawled upon the beds. They stretched their muscles on the floor. They gossiped about Kakapick, who existed beyond their understanding. They laughed at the rigidity of his jaw. "If he was ever to relax," said the Olympic sprinter, "he'd crumble apart." The religious swimmer asked, "Did you ever notice that tension line across his chin?"

In the expert view of Herndon coming awake, "The man's got a ramrod up his ass."

They laughed at Kakapick's black teeth. Rimrose closed his book and said, "We shouldn't laugh at a man's teeth, he should be having dental care, but he can't afford it, he's only a State Subsidy Student."

"Well, we won't laugh at his black teeth anymore," laughed the sarcastic basketball player.

The religious swimmer observed how furtively Kakapick negotiated the lavatories of Westby Hall, how invisibly he entered, how briefly he remained, how magically he left. "He's gone before you know he's there."

Nobody had ever seen him shower. Yet he was not dirty. He did not smell. But his body seemed to the athletes to be somewhat misshapen. "His shoulders are too high," the Olympic sprinter said. "He got no neck. His head shakes around like it was just set down there until he found a place to put it."

Herndon had noticed the very same thing. "He walks in a crouch," Herndon said. "He's one of your sneaker walkers, like he just picked your pocket."

The record-breaking hurdler said, "He walks from side to side like he can't stand the shock on his balls. He keeps lifting up his legs like he's walking on snowshoes."

The sprinter said, "He shines his teeth with shoe polish."

"He's a very neat dresser," Rimrose said, looking for something positive.

"He don't wear socks," Herndon said.

"What the hell, he wears shoes," said the record-breaking hurdler.

"Did you ever notice how it's like he *hides* in his clothes?" the religious swimmer said.

"He showers in the middle of the night," said the sprinter. "He don't sing."

"He don't like to appear naked," the basketball player said.

"Lots of people grow fur and call themselves animals," the sprinter said.

"He is an animal. That's what his name means," Herndon said, "translated from the original native language."

"What original native language was that?" Rimrose inquired. He loved his roommate's thinking. It was fun. It relaxed him from his studies.

"Translated from the original native Barbarian," Herndon replied. "It means pig-fucker."

"That's what he does," the Olympic sprinter said.

"You guys are really far from reality," Rimrose said.

"Don't get us wrong," said the record-breaking hurdler, "we're not saying he's a rooster-fucker or anything like that."

"Only exclusively a pig-fucker," Herndon said.

"We wouldn't live in the same house with a rooster-fucker," the hurdler said.

"Nobody would," said Herndon.

"He's a *natural* pig-fucker," the record-breaking hurdler said. "There's nothing unnatural about Kakapick."

"I'll tell you what Kakapick is," Herndon said, introducing a new topic. "When all is said and done, Kakapick's a jock-sniffer."

"You bet," said the sprinter. "He's always there."

"He's always where?" Rimrose asked.

"He's always at practice. He's always lurking around there in a seat by himself. He's always by himself," the hurdler said. "He's always alone. He never had a friend."

"He might have had a friend once," said the sarcastic basketball player.

"If he was to whiten up them black teeth he might acquire a friend," said the religious swimmer.

"He strolls into the locker room," said Herndon. "You can just tell a jock-sniffer when you see them. I mean he don't say nothing, he just stands around trying to look like he belongs there and after a while he goes away."

"We had kids like that in high school," Rimrose remembered.

"That's where they begin," Herndon said, "and work their way up their whole jock-sniffing life."

"Sometimes jock-sniffers steal things and go away," said the basketball player.

"Kakapick don't steal nothing," the hurdler said. "A jock-sniffer don't usually steal. He just likes to hang around and listen and watch you and gaze on you and tell people that he knows you personally and tell some anecdotes about you, him and you did this and that."

"Jock-sniffers would never *make up* anecdotes about you," said the sarcastic basketball player.

"I never thought of Kakapick as somebody that goes to sports events," Rimrose said.

"He don't go to them, he hangs *around* them. He wouldn't be a proper jock-sniffer if he didn't," the hurdler said. "He sniffs up your fame. He thinks you're famous. They love fame, that's what they love."

"If they're a girl they want people to understand that you fucked them," the sprinter said, glancing sideways at the religious swimmer.

"It's because they don't love God," the swimmer replied.

"A jock-sniffer hangs around athletes," Herndon said. "He goes in the locker room. We'll see him out of town. You look around and there he'll be."

"That's rather queer."

"No, he ain't necessarily queer. He just likes athletes. He likes to know people that got their picture in the magazines. He admires you from a distance. When he sees somebody he saw on TV he lays awake all night in excitement. He shows up. He'll catch a ride on the team bus. He'll worm his way in. He doesn't bother anybody."

"He'd bother you if he could," the basketball player said. "He hates you."

The Olympic sprinter said, "I once saw a jock-sniffer pay one hundred dollars once for a seat on the team bus. He just likes to come in a room and listen to us talk. That's what a jock-sniffer is and that's all there is to it."

"Then I must be a jock-sniffer too," Rimrose said, "because here I am sitting around in the room listening to all you jocks."

Herndon spoke in a hurry. He reassured Rimrose as promptly as possible. "No, no, you didn't go to their room. They came here to your room because you're here and you're one of the best fellows in the world. You're no jock-sniffer. A jock-sniffer is somebody that just wishes he was you, he thinks he should be you, he hates you because you're you and he ain't you, he'll kill you if he can only raise up the energy and do it, meanwhile he can't do nothing himself but stand around and gape and gaze on you. He's like one of them eunuchs you hear about from history, he can watch you do it but he can't do it."

Befuddled or sleepless or anxious or tossed by the latest *Sentinel* crisis, Rimrose nevertheless attended every class. It was his obligation to his father. Of all his classes he enjoyed literature most. For his teachers he read backward from Faulkner to Homer. For purest recreation he read many popular best-selling books his mother sent him. His peculiar Westby Hall acquaintance Kakapick defined as literature only those books taught in universities, but Rimrose doubted that idea. It was all one education.

Polly Anne Cathcart irregularly attended class. She read books when she was sick in bed. When she was well she was too busy. She was the newshawk, whiz and sleuth, uncovering hidden truths her public ought to learn. She and Rimrose prowled, they dug, they schemed, they haunted the annals of the university library and the morgues of the University City newspapers. They knew the local past. They exhausted themselves with their desire to emancipate their readers from falsehood.

One October weekend with two hundred other students they rode a bus to Washington to rally for civil rights.

In November President Kennedy was assassinated.

One spring week she went home with him to meet his mother and his father and assorted citizens of Zygmont, and to follow the operations of the *Herald*. She envied Rimrose the lifetime job awaiting him in the warmth of his family, his family's newspaper, and his family's town. She had no such place awaiting her. Rimrose's father said to her, "Come to Zygmont and help us run the paper," on the old-fashioned supposition that two young people packed in a single suitcase intended to dwell together forever.

During his first summer vacation Rimrose occupied several important positions for his father home at the *Herald*. He wrote sports articles for vacationing sportswriters, general news and social notes. He startled political Zygmont by taking it into his head to attend "off the record" meetings of the Aldermanic Council. The council made a welcoming fuss over the son of the *Herald* editor, but Rimrose wore out his welcome with short true incendiary articles reporting the antics of the council.

When his father praised him for his innovation, his speed, his skill at his tasks, Rimrose winced. The time was coming when he was going to be compelled to inform his father of something he had learned, if nothing else, in one year at college: he was not coming home to Zygmont. He was *never* coming home to Zygmont. He did not know where he was going, but wherever it was it was not Zygmont because—why? One reason was that the Zygmont *Herald* could never be his idea of a newspaper. Good of its kind, it was local, it was provincial, it believed above every other truth his father's guiding policy, that a dog fight on Mountain Avenue was bigger news than a revolution in China. In University City, within an easy distance of Westby Hall, Rimrose could buy international newspapers, attend stage plays, see foreign films, stroll through galleries of art.

Still, the future was the future, today was today, and the beauty of the season was his love affair with Angelica Vanenglenhoven, whom he flattered by remembering so well from high school. Or so he said, and so she said, too—they spoke of the depths of their memories of each other though they remembered almost nothing.

For what was to be gained by confessing to each other that their love might be nothing more than a coincidence of summer employment? Angelica was also on summer vacation from the university, working for *her* father at the venerable First Town Bank and Trust. She was beautifully well and healthy, robust and glowing. Rimrose could not help but compare her in his mind to Polly Anne, always so unwell, always suffering. He admired Angelica's athletic enthusiasm, her sturdiness, her strength, her endurance, her being so wide-awake, so energetic. She was a fast and tireless barefoot runner back and forth across the beach, a crackerjack volleyball player, and superior at tennis. She and Rimrose swam and canoed on Zygmont Lake in July.

On the beach they made love in August. Rimrose's father, who had feared the boy's succumbing to profligate diseased women in the sordid university district, was cheered to hear the rumor that his son in the Zygmont slang was "running the waves" with the banker's daughter.

At summer's end she was thrilled, she said, "excited and really flying high" thinking about seeing Rimrose "every day and every night" back at school far from the spying eyes of the busybodies of Zygmont.

* * *

But the actuality of autumn produced for Rimrose only gloom and a sunken heart. In September when he left messages for Angelica at her dormitory, she neglected to reply, nor did she reply to his October messages either, nor in November.

One day his father called him at *Sentinel.* "Son," said Rimrose's father on the line, "you know I wouldn't call you if something wasn't bugging me. I know you're busy yourself—"

"What's on your mind, dad?"

"Only this," his father said, introducing a complaint his mind was unable to dismiss. "Now here's your tuition bill in front of me again, and once again I'm staring down at this Student Annual Adjunct Assessment Rate. Why do I pay it? What is this goddamn thing for? It's just something that irks the hell out of me. How do you as a student benefit from this? We shouldn't be paying for things we don't know what they're for. I don't do it in my business. Don't get me wrong, I'm not complaining about the tuition, you're in college and that's all behind us now. I just want to know what this figure represents."

"All right," said Rimrose, "we'll find out if we can. We can find almost everything out."

"You're a digger," his father said.

"Herald to *Sentinel,"* Rimrose said, "it's in the blood."

The Student Annual Adjunct Assessment Rate, popularly known as the Indian Fee, was robbery, theft. It was a heavy charge, forty dollars on the current bill, a staggering sum in those quaint days, fluctuating with the Rate. The Rate depended upon—well, nobody knew *what* it depended on? Everyone knew where the money came from, but nobody knew where it went. The Rate had accelerated pennies a year every year for sixty years. By what authority nobody knew.

The Rate must buy *something,* people said, "the university must know what it's doing." Oh, did it though? Rimrose and Polly Anne tracked the matter as well as they could through codes and statutes and university rules and regulations and fiduciary declarations and tax interpretations and the minutes of meetings of university committees long since dissolved. They searched for weeks without finding anywhere the rationale or intention for the Student Annual Adjunct Assessment Rate.

Crusading *Sentinel,* led by Rimrose and Polly Anne, discovered that the Indian Fee was lopped from student tuition and delivered to the budget of the university Office of Savings and Economy (OSE). The director of OSE was Oliver Guitar, whom Rimrose interviewed for twenty minutes and vividly remembered always. Mr. Guitar served Rimrose as a model for characters in several stories as a prophet or seer, presumably a voice of composure but invariably suffering from a facial defect betraying his unease. In "The Bank" he appears as "a funny old face hardened in tension." In "Mortgaging the Sausage" he "chomped his lower lip so hard his eyelids fluttered." In "Yet Another" his nose is "massive and red, and one imagined he drank, which in its way was true: he drank water all day long in every season. His desk was adorned with drinking glasses of various sizes and shapes, bearing affectionate messages, presented to him by friends or associates on one occasion or another, for he was famous for his water-drinking."

"How's my friend Polly Anne Cathcart?" Mr. Guitar inquired of Rimrose. "Sit down and make yourself comfortable."

"She's perfect," Rimrose said. "She runs us all ragged all day and all night."

"I'm delighted," said Mr. Guitar. "I'll tell you something, too. I've admired her for what she's done for the university. She keeps this place alive. I mean to write her a little note sometime before I die and thank her for everything."

"For a long time now," said Rimrose, under the impression that a few weeks was a long time, "we've been trying to unearth any information we can get pertaining to the whole idea of the Indian Fee."

"The Student Annual Adjunct Assessment Rate."

"All right, call it that," said Rimrose. "What I'm wondering about is whether you can tell me what the OSE does with the enormous sum of money it collects for the Indian Fee."

"We don't collect it," said Mr. Guitar.

"It goes into your budget."

"We just keep a track of it," said Mr. Guitar. "We keep it in a safe place." He drank a glass of water.

"Can you tell me where the safe place is?"

"I can tell you anything you want me to tell you. I don't want to misinstruct you about the truth of life. The idea of the university is to tell students the truth about things. A lot of people around here think that the idea of the university is to make money and save it and never spend it and never give it away, just hang on to it and watch it grow. People like big numbers. They haven't any idea that a university is supposed to be educational."

"But you haven't told me where the money is," said Rimrose.

"I won't tell you."

"I thought you believed in telling students the truth about things."

"What's the question?"

"Where's the money?"

"The answer to your question is that I won't tell you," Mr. Guitar replied, "and that's the truth."

"We're going to get a subpoena to examine your records."

"I heard that you were," said Mr. Guitar.

"How did you hear that? I've heard that you tap our telephone."

"You don't need a subpoena. Examine everything right now. Help yourself. Take your time. Open up the drawers and

19

look in our files. You can track it here but you can't find it here. Here's where the trail disappears."

"People aren't going to stand for this forever," Rimrose bravely said.

"Oh, people don't mind. Lots of people just think of it as a gift to the university. It makes them think they're rich donors. It's you and Polly Anne that won't stand for it. You've got the good old indignation. Your father's the crusading editor of the paper up there in Zygmont."

"You looked me up?"

"Of course we looked you up. It's exactly like you say, it's a great deal of money. If it wasn't a great deal of money we wouldn't look you up because we wouldn't care who you are. People have always paid the Student Annual Adjunct Assessment Rate and they're going to go on paying it like it's a holy thing."

"I'd think people would want to overthrow a tradition that's costing them money," Rimrose said.

"I'd think so, too. But nobody's upset but you and Polly Anne."

"My father's upset."

"Your father's upset because it's coming out of his pocket. When you're no longer a student your father won't be upset anymore. It may not be a matter of principle with him."

"It's principle with me. How did we manage to change the name of the Chapel of God and can't rescind the Indian Fee?"

"This campus is ready to overthrow God but not money. Now think about yourself this way," said Mr. Guitar, "you're a smart student and you're going to grow up and be a smart man. We'd rather have you on our side than on somebody else's side. When you graduate you can come and work for OSE. If you can't lick 'em, join 'em."

"I wouldn't work for the OSE," Rimrose said.

"You might."

Rimrose wrote up his interview with Mr. Guitar. Polly

Anne commended his article, featuring it on page one, once again praising her star reporter for his art and persistence and inviting him to follow up with an editorial in the style of Rimrose Roving.

Rimrose Roving dropped around to see Oliver Guitar, keeper of the premises at the Office of Savings and Economy (OSE), asking him where the money from the Indian Fee goes. Mr. Guitar won't call it the Indian Fee, for that suggests people scalping people. He breathes the name like music, "The Student Annual Adjunct Assessment Rate."

Rimrose Roving through the office of the OSE was shown all the records. Mr. Guitar proved to him that the money came in. Rimrose Retorting told Mr. Guitar that *Sentinel* already knew that the money came in. We wanted to know where it went out.

Mr. Guitar explained that we lowly students are actually philanthropists supporting the university. Rimrose Reacting did not know that. Did you? Now you do. This tax is a donation we as students make to the university as if we were philanthropists, but with this difference: philanthropists such as your Fords and your Rockefellers give their philanthropy freely and willingly. They are not *coerced.* They are told where their money goes.

With all apologies to our worthy friends, the Indians, the Student Annual Adjunct Assessment Rate is properly associated with scalping, stealing and thievery. It is also akin to the tax levied against the early settlers of America by the British.

Let us have a Boston Tea Party right here.

Students! Rimrose Reacting urges you to circulate petitions all over campus, all over University City, into your family homes. Organize! Year after year we hear the students grumbling about this tax. Their parents complain of it.

But nobody does anything about it.

Who will fire the shot to be heard 'round the Office of Savings and Economy (OSE)? Your fathers are unjustly and dishonestly taxed. Get your parents to consult their lawyers. Get your parents to light fires under their congressmen. Talk it over with the editor of your local newspaper. Refuse to pay the Indian Fee.

Nothing happened. It was as Mr. Guitar had said it would be. Nobody was outraged. Nobody brought suit against the university. The issue failed among everyone in whose interest it was. Nobody cared but Rimrose's father and Rimrose himself and Polly Anne. Nothing had come of weeks of investigation except a lifeless truth—no Boston Tea Party, no petitions, no outrage, no indignation, only silence and passivity. The issue died, or so it seemed.

Rimrose received this silence on the issue of the Indian Fee in the most personal way, as if he himself had been scorned. He felt that Mr. Guitar had walked all over him. For several weeks he was depressed, having sent a message and been unacknowledged. He felt himself powerless.

Rimrose gazed from his window at a thunderstorm washing away the disappointments of his year. He was awaiting Polly Anne, who arrived sooner than he had expected and leaped from her car and ran through the rain into the entryway of Westby Second East, where Rimrose arrived from above, pulling his necktie snug. Quite by chance Kakapick arrived at the entryway at the same moment. With his eyes on Polly Anne he said to Rimrose, "I suppose you're off somewhere."

"We're off to celebrate her graduation," Rimrose said. He introduced Kakapick to Polly Anne.

"Rim has told me lots about you," she said.

"I wonder what he told you," Kakapick said.

"Oh, it was all good," she said. Of course she knew he'd know it wasn't. The guiding truth of his life was that nobody liked him, nothing good could be said about him. That was who he was and that was the truth he was learning to prosper with. She asked him to join them for dinner. He said he could not go with them for dinner. "Pleading bankruptcy, Your Honor," he said. He was a State Subsidy Student.

How awful his teeth were! "It's all right," she said, "don't give it a second thought, I've got heaps of money. Go back and get dressed and come to dinner with us."

He obeyed her. He was grateful to her for having given him a command. For Kakapick this was something new. Nobody took him to dinner. Not yet. But he visualized a future when people would compete for his company. Polly Anne's kind invitation was a start, an omen. He returned to his room as he had been instructed and came back soon in a clean white shirt and a bright red tie, carrying a broken umbrella. In his workaday trousers he looked only half-dressed. He would not have been especially surprised nor even dejected had he found they had fled. But there they were, and away they all sped in the rain.

They dined at the Delhi, formerly the Old Delhi, yet to become the New Delhi. People sometimes confused it with the idea of a delicatessen—a "deli." It represented itself as being Under New Management but it had always been under the same old management of the same sweet brown family long gone from Delhi to America. The Delhi was inexpensive but on the other hand a little more elegant than the generality of student joints. With wine they toasted Polly Anne's graduation.

Kakapick had never been there or almost anywhere. He dined alone three times a day on his State Subsidy cafeteria meal ticket. He expressed his enormous gratitude to Polly Anne for her kindness in having invited him. "Very few people invite me anywhere," he said.

"What an awful thing to confess," she said.

"It's true," he said, "ask Rimrose."

"You don't seek it," Rimrose said.

"I don't want it. I don't need it."

"Everyone needs it," Rimrose said, but even as he said it the idea crossed his mind that perhaps Kakapick was the gruesome exception. "You don't invite it, you act too independent, as if you don't need anybody."

"I *don't* need anybody."

"That's what I mean. You say it so firmly anybody hearing you say it says 'What the hell, I'll find somebody that does.' "

Polly Anne understood easily why so few people were kind to Kakapick. He was proud of being crude and selfish and unprepossessing and not very attractive, gauche and stingy. She was interested to have met him at last. He sounded to her like one of those genius-killers so often in the news. He was hidden. He was obsessed by his determination to try theories on the world. "At the moment my project is the unification of the world," he said. He held his menu before his mouth to hide his teeth.

"It needs it something awful," said Polly Anne, "although I can think of a lot of people I'd as soon not be unified with."

"I'm drawing up a list of the world's best titles," he said.

"You've been drawing up your list for two years," Rimrose said.

"It's getting there," said Kakapick.

This had been the subject of Rimrose's first conversation with Kakapick, and it had engaged them since from time to time in the hallway at Westby. That is to say, Rimrose had *listened* to Kakapick as he listened all over the university to a variety of cracked theorists devising social machinery to emancipate mankind. Rimrose was a listener, usually with a generous tolerance for irritating people like Kakapick. This evening, however, Rimrose was confused to feel the good vibrations passing between Kakapick and Polly Anne. She liked him.

"Who are you going to give this list to?" she asked with real interest, drinking wine very fast and smiling at Kakapick. He released her from Rimrose, who was sometimes too morally unrelaxed for her, too serious. So at least she felt when she was much in wine.

"I've got about two hundred titles right now," said Kakapick. "I'm boiling them down every day. I want to get down under a hundred, maybe ninety-six or eighty-nine, I don't want a big round figure. I want an uneven figure."

"Yes, they sound more specific," she agreed, "like you worked hard at it for a long time."

"I did," he said.

"Come on, it's more or less a fraud," Rimrose said. "You've been working forever on this thing and you haven't got anywhere."

"Don't you object to his saying it's a fraud?"

"Not too much. He says it all the time. We're good friends."

Polly Anne glanced at Rimrose. It had not been her understanding that he and Kakapick were good friends.

"I can't stand your calling books *titles*," Rimrose said.

"They're the greatest titles of literature," Kakapick said.

"They're the *books* of literature," Rimrose said, "and we don't know what's greatest and what's not. A title is only a label for a book. The trouble is you don't go much for the insides of books. You don't *read* books."

"I only care about their reputation," Kakapick said.

Kakapick's plan was soon to decide how many of the best titles of literature he was to choose for the people of the world to read and get it over with. People could then stop worrying whether they had missed anything. He imagined his plan as a wonderful convenience to mankind. Polly Anne asked him the question Rimrose had asked him on the first day they had met, "How do you know what's literature?" and he replied to her as he had replied to Rimrose, "Literature is what's established in the university."

"At *our* university?" she asked. "Poor little literature."

But from the beginning she was fond of him, she did like him, he did intrigue her, he did interest her. He was keenly ambitious, as she was, ambitious to succeed in a large way not by playing the world's game but his own, beating the world's system. She saw that he was half a fraud, recommending to the world for its own salvation ninety-six or eighty-nine books it must absolutely read although he hadn't the least intention of reading them himself. Too bad about his teeth, she thought. Surely he could get help for them.

But how and why and in what way and for what purpose did he wish to unify the world? Kakapick was unclear about this. "It's just a good thing to unify the world. Don't you think so? The world is just going to be a better place when we get everybody sitting down together, reading the same titles."

"He doesn't want to unify the world," Rimrose said. "He just wants to be famous for doing it."

"Oh, yes," said Kakapick, "you bet I do."

"You'd just as soon invent a flamethrower as unify the world," Rimrose said.

"Whatever it takes, I'll do it," said Kakapick.

"I see what you're saying," she said. "If you unify the world people will have to treat you right, be pleasant to you, friendly and kind, and take you to dinner."

The thunderstorm had reduced itself to a steady rain. In the Delhi the ceiling leaked. The proprietor and his family ran about in straw sandals catching the leaking ceiling in buckets. Rimrose felt a sense of peace and serenity tonight. "This evening is turning out very well," he said. "I should have thought of it myself."

"We'll do it again," Polly Anne said.

"What have we done?" Kakapick asked.

"We've brought you and me together," she said. "Two friendless people."

"I have lots of friends," said Kakapick.

Rimrose was surprised to hear this. "Who?" he asked.

"Why, everybody in Westby. All the fellows."

"What fellows?"

"All the fellows down your end of the hall. All the athletes. All the jocks."

"All the jocks are friends of yours?"

"They all like me. I'm convinced of that. I gravitate to famous people. I'm really overwhelmed by your asking me to dine with you."

"You have a crazy thing about fame," said Polly Anne. "I've

interviewed a lot of famous people passing through this town and there aren't two of them I'd cross the street to talk to again."

"The editor of *Sentinel* is automatically famous," he said.

"Rim's going to be editor next year," she said.

"Then he'll be famous, too." By Kakapick's standard almost everyone was famous except him. Anybody who had had his name in the newspaper twice was famous. The editor of *Sentinel* was *ex officio* famous. "Rimrose, I congratulate you, I'm sitting here with two *Sentinel* editors. Who would have thought such a thing could happen? I'd love to be famous," he said. "I'd have so many friends if I were famous, you wouldn't be able to count them. You think I don't have friends. When I have power I'll have friends."

"The way to power is to have your teeth fixed," she said. "All the famous people I've met have shiny white teeth. No kidding."

It was not as if he had not thought of it. "I admire you for having met so many people," he said, "and I know it's true what you say about their teeth. I envy people who know people. I'd love to be able to put things together like you do. Like that professor—" She had said of a young professor entering the restaurant, "Oh, he's in Communication Skills, something like that, he's new, it was his wife they really wanted." Kakapick would have loved to be able to say that sort of thing, to identify people, to know the ropes, to know how things were organized, where the power was, to be known, be famous, be extraordinary, be somebody everybody recognized on sight, be one of those people seated instantly in restaurants.

"We were seated instantly," Rimrose sulkily said.

"I'm talking about high-fashion places," Kakapick said.

"I know what you mean," said Polly Anne, who seemed to Rimrose always to be taking Kakapick's side.

"I'd like to be powerful," Kakapick said.

"You'd like to be able to order people around," she said. "You'd love to have everybody's cock in your pocket."

"Somebody's got to do the ordering," said Kakapick.

"Why not?" said Polly Anne. "I've enjoyed ordering people around at *Sentinel.*"

They liked each other, Polly Anne and Kakapick, neither of whom had ever been liked by anybody much except by a few sane, stable good tolerant eclectic citizens immunized like Rimrose against the merest niceness. Rimrose saw how perfectly matched they were. He felt he should have been able to guess that Polly Anne and Kakapick would have attracted each other. Clearly she was *interested* in Kakapick. He was intriguing to her.

When at the time of her graduation Polly Anne Cathcart exercised her option to select her successor as editor, she bequeathed her title to Rimrose.

For her entry in the annual graduation volume *Big Green* she named the *World Almanac* as "my favorite book," revealed that "my favorite sport is drinking the hard stuff, my favorite wearing apparel is my skin, my favorite meal is my birth-control pill, my favorite university activity was spending four years on *Sentinel* exposing this joint for the prejudiced racketeering sons of bitches they are, and I dare *Big Green* to print this."

Big Green printed it. Not a problem. The language of print was loosening. To that process the editor of *Sentinel* had made her contribution. In an editorial opposing censorship she had written, "If we can be so vulgar as to send our students to set fire to Vietnamese villages we can write *fuck* in our student newspaper."

Regarding her "career objective," she said, "I'm going to get as far away from this ivy-covered cesspool as I possibly can and never come back."

* * *

Editor Rimrose began by conducting the hard business of *Sentinel* much in the style of Polly Anne before him, often in the style of his father at the Zygmont *Herald,* and finally in a style of his own.

Sentinel under Rimrose fulfilled the best purposes of a newspaper. It accurately and truthfully told the news it chose to cover. It operated efficiently. Polly Anne had run it in the red. Rimrose ran it in the black. He never raised his voice. Under deadline pressure he sometimes called someone "half-assed, half-educated." He enjoyed the sensation of being a teacherly editor, of conveying a good idea out of his own head into another.

Sometimes he thought he might take up teaching. He improved the style and literacy of the paper. He taught his young journalists to write sparely and subtly, to spell, to punctuate, and to hyphenate their compound adjectives. He taught them to distinguish in their writing among fact, hearsay and the mere unattributed opinions of so-called experts and officials. He taught them to use the word *I* rather than to hide behind the cowardly *we.*

He wisely hired and seldom fired. His staff admired him and respected him, and for his twenty-first birthday presented him with a new Underwood typewriter and a greeting card inscribed to "our red-blooded hard-working compound-adjectivizing editor, from his half-assed half-educated staff."

He carried forward small campaigns against inequity—none so prolonged as the campaign against the Indian Fee, but none for mischief or mere sensation. *Sentinel* befriended penniless unregistered students, unwed student mothers, foreign students seeking haven in America, the university chapter of American Nude Swimmers, bicyclists, skateboarders and stray animals.

One of his journalistic ventures created immense stir, fuss, indignation and consternation beyond anything he could have anticipated. Nearly twenty years after he graduated from the university it returned to smite him. He had meant it as a week's playfulness to make a social point not too subtly, but the week he had chosen was wrong—Homecoming Week, occasion of the annual climactic UBD football game.

During this week, in place of long articles about football, *Sentinel* featured the Women's Archery Team on the eve of its match with Saint Mary's, Monday through Friday with complete reports, charts, diagrams and an exclusive wind flow performance chart dissecting the proposed strategies of the archers as their big shoot approached, detailed medical analyses of the archers' injuries and prospects for recovery, minute examinations of the bows and arrows the archers would carry to the contest, interviews with archers' mothers, fathers, sisters, brothers and lovers, speculations on the sizes of the bonuses to be offered to All-American bowpersons by member clubs of the Women's Archer League, statistical and astrological analyses of every archer's every performance, and a compendium of profound or inspirational remarks uttered by the archers as they approached in their minds the meaning of archery and the relationship between archery and fate.

Sentinel sent one female reporter to the UBD football game.

It sent ten reporters to the Women's Archery Shoot sheltered from the wind in Daley's Hollow three miles north of the football stadium. Each reporter interviewed two of the twenty spectators who attended the shoot.

Monday after the shoot, in a blazing editorial celebrating the victory of the archers, Rimrose recommended an increase in annual salary for the archery coach from her present wage of $12,500 as assistant professor of Exercise Science to $220,000 plus perquisites, benefits, long-term loans, personal services and contingent bonuses. *Sentinel* printed seventeen lines about the UBD football game, illustrated by one blurred photograph showing an unidentified player plunging into a mass of other teammates.

During Homecoming Week and for a week thereafter in

Rimrose's junior year, he was famous throughout the state. He was in the news. He inspired editorials. His face was caricatured by cartoonists. A sports fan in Terhune threatened to kill him.

He declined all media interviews except one thirty-minute telephone session with a reporter for the Zygmont *Herald.* In his Zygmont interview he revealed that he had never learned to drive a car. This news sped around the state. A Sunday editorial on the first page of the White City *Citizen-Vigilant* viewed it as proof that "this young man has been out of his mind all along. A young man who cannot take the wheel of a car should not be at the helm of the university student newspaper with 30,000 circulation." Two schools of driver education offered at no charge to teach Rimrose the art of driving. One alumni association called for his removal as editor of *Sentinel,* and another for his expulsion from the university.

One afternoon about that time Kakapick came down the long hallway and knocked at Rimrose's door. Rimrose opened his door and said in his father's style, "Ho, Kakapick, what's new, what have you got?"

Kakapick entered the room. He heard Herndon snoring and he said, "How can you stand that snoring going on?"

"I turn it off," said Rimrose. He called softly across the room, "Herndon," and Herndon stopped snoring for a while.

"Can we talk?" Kakapick asked. "Can he hear us?"

"He can't hear a thing."

"I hope you're sure," said Kakapick. "I've got a really neat idea. This is a suggestion I've been meaning to present to you for some time."

"The suspense is killing me," said Rimrose.

"You and I should be roommates," Kakapick said.

"Wow," Rimrose said. Kakapick's suggestion astonished him. He could not imagine anyone less likely for himself than Kakapick. "I'm really terrifically flattered by your offer, but I already have a roommate. I wouldn't want to change off from Herndon. Nobody could be better."

"I'd be more suitable."

"Suitable for what? I haven't the least complaint in the world against him. First of all he's gone half the time and when he's here he rests his eyes most of the time. Sometimes he's gone all night. I can't get a roommate quieter than that."

"Where does he go all night?" Kakapick asked, deeply curious.

"I don't know. With the jocks. They never take me with them."

"I wouldn't go with them if they asked me," Kakapick said.

"I'd go if they asked me," Rimrose said.

In a lower voice Kakapick said, "These athletes are stupid."

"I thought you liked them. That's their impression."

"He's not very intellectual. I was thinking you'd much rather have somebody like me than somebody like him. We'd pool our titles. We'd have all our titles in the one room. We'd have more titles than any room in Westby. But you don't want me for a roommate."

"I wouldn't want to say I don't *want* you," Rimrose tactfully said. "I'm only saying it's awfully nice of you to ask, but you took me by surprise. I must admit I'm surprised. I never expected you to ask me such a thing. You and I aren't really even that well acquainted."

"Oh, we're acquainted," said Kakapick. "You used to drop down to my room all the time." When Rimrose did not immediately deny this, Kakapick added, "You've been in my room lots of times."

Rimrose thought that over. "I was in your room only once in my life. I only poked my head in your room one time when I was passing by your door—I saw your books—"

"You should have stopped in."

"I did stop in, I poked my head in but I poked it out again—you didn't seem too cordial. That's okay, I didn't mind."

"Did you want to borrow a title? I can lend you a title any-time."

"You said you didn't lend them," Rimrose said.

"When was that?"

"When I poked my head in."

"I didn't know who you were. Everything's changed now. We've—well, you know, we go out to dinner at the Delhi—"

"We went once to the Delhi," Rimrose said.

"We share the same woman."

Rimrose was shocked. "We what?"

"A thing like this is a bond between us."

"I think you're a little bit off the track there. Maybe even a mile or two off the track there. We don't share any woman. Who do you have in mind? You shouldn't say anything like that, actually. What woman?"

"You know what woman. Polly Anne."

"You're out of your mind."

Maybe he was. Kakapick created truths as it pleased him to do so. In this he was like a writer of fiction, except that Kakapick believed the events he invented were true. On the other hand, if someone insisted his truth was untrue he in-stantly confessed that he had lied or been mistaken. "I guess I'm getting something mixed up," he said, gazing at Rimrose's angry face with the deepest fear and interest. He saw the reso-lution in it. He saw the big man on campus, the figure of importance. "I'm sorry if I offended you when you came to my room. You weren't anybody then. You're famous—the edi-tor of *Sentinel* is always famous. Listen, if I was rude to you I didn't mean it."

"Maybe I'm making too much of it," Rimrose said.

"Right, the past is past. Come down to my room and just look things over. We don't have to go in together. I've always got chocolate cake in my room, so you come down as soon as you can and we'll fill up on tea and chocolate cake, that's what I serve."

"I kill for chocolate cake," Rimrose said. He moved with Kakapick toward the door.

"And borrow as many titles as you like."

"Right, I'll drop by, I really will."

"Will you?"

"Sure, if I say so I will. I love tea and cake and I love looking at books on other people's bookshelves. What else is there?"

One evening, thinking books and chocolate cake, Rimrose dropped in to visit Kakapick.

Books and three-by-five index cards lay strewn all over Kakapick's room. (No sign of the cake.) The books were mostly from the university library, and they appeared to be overdue. Kakapick's room was spare, sparse, stark. It was a workroom only but for the island of the bed in the middle. Kakapick's walls were wholly unadorned, bare of posters, banners, pennants, slogans, mottos, political statements—for he had none of the customary allegiances—and photographs of family or admired friends or beloved girls in swimming suits.

He was in the process of evaluating titles, as he had been ever since he entered college. This was the project of his life, his plan, as he had told it at dinner at the Delhi last May, to reduce the thousands of important titles to a manageable number such as eighty-nine or ninety-six, thereby to unify the world. "What I've got in preparation," Kakapick told Rimrose, "is a foolproof system that's going to take all the guesswork out of literary evaluation. People are going to know where they stand. They're going to know what titles are better than others, they're not going to get bogged down in time-wasting reading."

"I don't mind a little time-wasting reading now and then," Rimrose said. "I don't feel bogged down. Right now I'm reading a really very good book, number-one on the best-seller list —*The Spy Who Came in From the Cold.*"

"I never heard of it. Is it literature?"

"I don't know. My mother sent it to me. I never heard of it either until she sent it to me. It's a new book, just out."

"It's trash."

"Well, that's a quick opinion," said Rimrose, "considering you never heard of it until a few seconds ago. It's not a bad book, actually. It's keeping me interested. I'll tell you one thing I'm wondering about—I don't see any sign of that chocolate cake and tea you said you keep on hand for visitors like me."

Kakapick did not hear this plea. He invited Rimrose on a tour of his room, as if it were an unfolding space. But it was Kakapick who toured and Rimrose who stood in place listening. "We want to save the world from reading its eyes out on titles that are just too damn irrelevant and wasteful and just plain sappy and full of shit." Kakapick was terribly impatient of the idea of so many books in the world, so much frantic writing, so many printing houses pouring out titles. He would demolish the whole enterprise. Those titles he had chosen as candidates for survival he had committed to his mind and to his index cards. He could not refrain from explaining his index to Rimrose.

Poor Rimrose foresaw a long evening. Lately he had recognized himself as—well, speaking of time-wasting, a time-wasting pushover for other people's narratives of their frustrating lives. People viewed him as someone who listened readily to tales nobody else cared to hear.

At this moment he thought *I should have gone directly to the Sweet Shop* but in the next moment he was seized by one of the most consequential ideas he had ever had. He would turn Kakapick's monologue to better use. "You know what let's do," he said. "My taste buds came here expecting chocolate cake. I'm going to run out bareheaded through the snow to the Sweet Shop and *buy* a chocolate cake and bring it back here so you can tell me about your foolproof system in comfort. I'll write it up for *Sentinel.* That way I'll at least get a feature out of it—I won't feel that I've wasted this whole evening merely bullshitting."

Kakapick lit up. "For *Sentinel?"* he asked. "I'm ready." No prospect could have brought him greater pleasure. He fingered his shirtfront to be sure he was buttoned up for Fame knocking at his door. "Will it get printed?"

"I'm the editor," Rimrose said.

Soon Rimrose returned with one whole large chocolate cake on a Sweet Shop tray, quarts of hot tea and his notepad. He interviewed Kakapick until half-past one in the morning.

As they talked, Rimrose's article about Kakapick took form in his mind as humor. It would amuse his readers in proportion to their sophistication. Some *Sentinel* readers would smile at Kakapick's innocence even as others would cheer the visionary Kakapick to the fame he said he sought. Kakapick himself would relish it, oblivious to the ironies.

On the following day the businesslike, thorough, conscientious journalist Rimrose trudged through a snowstorm to the tiny office of Professor Struther in Humane Studies. Professor Struther complained that the day was Friday and he wanted to go home. He smiled at the mention of Kakapick, whom he had "enjoyed" as a student in a course called World Literature, Ancient to Present. "He's a plodder," the professor said, taking a roll book from his shelf to see the grade he had given Kakapick, nodding to himself meaning yes, he'd given the boy an *A* for regular punctual plodding. "He's not a wit," he said. "He doesn't receive wit. To receive wit you've got to have wit of your own."

Yes, the professor said, he remembered very well Kakapick's ambitious term project. The earnest boy had drawn up a list of books everybody should read and written an essay telling why. Professor Struther recalled having criticized the list as being strictly an English-language menu of Western immortals.

Thereupon Kakapick had worked further on the list, but unsuccessfully. His new list contained different books but the same basic error. Kakapick had missed the point. Professor Struther had reiterated his objection. Kakapick *now* seemed to understand the point the professor was making, and he vowed to overcome his deficiency by mastering "the key languages of the world."

The professor could not say (here he smiled at Rimrose) whether Kakapick had mastered the key languages since last year. "I wished him luck," said Professor Struther and he wished Rimrose luck too, and said, "Do you mind if I go home, it's Friday."

Rimrose returned through the snow to *Sentinel* and wrote his Kakapick article in thirty minutes at a single sitting with his usual speed, accuracy and good humor. He began, as it turned out, with a description of Kakapick's plan. Kakapick intended to establish a list of the world's indisputably best titles—never books, always titles. In his solitary room in Westby Second East day and night during this cold winter season Kakapick was saving mankind time and effort by selecting its future reading. He had kindly provided *Sentinel* with a list of 750 titles which had survived his "first cut." Rimrose quoted Kakapick: "More people should be doing what I'm doing. I'm crusading against guesswork."

Those titles which had not survived Kakapick's first cut were now dead forever. Many more would die as he reduced the books of the world to his magic figure of ninety-six or eighty-nine. "Mr. Kakapick is big on the death criterion," Rimrose observed. "The authors of all selected books must be dead. Mr. Kakapick insists upon it. On his index cards scattered everywhere in his room Mr. Kakapick has written the word *dead* in a corner of every card keyed to the name of an author, flanking the word with two checkmarks fore and aft certifying the author dead."

Kakapick's plan "is a grand idea," Rimrose wrote, shifting his Underwood into editorial gear:

> God knows our poor dear bleeding globe needs the right sort of unifying. Mr. Kakapick intends to relieve our disunified world of vexing questions of comparison. He will end debates and arguments. He will settle once and forever questions of curriculum. He will institute conformity. All our bookshelves will be identical. Everyone will read the same "best titles." The work of the libraries will be simplified. Librarians will need to know nothing about books and can devote themselves exclusively to their proper business of answering quiz-show questions. This will save the taxpayers millions of dollars. Children will memorize Mr. Kakapick's list and know what to read. The world will be grateful for Mr. Kakapick's having simplified its ancient quest, reducing our infinite library to a convenient short list anyone can carry in pocket or purse.

Editor Rimrose assigned a creative *Sentinel* photographer named Anna Brown to photograph Kakapick, "maybe standing with his books all around him," Rimrose suggested, "maybe leaning up against his bookshelves looking visionary, maybe sprawling on the bed holding a couple of dozen books in his arms, flipping his index cards, something like that, you'll do it."

Two weeks later the funny student writing *Sentinel* weather reported "four hundred million degrees below zero." On this chilly Friday Rimrose's article on Kakapick appeared on the feature page of *Sentinel,* bringing down upon its subject's head a calamity far different from the blessing he had been awaiting. The creative *Sentinel* photographer Anna Brown had produced a lovely picture showing Kakapick in his room bearing a serving tray piled with books and index cards. The tray was the tray on which Rimrose had brought chocolate cake and hot tea from the Sweet Shop. So far so good. But the books were perceived by a university librarian to be stolen goods. Kakapick's fame was beginning.

*   *   *

Kakapick was arrested in bed at six o'clock on Monday morning, released by Security at ten o'clock on his own recogni-
zance, and a few minutes later appeared at *Sentinel* coatless
and dizzy with fear.

The news of his arrest had not yet reached Rimrose. When
he saw Kakapick's desperation, he assumed that something
about the article had displeased him. Rimrose had not
thought that would happen. He had thought the article too
nicely double-edged, too subtly ambiguous to trouble its hu-
morless subject.

Kakapick begged Rimrose to step out of the office with him.
"I'm in the deepest crisis of my life," he said. They hurried
down the hall to a warm radiator. Rimrose sat on it, and
Kakapick in his agitation danced around it. Not his crime but
his publicity troubled him. "Your article got me arrested," he
said. "They're accusing me of stealing books. They arrested
me." He held out his hands to prove it. Prove what? Arrested
for what? "Fill me in," Rimrose said. "Do you mean they
handcuffed you?" "No, look at my fingers." His fingertips
were inkstained. He had been fingerprinted. "You've got to
keep it out of the paper," he said. His voice was pitched high.
In his distress he had lost control of its natural depths. "I was
only trying to help you out. Don't let them print anything
about it or I'm dead. I'm a State Subsidy Student."

"How were you helping me out?"

"Posing for a picture for your paper."

"Did you steal them?"

"Never. I don't steal. I borrowed them."

"How many books did you borrow? It looked to me as if you
had an awful lot of books in your room."

"Isn't that what a library's for? In a few days I was going to
take them back. We're old friends," Kakapick said. "We hang
around together. You know that. We go to dinner together. We

went to dinner with—" He tried it again: "—with the woman we've shared."

"We never shared a woman."

"If it was you, you'd figure out a way to keep yourself out."

"I don't know. Maybe I would. I can't say I wouldn't. This is something new to me."

"Don't you think it's new to me, too? Do I look like a thief? What's going to happen to me if I turn up in the paper? I'll lose my subsidy. I'll give you fifty dollars. I'll give you any amount of money you ask. You name it." He held his wallet open before Rimrose. His wallet was empty. "I can get it," he said.

"This is terrible," Rimrose said. "It's not right. The more you talk, the worse you make it. I don't think I know how to handle a thing like this."

"How much do you want?"

"I don't want any. I want to get back to my desk and get the paper on the street." He sounded to himself like his father.

"Think about it. Don't let me down." Kakapick detained him, clinging to him. "Just make me one promise. Think it over. Ask yourself what you'd want somebody to do if you were me."

When Rimrose returned to his desk he fulfilled his promise to Kakapick to think it over. He could not help himself. He could think of nothing else. He obtained the blotter from the police reporter. The blotter named two students arrested and released for "fisticuffs with intention to harm," one student arrested and detained for stealing a car battery, one student arrested and released for window-peeping with binoculars, three students arrested and released for "drunk and intoxicated," and Kakapick arrested and released on suspicion of theft of books from the university library.

Rimrose studied the photograph which had accompanied the *Sentinel* article. Was that the tray he had brought to Kakapick's room from the Sweet Shop? It could be, couldn't it? And hadn't he borrowed the tray, just as Kakapick had borrowed the books? And hadn't he intended to return the tray to the Sweet Shop, too, just as Kakapick intended to return the books to the library? Were the two crimes of the same order?

All day he thought about Kakapick and the police blotter. In his mind he removed Kakapick's name from the record. Then he restored it. Off and on. The question was vexing though the right answer was clear. It was the paper's policy to report the names of students who were arrested. The policy preceded Rimrose and had preceded Polly Anne Cathcart and admitted no exceptions. There was no way around it. He recalled occasions of his father's coming home with tales of someone's asking him to keep something out of the *Herald*. His father never protected anyone, friend or family. Rimrose liked to think of himself as being capable of playing as straight and as fair as his father. Or did his father always? An image flew into Rimrose's mind—he had seen something and never known what to make of it—of his father's kissing a reporter named Valerie Eischberg, of the numerous family of Zygmont Eischbergs, beside the teletypes at the *Herald*.

At six o'clock a cheer rose in the *Sentinel* newsroom. Polly Anne had entered. The young reporters embraced her, and when they freed her she came to Rimrose at her desk—now his desk. She had driven to campus over ice and snow to plead for Kakapick. "You mustn't put his name in the blotter," she said. It was a command, but in the moment of her commanding she became aware that she hadn't the power to command the editor. He was his own editor now. She was beloved in the shop but without authority.

"We print everybody's name who's arrested," Rimrose said.

"Why do you want to ruin him?" she said.

"Mad talk, Polly, mad talk, I don't want to ruin anybody."

"It'll ruin him," she said. "He'll lose his state subsidy."

"He was only arrested. We only report arrests, we don't convict people."

"He borrowed them," she said. "He was planning to return

them. He's got a big project going. You know, he doesn't have a lot of money, but he gave me a hundred dollars to give you." Rimrose pretended not to have heard her, and she pretended not to have said it. She surveyed the newsroom as if she had never seen it. "What a little dump this is," she said.

Rimrose was hurt. "It's no dump," he said in anger, "it's a good honest hardworking shop."

"If you keep his name out of the blotter I'll do something good for you," she said.

He wanted to say *What? What can you do for me?* He was curious to know what she had in mind, but he caught himself before he asked. "I didn't know you and he were this close."

"Terribly close," she said. She lowered her voice and spoke confidentially. "Everything in his life depends on this. Everything depends on you now. Take my word for it. He'll be ruined."

"He didn't tell me how many books he borrowed," Rimrose said.

"What does it matter?" she said, but she wouldn't tell him either.

"Somebody said a hundred books."

"More than that," said Polly Anne, as if the mere *number* of books were irrelevant, as if she knew much more than Rimrose about the whole matter—as if the last thing that mattered was this theft itself, as if there were something much deeper which Rimrose might understand someday as he grew older. It was a shrewd direction for her to take, her best argument, for Rimrose was already convinced she knew more about everything than he.

At the Student Union they sat at the *Sentinel* table. They had not seen each other since the week of her graduation. "It's a tragedy," she said. "I used to see you every day."

"You're busy," he said.

"No," she said, "I'm not busy, I'm just in a state of being stupidly occupied. I work all week so I can stay in bed all weekend. I'm not very well. Maybe I'm diseased."

"With what disease now?"

Old age, she said, feeling suddenly very old among these college youths, and she was always ill, always fearful that she was coming down with something. She was living on the west side. Doing what on the west side? She was slaving away like a moron, she said, for a neighborhood newspaper called the *West Side News.*

"I never heard of it," said Rimrose.

"It's a throwaway," she said. "If you ever get your hands on a copy, throw it away. It's a horrible abortion of a thing, in case you don't dig what I'm saying. It's totally advertising. They print with some kind of substance in the office that's making me sick. It's a poison ink—it poisons employees but saves the company money."

"You're psychosomatic," Rimrose said.

"That's right, you're still in school. When you're out in the world you can't afford to think about psychosomatic this or that. Out there you either go to work or you don't get paid. It's the shits out there. If this was last year I'd have gone to the infirmary by now. I've got no more Health Plan now. Either I should marry a rich boy and put all this poverty behind me, or I should get a job at the university and get back on the plan."

"This sounds like the moment for me to say 'Marry me,' " he boldly said. "Only I'm not rich. I've got about ten dollars right now. It's terrible to think that somebody as brilliant and smart and creative as you is ready to sell her soul for a medical plan."

"Try me."

They spoke not a word of Kakapick. When Rimrose returned to *Sentinel* he retrieved the blotter and deleted the news of Kakapick's alleged crime. But he was not satisfied with having done that. Therefore he restored it, but he was not satisfied with that, either. Therefore he once again removed Kakapick's name and the notice of his alleged crime, and with strokes of his broad black pencil he also deleted the news of the fist-fighters, the drinkers, the window-peeper and the battery thief. The blotter was blank and he dropped it into the wastebasket.

Two university laborers with strong backs, two university Security officers with a warrant, and two university librarians pushing book carts arrived at Westby Second East at midnight, and upon the warrant of Security removed from Kakapick's room all the books he had stolen from the library.

The warrant specified two hundred books in mistaken contradiction to Kakapick's own close and careful record preserved on color-coded index cards specifying two hundred and fifty "titles," as he called them. Screaming and cursing, he insisted to the last that they were his property. In spite of all appearances he owned them. His logic was shadowy. "See my name in the front." He seized books and shook them open and showed his name where he had stamped it. When he stamped his name in a book the book became his. "I'm a student of the university," he shouted, "I have a right to borrow as many titles as I want. I own them." His neighbors of Westby Second East came running to the scene of this excitement. His fury lent him strength. A Security officer closed his door against the gathering public, but the All-America linebacker with thighs like tree trunks wrestled it open.

"You tell it, Kaka," called the Olympic sprinter.

"I only forgot to return them," Kakapick replied high in hysteria. "I simply borrowed them." The athletes cheered his report. He did not know that they were mocking him. Kakapick was joyful in his righteous anger. "You're all my friends," he called. "You all care for me. You all came to my defense. You all came and supported me," but they had come only for the fun. When the first laborer with a strong back began to wheel away books on a library cart, the athletes cheered him, too, and whooped and hollered, "Kaka didn't do nothing, only stole a bunch of books."

Everyone but Herndon had awakened in Westby Second East, and a great many people even as far away as Second West. Kakapick's fame was spreading fast. The Security officer exhorted the athletes, "Come on now, you got to get the hell out of here, none of this is any of your business," but nobody retreated, least of all the football tackle with thighs like tree trunks, who cried out, "We're standing by old Kaka to the death."

"Kakapick been falsely accused," cried the record-breaking hurdler.

"Never say Kakapick's no rooster-fucker," cried the Olympic sprinter.

"No, sir, he was never a rooster-fucker," the sarcastic basketball player shouted. "Say what you want, he was only a pig-fucker."

"Give him back his books," cried the record-breaking hurdler, fist-pumping the heavens, "he stole them fair and square."

"It was all in fun, he was only playing a joke on the library," the religious swimmer argued.

The night expanded. The crowd grew larger and larger.

"I'm not afraid of any man," Kakapick called.

The jocks laughed, the crowd laughed, everybody laughed except Rimrose from *Sentinel,* who had just arrived and was standing alone in the corridor in his bathrobe angling to write things down in his sky-blue notebook. The Security policeman said to him, "Midnight was the wrong time for this. We should have did it at noon when these damn jocks are all asleep." A photographer from *Sentinel* arrived, shooting his flash as fast as he could.

This was sure to go down in legend as one of the biggest nights in the long history of rowdy unruly behavior in Westby Second East. Kakapick had become a midnight success. He had gathered a crowd. He had brought everybody here. He had made something happen to relieve the boredom of education. The famous athletes had boosted his confidence by so loyally turning out to cheer him. He folded his arms and smoked a cigarette and addressed the crowd at his doorway. "I was fully intending to return all those damn titles. I told them so," and the athletes chanted "You told 'em, Kaka," and the religious swimmer cried out to him, "Yeah, we believe you, Kaka, you're a hero," and the Security officer pleaded, "All right, you guys, come on now, out of the way, open the path."

Soon all his books had been removed from his shelves, gathered from the corners of his room and lined in rows on the library carts immobilized in his doorway.

"Well, Kaka, anyhow you tried," Rimrose's roommate Herndon called, arriving late from sleep, "nobody can't succeed at everything." Then even the athletes, tired of their exuberance, relented, fell back and cheered the university laborers wheeling away Kakapick's books. "Now they're all gone— all my work carried away," Kakapick wailed. His shelves were bare. He had been plundered. Where he had possessed hundreds of books there were none. "Now you're just like us," said the Olympic sprinter. "We got no books, either."

"Two hundred and fifty books gone like the wind," mourned the All-America linebacker.

"All Kaka done was borrow a few books," said the sarcastic basketball player.

Polly Anne Cathcart, former editor of *Sentinel,* testified under oath before the Liberal Arts Disciplinary Committee that Kakapick had in point of fact only *borrowed* the books, that he had planned to return them, that he had lately been, she observed, under extraordinary pressure of academic work and personal stress.

The always very liberal Liberal Arts Student Disciplinary Committee suspended Kakapick's library privileges for thirty days, effective immediately, with the right of appeal. Kakapick took up the appeal. He sought a ninety-day suspension of his sentence to carry him to the end of the term, when he would no longer require the use of the library. This appeal was sympathetically granted on the grounds that he was a State Subsidy Student with no prior Security record. His bookshelves were empty, but he soon filled them again.

Christmas came, and spring. Rimrose was regularly in love for days at a time with young women he spied in classes or who worked for him at *Sentinel,* but these romances were over almost before they began. He was doing something wrong. He began to think he was in need of some sort of instruction in romantic life. No vision reappeared like the vision of Angelica Vanenglenhoven in the moonlight on the beach at Zygmont Lake. But Angelica had been only a morsel of hometown good luck.

Perhaps it was a car he needed. He thought he'd buy a car, but he had no money to buy a car, and he couldn't have driven it if he had it. He could learn, he supposed. He could get a girl to teach him. Polly Anne would surely teach him. His roommate Delbert Herndon said to him, "There's ten million Chinamen in their ignorance driving a car and so can you."

Herndon also said to him, "Did you ever stop and count up there's twenty-two hundred million women on the earth and you ain't fuckin' a one of them?"

He missed Polly Anne. She seemed to have fallen out of his life. He phoned her at the *West Side News* but he could not reach her. He tried her again. He tried her several times. He wrote her a postcard. He left messages for her with a young woman and thought at last to ask the young woman if Polly Anne actually still *worked* there, and the woman said no, basically not, hard to tell, "We think she's gone, it's incredible."

"In what way incredible?"

"She just disappeared and never came back and here's the incredible part—she left a whole carton of cigarettes behind."

It was a mystery. He decided he'd cease to think of her. But the very next day Kakapick came to his room and asked him a question to which Kakapick very well knew the answer, "Did I hear that you're trying to track Polly Anne down?"

"Do you know where she is these days?" Rimrose asked.

Kakapick was dying to tell Rimrose he knew where she was, all right, and much more too, dying to tell him everything he knew about the girl they "shared"—that's how he put it. "Sure I know where she is," said Kakapick, "and I expect to see her tonight. I'll deliver her a message if any." He looked at his watch and he looked up from his watch into Rimrose's eyes to see whether Rimrose was seizing his meaning.

"I'd love it if she gave me a call," Rimrose said, painful as it was to ask Kakapick to carry his message.

She called him one evening at *Sentinel.* She had found a better job than the one at *West Side News.*

"Doing what?"

"At the university," she said.

"Doing what at the university?"

"Thank God back on the Health Plan," she said.

"But doing what—what job?" Rimrose asked. "Come on, don't be secretive, when somebody gets a job everybody at *Sentinel* wants to know what it is and how you got it."

"I'll tell you all about it. Let's have dinner," she said.

"Perfect," he said. "And I want you to give me driving lessons."

"I'll be coming by bike," she said. She was living west of campus. It wasn't the west side of town, but it was still a mean distance.

"I already know how to bike," he said.

Her driver's license had been suspended for "suspicion of reckless operation."

"Then it sounds like you're probably not the person to teach me to drive," he said.

She came to *Sentinel* by bicycle one cold April Saturday. She hated bicycles because they had no heaters, no radios. "Hard as hell to light a cigarette when I'm riding a bike," she said. She was wrapped in a woollen poncho replicating an American flag, a helmet and goggles. They sat until dinnertime with their feet on his (formerly her) desk, where he told her, among many other things, how unhappy she had made him when she called this *Sentinel* office "a little dump."

"Did I say that?" she asked. She knew she had. She had seen the shock pass through him at the time. "Maybe I was feeling bitter."

"You were going to flee this ivy-covered cesspool."

"And never come back," she said. "When I was editor I didn't know I had it so good. When you're the editor you're the boss. So enjoy it. The day the job ends you suddenly become promoted to nobody. You're out on the street and you're broke. You'd have been bitter, too, on the *West Side News.* I mean, of all the work a distinguished college graduate like me could get to do—editor of a major national university daily—the *West Side News* took the cake for shit. You wouldn't understand this. You'll never face it, I guess. You've got your cozy family newspaper to go home to, your boss is your father and your father is your boss, you can't begin to imagine how much I envy you. That's what I call making it in a big way."

She believed that she had thrown four years away. Nothing had come of anything. Think of all the money she could have earned in four years! Think of their squandered idealism! She could almost weep, she said, to think how little had come of their hard campaign against the Indian Fee. The university crooks had outlasted all *Sentinel* sleuthing, all the undercover work, all the articles exposing the fraud of it all, all the editorials, all the letters to the editors *Sentinel* had evoked. She and Rimrose had worked themselves into exhaustion, and nothing had come of their labors.

"I don't feel that way at all," Rimrose said. "Those were the greatest years of my life."

She smiled a superior smile. "You haven't got a lot of years to compare them to." She felt herself to be an old veteran of a forgotten war. "I went all through it for certain principles and I got my legs shot off and nothing has changed. Not one single thing."

"Oh, come on," he said, "we abolished the Chapel of God, we put up a good fight against the Indian Fee, we brought the OSE out in the open—"

"That's where my new job is at," she said.

"Where?"

"For the OSE."

"You're kidding me," he said, but instantly he saw that he might have expected it. "If you can't beat 'em, join 'em," he ruefully said. "Do you work for that Mr. Guitar?"

"He hired me," she said. "At OSE you don't know *who* you're working for. He'll be trying to hire you too one of these days."

"I can't believe it, you took such a job."

"Well, it's as true as it can be."

"It seems to me," he said, "you're joining up with everything you always hated. But then maybe you didn't hate it. You loved discovering things furtively. You loved the undercover game."

"Still do," she said, "especially when I'm getting paid for it."

"You encouraged us to get people's secrets out of their wastepaper baskets. I could never go for that. I don't know, somehow I felt my father would say that fishing in wastebaskets wasn't newspapering. Have you acquired the art of tapping telephones?" But he was not angry. He was only disappointed.

When she saw he was not angry, she smiled and said, "I've got to confess I can find out almost anything in creation by telephone. If I can't find it out it didn't happen. When you can get a job where the work is play you've got to take it. I love stealing people's secrets, copying mail, forging documents, duplicating keys, breaking and entering, spying, extorting and blackmailing."

"I'm sure you must be kidding."

"I love having everybody's cock in my pocket. I thought you might not like it," she said. "I almost didn't tell you."

"I'd have found out sooner or later."

"Not necessarily," she said.

He said, "She sold her soul to get herself on the Health Plan."

"I never had a soul. Two days after I got the job I came down with a bad attack of my good old asthma, and I went to the clinic and flashed my health card and they put me out of my misery. You know how much it cost me?"

"One dollar," he said.

"Ninety-nine cents," she said. "Nobody sends me money from Zygmont."

They dined at the Mermaid Tavern. He walked with her through the night to her bicycle. At the *Sentinel* rack she unchained her bike and wrapped herself in her scarf and strapped up her helmet and goggles and smoked one last cigarette to sustain her through the smokeless quarter-hour ahead.

"It was good of Kakapick to get my message to you," Rimrose said.

"He never got any message to me," she said.

"He said he would."

"Well, he didn't."

But whether Kakapick did or didn't, Rimrose would never know. Kakapick had said he would, and when she phoned Rimrose she said he had, but now she preferred another version of things. These were the lies that baffled him, that didn't make any sense because they didn't make any sense. She lied to be lying. "Then you got my message by mental telepathy."

"I don't need a message to call you, Rim. I called you because I hadn't talked to you in a long time and I wanted to talk to you and see you and bullshit the happy hours away."

"Not that it matters. I don't mean to be petty. I'm sure I should start acting grownup about these things. Do you— what do we say these days? Do you—?"

"Do I see Kaka? A lot," she said.

"You're close." In his mind he saw Kakapick's face above Polly Anne's, Kakapick smiling down at her with his black teeth.

"Horribly close," she said. "What's the mystery? You introduced us."

"I didn't *introduce* you. You and I were going someplace and he came along in the rain."

"And you introduced us."

"Well, all right, if that's what you mean by *introduced*— accidentally bumping into somebody in the rain. Do you want to hear something? He tells people we *shared* you, we share the same girl, not that that's any of my business either, not that you're under any obligation to tell me anything, but he says he and I *share* you. You should tell him he shouldn't say that."

"Don't be so straight-arrow. The straight arrow from Zygmont. Who the fuck cares who the fuck fucked who?"

"Then you don't mind if people think you and I—well— fucked," he said.

"All the boys and girls on *Sentinel* always assumed so anyhow," she said. "Don't you know that? We'd been to bed together, fucked or shortly would or certainly should have if we hadn't. What in the world were we waiting for? Two such attractive people! A natural team!"

"We got to know each other too well too fast," Rimrose said.

"I think so," she said. "That's a damn smart analysis. You're a damn smart kid. The fact was, the truth was, given all the crises we lived through at *Sentinel* and all the late hours and all the overnights we endured, you and I were too much business and too little play. I don't care what Kakapick thinks or what he wants people to think. He's just up to tricks of his own. Kakapick wants people to think something and put two and two together and come up with the three of us. He wants people to think you and he are fucking the same girl. I understand that. He's a boaster, he's a braggart, he thrives on claiming association. Look at me, ma, I'm going to bed with the former editor of *Sentinel,* she goes to bed with the present editor of *Sentinel,* doesn't that make me the fucking Czar Kakapick of Russia?"

"That's a lot of fame rubbing off on Kakapick."

"I'll say."

"It's creepy living that way," Rimrose said.

"Oh, I don't know, I do that kind of thing myself," Polly Anne said, and away she glided on her bicycle.

Fifty stories swarmed in Rimrose's head—not newspaper stories but others. At first he did not dare to call them fiction or literature, in the style of the literature his mother read—"your Mark Twain," as she said, your Tolstoy, Salinger, Mann, Updike, Baldwin, Maugham, Sherwood Anderson, A. E. Coppard, Saroyan, Melville, your Hawthorne, your Henry James, your Flannery O'Connor, your Welty, Mary McCarthy, Thurber, Maupassant, Bellow, Chekhov, Stevenson, Steinbeck, Faulkner, Caldwell, Joyce, Wilde, Lardner, Runyon, Fitzgerald, Mansfield, Wharton, Porter, your John O'Hara, your Hemingway, your Conan Doyle, your Cather—but as his writing grew bolder he called them fiction. What the hell.

He began by sitting before his birthday Underwood at his table in his room in Westby Second East in the echoing silence of everyone's having gone off to summer. Herndon snored *in absentia* in the empty bed. Hardly a word came to paper.

Rimrose's presence in his room violated Security regulations. Security locked the building. Rimrose came and went through a window. Security turned off the air-conditioning.

Food service had been suspended. He dined on stale leavings in coin machines. Summer was cool until it heated up, and the breeze through his room cheered him until it abandoned him to doldrums.

What a fool he was! He could have been home working for his father so comfortably at the *Herald,* covering the Fourth of July and the fraternal picnics. His father so ardently wished he were there he had made summer plans without quite consulting the boy. It was a family crisis, mediated by his mother with the help of his brother Alf on the long-distance phone from Bangor.

Look at the summer splendor he was missing. After the day's hot work he could be running the waves at Zygmont Lake in the moonlight, renewing his idyll with Angelica Vanenglenhoven.

Anyhow, with *somebody.* Anybody was better than this loneliness. He covered his Underwood and stowed it away. He packed a summer of clothes in the big battered green war-surplus footlocker he and his father had carried into Westby three years earlier. But the problem remained how to transport the footlocker from Westby back into the world. Security had locked the doors. Therefore Rimrose slid the footlocker out of his window. It landed beautifully upright, green footlocker on the green grass, and Rimrose jumped out of the window after it. He struggled across campus, intending to return to Zygmont by bus.

The footlocker was heavier than he remembered its having been—well, of course, his father had carried one end. He saw summer-school students arriving. Hey, if summer-school students were here, food service could not be far behind. The Sweet Shop would reopen. The post office this very moment was raising its flag. In the mail came postage stamps from his mother. Life was on again. He corrected his course and soon arrived at *Sentinel.*

There he parked his footlocker, and there it remained for fifteen years. It was employed over the years by *Sentinel* staff

as table, bench and chair. People played cards on it, carved
their names on it, blackened it with cigarette burns. For a
while it was propped on end to serve as a dictionary stand.
Moved here and there about the office, it never traveled farther than twenty feet from the spot where Rimrose had
plunked it down that summer day. For the year remaining of
his editorship he became so accustomed to its presence he
forgot it was his. For five years thereafter everyone assumed it
was locked. When someone propped it on end to serve as a
dictionary stand it flew open to reveal nothing much besides
old story manuscripts somebody had chucked out of his or
her life, and odds and ends of sports apparel and equipment.
People wondered whose manuscripts they were. Then somebody shut the lid again for another ten years.

The *Sentinel* office, on the day Rimrose entered with his
footlocker, was airless and abandoned. But he had not come
for the climate. His faith lay in the idea that one of the old
office Underwoods would get him started. He was confident
he could write fiction if only he could remember the stories
he had intended. The silence appalled him. He was alone
and he was thirsty. He fetched a bucket of ice from the Sweet
Shop. He switched on the UPI teletype. Its pounding assisted
his mind.

The virtue of *stories,* he had thought, as opposed to newspaper *articles,* was the opportunity to go back in life longer
ago than yesterday. But in the airless heat, in spite of the
comfort of the song of the teletype, he could think of nothing
to write about but the immediate oppressive present. The *Sentinel* office confined him. The walls closed in. He wrote a
weird gruesome supernatural sci-fi story about a young man
trying to write stories on an old typewriter in his college
newspaper office. The office was an oven turned on high. The
young man melted. That puddle on the floor was him. When
the students returned in the autumn they mopped him up,
sweeping his abandoned manuscripts into the waste. Rimrose
entitled this story "The Airless Furnace, or Buckets of Melted

Ice," stamped it with stamps his mother sent him, and mailed it to a sci-fi magazine called *Gyroscope.*

Stories were everywhere if one was wide awake, his father said. Look around, keep your ears open. Rimrose began to teach himself to make plot, drama, incident, suspense out of moments suggested to his mind, to begin with things known and inventing their undiscovered depths. His father thought "stories" meant newspaper articles. The principle was different.

Rimrose, having completed "The Airless Furnace, or Buckets of Melted Ice," needed to look no farther than his footlocker on the *Sentinel* floor. He began a story about his footlocker that turned into a story about his father the day his father had driven him down from Zygmont. Rimrose aimed the climax of his story at the remembered moment of his parting from his father. His father's hand was clawing at his back, trying to recapture him, take him home. Rimrose felt it yet. He would feel it forever. He suspected now that he had known in that moment he would never go home to Zygmont. Write a story about that, he thought.

Or write a story about Polly Anne's going to work for the Office of Savings and Economy. He tried. It became too complicated. He could not make it go right. The more he wrote, the less he had. He tore it up. He would be a while learning the sequence of composition. Sometimes a title came, sometimes a place, sometimes a person, sometimes a situation, it was hateful, arbitrary, accursed, and yet it was all he cared to do that summer. It was tricky. It was nonsense. It was healing, self-revelation, world illumination. Give the son of a bitch a try.

He was stuck. Oh, it was very damn hard, this shit. He hated it. Journalism was easier. He'd go home and pound out the copy for his father and swim the summer through. Instead, he bought an electric fan.

He wrote several stories he was unable to complete. It was a mystery the way stories resisted him. It was crazy. In journalism one printed everything one wrote. His father would sneer at this rewriting, this copying over, and Rimrose did not enjoy it, either, starting every goddamn thing all over again.

And yet he did it. To the sound of the whistling steel blades of his new electric fan Rimrose wrote a story about his father's objections to stories unless they were newspaper stories, and his mother's objections to his father's objections, ending in a screaming match late at night between the father and the mother while the boy lay abed, listening. The boy, knowing that he had been the cause of the argument, leaped from his bed—But what would the boy do now that he had leaped? Rimrose could not figure out how to go forward, and there the boy remains to this day . . .

He tried a story about Kakapick. Once upon a time this boy with black teeth entered college as a State Subsidy Student. Well, wasn't that getting a little too close? Okay, forget Kakapick, make him Jones, make him an athlete with shining white teeth who had lost the heart for sports. Yet on the other hand he was determined to play sports to assist his father to pay the college tuition. He wished to be loyal and helpful to his father, and yet he also wished to be loyal to himself. One day Jones's father and mother came down to visit him thinking he was going to play in the big Homecoming Game. There they sat in the grandstand waving their pennants . . . but Rimrose could not go on, and there they remain to this day.

He tried yet another story about Kakapick. Diving one night into his airless furnace in the *Sentinel* office, Rimrose wrote a story about a newspaper editor who accommodates a friend by suppressing the news of his friend's arrest for theft. The editor's action distresses him. He has violated journalistic ethics. In a sense, he has taken a payoff, a bribe, he should be punished. He should not have protected his friend. He writes a confession which he intends to publish on the front page of his newspaper, but at the last minute he changes his mind.

Rimrose mailed this story to the New Yorker magazine, which returned it with a printed rejection slip upon which an editor had added a handwritten message, "Nicely written but we are overstocked with stories about moral dilemmas."

Even when summer was over he continued to write stories. He edited *Sentinel* and he wrote fiction. How did he do it? People marveled at his energy. Rimrose was fecund. He was industrious and disciplined. He was his father's son and his mother's son, having inherited the best of everything.

His staff at *Sentinel* was never wholly certain whether Rimrose at the Underwood was at any given moment writing fiction or newspaper copy. The paper in his machine could be a clue. He wrote *Sentinel* stuff on half-sheets and fiction on full-size eight-and-a-half-by-eleven-inch sheets, although there were moments when thoughts popped with such rapidity into his mind that he didn't have time to choose his paper.

Rimrose maintained a good scholastic average, played intra-mural basketball and touch football and worried what would become of him in life. Would he ever find a wife? Much as he worried, he never lost sleep. He managed on little enough. His roommate Herndon slept for two.

Rimrose so much enjoyed writing stories he could not stop. He passed his stories among his friends, who especially enjoyed them for their saucy parts, their naughty bits, in which the young hero of the story seduces the heroine. The hero undresses her, unbuttons her, unzips her, unclasps her, unstraps her. The author had not done much of this sort of thing himself, and certainly never with the finesse of the heroes of his tales, but he had developed a keen facility for imagining encounters.

The men of Westby Second East passed his stories around. One of their favorites was "Girls Will Be Girls," which became in a sense Rimrose's first published story—a limited edition that someone in Westby messily typed onto stencil and cranked out on mimeo.

When he completed a story he sent it to a magazine. Let

someone else enjoy it as he had. Too bad when the magazine rejected it—the world had missed a good yarn. He sent it to another. After a story had been rejected three or four times, he dropped it into his green war-surplus footlocker in the corner behind his desk at *Sentinel.*

The story "Getting to Class Regularly on Time" was universally read in Westby Second East. The student commanding the mimeo machine made many copies. Nobody missed this story—you can bet on that. Men of Westby who rarely read a word of fiction read this story.

Here's how it went. In "Getting to Class Regularly on Time" an ordinarily indolent student named Rutherford signs up for Professor Streetspitter's course called Microeconomic Principles 224. He seldom attends class, but on one of the rare occasions of his doing so he falls in love with Marigold across the aisle. He tries to follow her from class, but she is elusive and disappears. He plans to sit closer to her next time. In order to accomplish this he comes again to class—"What, Rutherford getting to class regularly on time two days in a row, I can't believe it," exclaims Professor Streetspitter.

Present, yes, but a bit tardy. Rutherford has not quite solved the problem. He realizes that he must arrive earlier at class if he wants to sit near Marigold. For the following session he arrives early. This is a strange and unusual experience for him, but he endures it. He must wait a long time alone in the empty classroom before the other students arrive.

To while away his idle minutes Rutherford engages in an act uncharacteristic of him. He begins to read in the textbook he has heretofore left unopened, *Microeconomic Principles,* edited by Doodoo, Rawface, Bahstid, Biche and Streetspitter.

Eyes alert beyond his textbook, Rutherford the early bird sights Marigold when she enters the classroom. He follows her to her chosen seat. He sits beside her. He charms her with his remarks pro and con on *Microeconomic Principles.* She is eager to hear him further on the subject. They arrange a date.

And it was basically Rimrose's narration of Rutherford's

date with Marigold which recommended the story to his peers in Westby East. Stories whose only dimension was microeconomics might not have moved them. But a story featuring Marigold the Naked was—well, a different story. For a few weeks she dominated the dream life of Westby Second East. Over and over the men of Westby read Rimrose's story for its undressing scene. They read it in solitude and they read it aloud to their roommates. They sent it to friends at faraway institutions of higher education and home to their baby brothers.

We may scarcely be surprised—although it perplexed Rimrose at the time—that most of the men of Westby missed the author's innovative comic ironical intellectual instruction: "Confront complexity. Try it. You'll like it." Rutherford in his early zeal to sit near Marigold had fallen in love with his textbook.

The struggling, groping author had dramatized this idea in the following way: during the undressing scene Marigold the Naked declares her love for Rutherford. Will he marry her? "Of course, yes, sure, why not?" For two weeks they arrive together, arms entwined, at Microeconomic Principles 224. But we the readers sense a rival in the wings. Rutherford seems to be changing his mind about Marigold. Before long he no longer cares even to *see* her. He wishes she would go away. She is bothering him, she is taking up his time, she will not leave him free to pursue the truest love of his life. "What is that?" she asks. "Damn it," he replies, "microeconomic principles. Haven't you ever heard of them? They're the salt of the earth. No matter what you might think of them, I've fallen in love with them, I adore them, I worship them, leave me alone with them."

One evening a troubling thing happened to Kakapick. He saw a resident of Westby Hall racing down the stairway. The student caught sight of Rimrose and shouted to him, "Hey, your story was great stuff, Rim, do another." This was painful for Kakapick to hear. Nobody ever hailed Kakapick on a stairway, nobody ever commended him, congratulated him for something he had done, shouted praise at him, "Hey, Kaka, keep those index cards coming." Not many people knew his name. Rimrose, however, had a kind of fame.

Kakapick, too, like everyone in Westby Hall East, had read Rimrose's story "Getting to Class Regularly on Time." It was the only story he had ever read. His problem was that he had no way of knowing how to feel about it. He was unable to bring to it any opinions or judgment, for he had never heard it discussed in a class, nor had he read analyses of it by critics.

Far into the night the thought of Rimrose as a prospect for fame kept Kakapick awake. He left his bed in a fury. He dressed in trousers and shirt and slipped his feet into his open-heeled step-in go-ahead slippers. Several questions about the story had vexed him. In what class had Rutherford (or Rimrose) met Marigold? Kakapick consulted his University Bulletin. He was unable to find a course called Microeconomic Principles 224, nor did any professor exist by the name of Streetspitter. He would have this out with Rimrose. He strode down the hall. How unfair things were! Who was that Marigold? What was her real name? Where had Rimrose met her?

Kakapick walked the long hall. His go-aheads made absurd flapping noises, slap-slap slap-slap on the old stone floor. The snoring of all Westby drifted through the walls. When Kakapick found himself before Rimrose's door, he knocked. When Rimrose did not answer, Kakapick knocked harder. Somewhere down the corridor someone's snoring ceased. Kakapick intended to knock as loud and as long as necessary, for he was in crisis, and at length he called, "I know you're there," to which Rimrose replied from within, "Where else would I be at this time of the night?"

"I don't mean to wake you up, I only came to discuss your story."

"I can't believe it." Rimrose opened the door. "Look at the time."

"Turn on the light."

"We don't need a light. You're leaving right away. Herndon's asleep."

"I'm dying to know who Marigold actually is," Kakapick said.

"She's nobody, she doesn't exist, I never met her," said Rimrose.

"You must have met her."

"Never. Go back to bed, you're a maniac. There's no Marigold. She's just made up. You're a moron. There's something wrong with you."

"You can't make a person up."

"Of course you can. That's how you write stories. You make people up."

"There's no such course as Microeconomic Principles."

"If there isn't, we better get one in a hurry," said Rimrose, "we're falling behind the Soviet Union. I can't believe you're saying what you're saying."

"It must have happened to you," said Kakapick. "You couldn't have made it up."

"You're giving me a royal pain in the ass," Rimrose said. "I'm very tired. I really need my sleep."

"I'd like to get a look at Marigold," Kakapick said.

"There's no Marigold," said Rimrose. "The whole thing didn't happen. It's all fictitious."

"It might have happened."

"Of course, certainly, it *might* have happened," Rimrose agreed. "It happens every day. That's what stories do. They take off from the things that happen every day. That's literature."

This was shocking to Kakapick. He could not believe what he was hearing. "You're not telling me your story is literature, are you? It's definitely not literature."

"Okay, it's not. I don't care if it's literature or not. I don't even care at noon in broad daylight, much less at three o'clock in the morning. I'm losing my patience with you."

"Literature is what's taught in the university."

"That's great. But somebody wrote it first. How do you think they got ahold of it if somebody didn't write it first? It was only a piece of paper at first. Keep your voice down. People are sleeping."

But Kakapick raised his voice instead of lowering it. "You'll never be literature, Rimrose. You're only—"

"I'm only what?"

"You're only a person. The things you write will never be literature. Everything is trash. I saw a guy the other day reading your story in the crapper. I don't read everything, I just read literature. You changed her name from something else."

At this point Herndon the football star, surfacing from sleep, cried out from his bed, "She's only a fucking story, Kaka," leaping from bed, charging at Kakapick, and seizing that poor fellow and twirling him around and thrusting him out of the door into the corridor, slamming the door behind him.

Rimrose met Lucy Revere in Marriage and the Family 424 conducted by Professor Markell. Two hundred and forty students swarmed to the dim auditorium in Chapel Arts, once upon a time the Chapel of God, whose name and function had been changed under pressure from *Sentinel*. Professor Markell now subbed for God.

On rainy days the stone walls seeped. The students sat alphabetically. For ease of notetaking their seats were equipped with frail lights attached to armrests. When Rimrose's light failed, he turned for help to Lucy Revere in the seat beside him.

In the first minutes of the first session of class Professor Markell addressed his students in the following way. "If you notice me on the street, just give me a wave but don't be surprised if I don't recognize you. There are too many of you to remember. Wave just the same. Here's how we do it." From his high platform before the class he waved to show how it was done, and his two hundred and forty students waved back.

His first minutes of every semester were his best. Never again could he reach those heights. He began by playing the role of the student. "Am I ready? I am a college student coming to the end of my undergraduate career. I am twenty-one years old, I am about to graduate from this institution I've loved and hated for four miserable inspiring years. During my period of attendance here I have been in love with a variety of specimens of the opposite sex, or at least I think it was love. Maybe it was only poison ivy. I have got to learn to distinguish between sexual itching and the truest love and affection while peering into the future to see if any of these relationships holds marriage for me. I am examining myself. The key expression in my head is the question, 'Am I ready?' Am I ready for the self-sacrifice of a shared life? Am I ready in my head? Am I ready in my body? Am I who only yesterday was a sniveling selfish child ready today to bring children of my own into this world? Am I ready to tell myself the *truth* about whether I am ready for a monogamous sexual life? Am I ready to accompany my prospective spouse in religious companionship or am I holding something back? Am I ready to depart from the house of my dear mother and father and prove to the world that, having read Thoreau and Emerson and Greek philosophers and continental authors and Freud and Marx, a college graduate can plumb his own toilet. Ready or not, here I come. Am I ready?"

The class applauded. The professor waved. When the class interrupted its applause to return the professor's wave, silence fell magically in Chapel Arts.

That was the last real exchange between Professor Markell and his students. To his captive audience he subsequently delivered lectures in a style characterized by extensive redundancy. He could have said it all on day one. He spoke monotonously. "If he played a musical instrument," said Lucy Revere, "it'd be the monotone."

His syllabus recommended no reading. After the second session of class Rimrose considered dropping the course. He did not require the mornings to follow—it was all, he thought, commonsense bullshit—but he returned day after day for the pleasure of sitting beside Lucy, who kept notes for him when his light failed. When Lucy's light failed too, she kept notes in the dark, squinting, struggling, contorting her face with such dedication and determination that Rimrose was moved as he had never been moved by anyone. It was all he could do to refrain from seizing her in the moment and covering her face with a thousand kisses of devotion.

Yet he had hardly spoken ten words to her. For many weeks they met only in class. He had no idea what she looked like standing up. When she was absent from class the hour was so unendurable to him that he departed in a state of alarm, fearing she would drop from his life like Angelica Vanenglenhoven.

They had been brought together by the alphabet. Suppose their names had not so nearly coincided. Would they have discovered each other nevertheless? Fate had assigned them their alphabetical places—they had not chosen their own names. Suppose someone had sat between them in the alphabetized row—would they have met nevertheless? Was existence free will or determined? Suppose one of them had enrolled for the course in autumn instead of spring?

Shortly before leaving *Sentinel* one morning for Marriage and the Family 424, Rimrose at his desk slit open an envelope from the office of the university president. It was a press release announcing with a brevity suggesting churlishness that the university, upon the basis of a "special study," and with the approval of the Board of Regents, "following a review of existing schedules, has elected to discontinue collection of the Student Annual Adjunct Assessment Fee."

Rimrose had expected no such news now or ever. It confused him, exhilarated him. This piece of paper in his hand was a trophy, an historical document, a message of victory, a conquest, a triumph. It belonged on the wall. His very breathing excited him. He regained himself.

He telephoned Polly Anne at OSE. She was not at her desk. He left her a message. He rolled his chair to his Underwood to write up the news. News today, editorial tomorrow. In his editorial he would not gloat. No, sir, not he, he'd do it his father's way, adopt the tone of the graceful winner. It was a long time coming after having been defeated. This proved that things happened, that virtue was rewarded.

He hadn't time to write the news. He'd go to class first. Damn it all, this *was* exciting. They had won, they had won, it proved democracy, it proved that *people* could win over monster bureaucracies.

He walked swiftly—he practically danced to class, his body bursting with triumph. *This* they had done at *Sentinel, this* they had made happen on their own little wobbling battered Underwoods. They had overturned injustice—not the world's bloodiest injustice, to be sure, but injustice all the same; they'd taken money out of the pockets of crooks and put it back into the pockets of regular modest moderate hardworking people. His father! Instead of going to class he'd telephone his father. This news proved the value of the press, the value of writing. It made journalism seem more worthwhile, more practical in the way of doing good. He would say to his rejoicing father, "Dad, I'm coming home to the paper."

In his own life his imagination had often been moved by the written word, and in the same way, simply by the power of his own writing, he had now moved other people to action. This man or boy was powerful. He could pound his chest like Tarzan. This boy wrote strong stuff. This boy moved people.

But he did not phone his father. He continued on his way to

class. Down the path he walked to Chapel Arts, knowing his
success, his power, his confidence, when he spied at the doorway of this building once devoted to God, now to Marriage
and the Family 424, his alphabetical partner Lucy Revere. She
was undecided whether to enter the building. She said afterward that if Rimrose had not appeared that day she'd never
have gone back. But he *did* appear, and he *did* seize her, not
to her absolute surprise, and he *did* cover her face with kisses,
not with a thousand but with two unexpected kisses arising
from his new confidence, two sudden kisses making his feel-
ings known, and he said, "You and I should get married," and
she replied, "Are we ready?"

As a graduation gift his loving, affectionate father presented
Rimrose with a lifetime subscription to the Zygmont *Herald.*
Joke. However, joke or not, that first-rate newspaper thereafter
came to Rimrose six times a week.

His mother presented him with a new Underwood. The first
words he wrote on it were his thank-you note to her. "I thank
you for this here machine. I now have two Underwoods and
no money."

Father and mother came down for graduation. They stayed
two nights at the University Sheraton Ramada. They took
Rimrose and Lucy to dinner one night at the elegant Hotel
Barcelona. When father heard that Lucy was from White City,
he said, "You've got a great paper there, your *Citizen-Vigilant.*" Rimrose reminded his father that the *Citizen-Vigilant*
had *crucified* him in the matter of the women archers. "Still a
great paper," his father said. Lucy had never dined so expen-
sively. The prices on the menu staggered her. She wasn't sure
she should eat.

Rimrose, in the language of the graduation ceremony, "presented himself to the faculty for the purpose of knowing its
decision whether to award him his degree." The ceremony

was tedious, sometimes ludicrous, sometimes moving. His mother criticized the orators for the banality of their language.

Father, mother, and Rimrose strolled on campus. He showed his parents exactly the spot in front of Chapel Arts where he had proposed marriage to Lucy. Father said, "Erect a monument, I'll make a speech."

Father and mother stopped at Westby Hall for a last goodbye on their way out of town. Rimrose asked his father whether he remembered carrying the footlocker into Westby the day they had come down from Zygmont. "That's what I remember about that day," Rimrose said. "I don't know why, but I do. In fact I wrote a story about that footlocker. I sent it to you."

"I don't remember it," his father said.

"It was a green footlocker," Rimrose said. "It cost four dollars or something like that."

"I remember the footlocker," his father said. "I don't remember the story."

"You read that story," mother said.

"All right, I read it but I don't remember it. I don't remember every story."

"Even when your son writes it?"

"Even when anybody writes it."

"Don't feel bad," said Rimrose's mother to her son. "Lots of people don't read stories. It's the way of the world."

"I remember other things," said father. "I was afraid this place was going to be just another playland, you'd take up crazy ideas and drinking, you'd race around in cars. It wasn't going to do you any good."

"He's going to be one of the great writers that never drank," his mother said hopefully.

"I'm hoping you'll come home to the paper," father said in a forlorn way. "Do you suppose you might? I suppose not. I have the feeling that your mind is made up to do something else. I don't know what. Of course we'll get along. We mustn't press you. You've got the right to do what you see fit."

"I'll know more soon," said his son.

"I wish you knew more now." Father started the motor. "None of them ever had the talent for the paper," father said, as if he were talking alone to mother. "This is the kid that could write. From the day his fingers were big enough to work the machine, he began banging away on it."

"He's writing," mother said.

"Stories," father said.

"He'll make his mind up," mother said.

"He could write for the paper all day and turn out those little fiction stories at night," father said. "Many of the guys in the shop write their stories at night."

"I never knew one," mother said.

In the morning, in Westby Second East, resting on his bare mattress in the sun-flooded room they were about to vacate forever, Herndon addressed his roommate Rimrose. "All right, I know you always worried about me laying in this fuckin' bed four years sleeping the whole time, and I never intellectually grasped shit out of a book while you were a fuckin' bolshevik revolutionary running around changing everything. But now on the day after graduation *you're* the one that's fuckin' worried what you're going to do in life, you're out of your mind with suffering and anxiety worrying if you're ever going to be somebody, whereas for me—" and he reached up from his mattress to shake Rimrose's hand—"I hope you're going to be whatever you want, buddy, and goodbye forever," he said, and he lay back for one final short nap before departure.

2

ONE of Rimrose's first published stories was "Listing House," for which the optimistic or deluded editor of Hearth and Home paid him $33 for first sale in conformance to the following formula: for a second sale to Hearth and Home he was to receive $66, for a third sale $132, and so forth, until for his tenth sale he was to receive $16,896, a fortune exceeding the assets of the magazine. Heaven! However, Rimrose never sold a second story to Hearth and Home nor did he ever receive from anyone else for anything he ever wrote any sum anywhere near $16,896.

Rimrose had not seen a copy of Hearth and Home until the day it arrived in the mail announcing "Listing House." By then he had more or less forgotten the story, which he now read standing just inside the doorway of Listing House itself. He tried to read it as if it were not his own. He liked it. Damn good story. The action came back to him as he read. It was funny and snappy and quick, moving along in a well-paced dramatic fashion. And yet it was hardly his own any more. He saw many of its flaws. He had done things in this story he would no longer do.

Only after he had reread the story did he register in his mind the unusual idea that the story he had just read standing by the door had been written a few feet away, right here in this house, this listing house, this odd peculiar sprawling unfinished house for which he and Lucy were gaining affection. To begin with, they had called their house Listing House be-

cause that was what the fast-talking man from the rental company called it—a house *listed* for rent was a listing house.
Clear enough. But Lucy and Rimrose soon applied a second
meaning of the word—the listed house was *listing.* It was falling over. It was cockeyed. This house needed their support.

Its listing gave it its distinction. Straight up and down it
would have been just an ordinary house. Who would have
looked twice at the Leaning Tower of Pisa if it hadn't been
leaning?

The rental agent was Norton Tree. He reappears as a figure
of fiction several times over the years in stories by Rimrose—
as Norbert Trunk, Norville Branch, Norwood Leaf, Norio Eda-
matsu, Norfolk Bark—always the hurrying commercial fellow
deeply denying the defects of his products. Mr. Tree denied
that the house listed. In court he would have sworn that the
plaintiff tenants had *caused* it to list. In Listing House in the
beginning the bathroom had no door. "People don't go in for
bathroom doors anymore," said Mr. Tree. When Rimrose complained to him of the failure of the furnace, Mr. Tree said,
"The winters are becoming mild, people don't go in for heat
in the winter anymore."

Young Rimrose was so busy you'd hardly have thought he had
time to make babies. But he did. He worked it in. Lucy and
Rimrose named their babies, in the order of their appearance,
for planets, beginning with Eartha.

Rimrose worked extraordinarily hard to make his writing
skillful, graceful, musical, and at the same time tell an important story about men, women, children and animals of character. His nose for news had become his nose for drama, for
people's perplexities, predicaments, scandals and heroism.
He told meaningful stories and told them well. He tried to be
a good critic of his own work. He had to admit that a few of
his stories were superb or exceptional. Of course, in the long

run every story was both somebody's favorite and somebody else's idea of disaster.

He could never write a bad sentence. That is to say, he never permitted a bad sentence to leave the house. If he wrote a bad sentence Lucy admonished him for cheating, and he took back his sentence and polished it. He felt himself to be a master workman, master carpenter, master architect and sweating day laborer, building sheltering structures known as stories. He loved to shape each part to make the whole resound.

Perhaps one of the first of his finer stories was "The Rat-Lover," in which a "recently pregnant recent college graduate living with her gallant husband in a little house on a little budget" finds herself unable to resist rescuing animals. (Sounds like Lucy.) She has a magic touch with animals. An animal within the range of her influence becomes peaceable, casts off traits of aggression and loves its enemies. The young woman, however, becomes unpopular in her neighborhood. People complain about her. People summon the police, the police summon the Health Department, and the Health Department summons the rat-catcher, who by the contagion of love falls in love with the rats—not only with white rats, for anyone can fall in love with a white rat, but with the gray and black rats of the sewers, supposed enemies of mankind.

Some scholarly commentators have hastily compared that story to "When In Doubt I Take Them In," in which a forlorn woman, projecting her own lonesome state, tumbles into the conviction that every animal walking the street is lost. She earns a reputation as the savior of animals not requiring saving. This story is often overinterpreted in the interest of one or another theological theory, but in truth it is only a sympathetic story about a lonesome person closely observed—probably the Rimroses' neighbor Millie Fishback, across the street from Listing House.

Rimrose's storywriting had begun with college settings, but after a while he turned to stories of childhood in a town not unlike Zygmont but sharing many features of White City and drawn from Lucy's accounts of a girl's life in that place. From the period of childhood he advanced to his Listing House stories of early marriage, and beyond Listing House to that series of interesting tales eventually gathered as *Mobilized Automobile Stories.* These automobile stories don't necessarily *feature* automobiles, but in every story at least one automobile appears, and on one occasion (in "On the Gas Line") 2,202 vehicles appear "all in a petrified row," as readers will recall.

The magazine world beyond Listing House was Lucy's domain. Magazines gave birth to themselves and lived long or died young. The magazine world was amazing. Lucy marveled how this strange business went. She had come upon Hearth and Home in the Periodicals Room of the university library, where she regularly went for exactly the purpose of understanding who was who in the universe of magazines. She made a brilliant study of it. Soon she knew more about magazines than anyone alive from a specialized point of view: where she could sell her husband's latest story. The country was alive in those days with many magazines publishing short fiction, often of good quality, and Lucy soon made the acquaintance of them all, writing detailed memoranda to herself about the tastes of their editors and recording their names and addresses.

It never occurred to Lucy to suggest to Rimrose that he write a story directly intended for one magazine or another. That was not his way. On the contrary, he wrote the story and Lucy found the magazine to suit it. She read stories by the thousands in magazines in the library, and when Rimrose completed each new story she knew where to send it. This was an art in itself—to match each story with its market. Into the mail it went.

In the early days of their career Lucy thought Rimrose

worked too hard, too fast, too confidently, on too many stories at once, smoked too many cigarettes and drank too much coffee. She said he wrote faster than she could read. He pounded and pounded on "mother's Underwood," as in moments of irritation she called it, and he never ceased his day's work until he had made a suitable number of "discoveries." Household time was measured by discoveries. "Time to go," said Lucy, who was chauffeur. "Just one more discovery," Rimrose begged. How long was a discovery? One never knew. Sometimes a discovery happened right away. Sometimes a discovery came to him in the night.

Lucy made many suggestions, spied new directions, solutions, conceptions, implications, moral dimensions Rimrose may have overlooked, ways of resolving the actions of stories. Her head burst with so many things at once, so many people, so many scenes, so many complicated plots to keep track of, so many connecting details that people sometimes wondered if now and again she had actually written some of her husband's stuff. "And how about you, Lucy, do you also write?" Oh, how tired she was of hearing that question! She replied, "One chauffeur in the family is enough." Lucy never wrote a word and was determined never to try. She vowed that no matter how long she lived she would never write a story.

At a grand family gathering of Reveres and Rimroses in White City one cold Easter season, Rimrose, having drunk two good hot whiskey toddies, toasted Lucy's mother and father, expressing his gratitude to them for having created her for him. He toasted his mother for having taught him to love stories. He toasted his father for having given him the confidence to write with the speed of light. He toasted Lucy for everything else, and Lucy replied, "But I couldn't have done it without you, Rim."

For many weeks Rimrose worked hard on a story about his college roommate Delbert Herndon. Then the story collapsed, defying every strategy of its hopeful author, refusing to continue.

The author took to the air. With Lucy, their daughter Eartha, and the baby Marco in his perambulator, Rimrose on a wind-blown Sunday afternoon strolled the university campus. He could not recall when he had last been here. He and Lucy were awed to notice, too, how in so few years the names of certain old university friends and acquaintances had slipped their minds. They struggled to recall the name of even such a crucial figure of their past as Professor Markell, in whose Marriage and the Family 424 the alphabet had brought them together. As they strolled with Eartha and Marco past Chapel Arts, the wind blew the professor's name back into their heads.

And at a moment's pausing in front of Westby Hall, Rimrose's stalled story about Herndon completed itself in his brain. He had for a long time had a title for it—"Playing Sports While Soundly Sleeping"—but until today he had never been able to round out the action. Now at last it was done in his mind, and after he had conveyed it from mind to paper he sent forth his narrative with these admired sentences for openers:

> The marvelous athlete Hurlburt Drinnon steadfastly maintained that the first rule of success was to perfect one's program of sleep. "Get yourself sideways for a real good night's sleep twice every day," he said, "and an afternoon nap."

Friends of literature, often innocent of commerce, have found it hard to believe that so fine a story as "Playing Sports While Soundly Sleeping" was a hard sell. Lucy had known it would be a hard sell—its complexity lay in its seeming simplicity. But she was determined to sell it hard or easy, simple or complex.

She sent it first to the best-paying magazines, and from there it worked its way down, or fell down, or stumbled down, or slid down from high-paying markets to low-paying markets. She spent more money in postage than hope could repay. Postage was already ten cents the first ounce and the greedy U.S. Postal Service was threatening to raise it.

Editors too were an obstacle, unspeakable brutes putrefying her husband's stories with their nosepick and their coffee spill, disgusting creatures, she hated them all for their filthy habits and their weak minds. Some editors complained that "Playing Sports While Soundly Sleeping" was "unclear." "This baffles me," an editor scribbled in his demented hand. One editor wrote, "Looks like to me that the footballer Drinnon kicked himself in the head." And from another maniac, "I find this too incremental."

Although the story was delicately and intricately plotted, one hurried editor wrote, "You must tell stories with stronger plots if you want to sell me. I am in business to give my readers plots." On the other hand a weak-minded editor dared to say, "I heard Rimrose was a great plotter, but there are too many plots in here. They confuse the reader."

No matter how critically severe those editors were, Lucy knew this story was superb. The idea was to get it into the light for the world to see. Whenever it came home she sent it right out again. Damn the postal cost. Damn the editorial ignorance. Rimrose's rejected story pained her eyes.

More than once "Playing Sports While Soundly Sleeping" came home too spotted and stained to go out again unrenewed. Lucy retyped dirty pages. From Rimrose's point of view this insult to Lucy was the most painful aspect of a hopeless process. Editors ought to respect Lucy. Editors were at liberty to reject manuscripts *Rimrose* had typed—that was the way of the business—but when editors insulted Lucy by rejecting a manuscript she had repaired with her own slender fingers, Rimrose's sinking heart filled with anger. He said to her one day, "Lucy, my good old pal, slave and partner, why don't you give it up—this story is a loser," but she refused to give up. "No story of yours is a loser," she said.

At such times of his life Rimrose saw himself quitting the business of storywriting. He'd go home to Zygmont and work for his father at the *Herald,* writing little news stories all day long, turning off his mind every evening at quitting time.

Then Lucy won the battle. After she had sent "Playing Sports While Soundly Sleeping" all over creation she began again, still convinced that some editor out there, wide awake on a Monday morning, would see that this was a story whose time had arrived. Whereupon on a Monday morning the fiction editor of Esquire magazine purchased it in a frenzy of deadline excitement by telephone. Nobody at Esquire mentioned having rejected it before, and Lucy respected their silence. The editor said, "Everybody laughed and cried all the way through. We love it."

The editor was under the impression he was talking to Rimrose's agent. Was $1,500 a right price? Send the check where? Lucy asked for $5,000. She'd have settled for $500. It had been around. The fucking postage alone . . . In her heart she had given up on it. The editor said, "We want to put Rimrose's name on the cover." He rose to $2,500 and Lucy took it.

How odd it was that Rimrose had never been able to complete a Kakapick story. He thought often about Kakapick. Of all the people he had known at the university, Kakapick was the most memorable for the reason of his having been the most— well, the most this and the most that, the most frightening (to Lucy), the most ludicrous (to Rimrose) with his plan for reducing all literature to a few "titles," the most dishonest (for he had stolen more books than anyone else), the most intolerant of every opinion except his own.

To these details Lucy contributed charges of her own drawn from memories she had over time shared with her husband. "The man with the foulest breath," she said, who had herself been breathed upon by several college men and knew the territory, "the man with the dampest hands, the man with the blackest teeth," for at the time of her courtship with Rimrose she had now and then felt Kakapick drawing close to her, his moist hand upon her, his sour breath in her face. Sometimes he rubbed against her, grazing her hip with his hand, leering, breathing on her through his dirty teeth. "He was truly nobody I enjoyed," she told Rimrose at last. "He wasn't the part of college I like to remember."

Now, for a while, Kakapick had been gone from their lives. Then Lucy encountered him one afternoon at the gasoline station. When Lucy drove up he drove up beside her. He said, "Hello, Marigold," greeting her through his open window by the name of the girl in the story—Marigold the Naked. Lucy replied, smiling unsuccessfully, "I'm Lucy, do you remember? How have you been?" He did not reply to her. He remained behind his wheel. She thought he had not heard her, and she asked him again, "How have you been?" but still he did not reply. When she drove from the station he followed her. She felt alarm stir within her. But somewhere along Mile Wide Avenue he dropped away.

In recent weeks he had again appeared several times out of nowhere, out of the air, out of the shadows, out of a doorway, around a corner, at night outside the library. Sometimes he seemed to see her, sometimes not.

Lucy felt that he was *stalking* her. It was the only word she could find to describe her sensation of threat. So it *felt,* she said at first, so she *knew,* she said finally. He was increasingly present in her path. She began to fear walking alone. Once as she emerged from Genuine Foods she saw him standing beside her car in the lot. She reentered the market and phoned the police. When the police arrived Kakapick was gone.

Lucy was pregnant with Vanessa when Kakapick appeared one night like a ghost out of the mist in the dim pedestrian tunnel north of the library. He called to her. "Where are you going, Marigold?" His voice bounced from the walls of the tunnel. Something terrible was about to happen. Then she thought *But it needn't,* and she dropped her books and ran back as fast as she could to the library.

Rimrose came for her by Yellow Cab, Eartha on the seat beside him, Marco in his arms. A young policeman from Campus Security also arrived. He looked thirteen, perhaps eleven. He asked her, "Who saw you in the tunnel?" Nobody had seen them in the tunnel. To the young policeman, then, it was not real.

To Lucy it was real and distressing, affecting her heart, which palpitated wildly for a week, and her head, which ached. In sleep she ground her teeth.

Rimrose asked the University City police if he might perhaps discuss the matter with someone a bit more experienced than the people at Campus Security. Detective Tharp came to Listing House to listen to Lucy's account, but he was not truly helpful. He asked her several questions, and he admired Eartha's lizards. "Lizards are man's best friend," he said. Lucy's complaint would be investigated, he assured her. Stalking, he said, was only one of many bad crimes in a college town. "If it *was* stalking in the first place," he added. "How sure can you really be that this creep in the tunnel is the same creep you're thinking about?"

"He called me Marigold," she said.

"That's not your name," the detective said.

"My name is Lucy," Lucy said.

"Then he didn't know you. I thought you said he knew you."

"He likes to call me Marigold. It's the name of a girl in a story by my husband. She's—"

"What?"

"She's often naked," Lucy shyly said.

When Detective Tharp left Listing House he said, "Sit tight." Weeks later he returned to tell Lucy and Rimrose that "we"—by whom he meant himself—had interrogated, naming no names, "this Kakapick," who was at a loss to explain why anyone should say she had seen him in the library tunnel on the night in question.

This Kakapick said he never used the library tunnel. Detective Tharp had found him a persuasive and honest fellow, he said. "This Kakapick is credible," he said. He had himself begun to believe, as the younger policeman had believed, that the event may have been unreal, it may never have happened, that Mrs. Rimrose had not experienced the incident she appeared to believe she had experienced; she was, after all, pregnant at the time. "Isn't that true?" he asked.

True but irrelevant, Rimrose replied. His wife knew reality if anyone did—"She's the perfect student of reality," he said.

"I don't hallucinate when I'm pregnant," said Lucy, "the thing that happened happened just exactly as I told you, he scared me horribly."

Rimrose perceived that at this point in their account Lucy and he had lost credibility in the mind of Detective Tharp, who suffered serious doubts about a man who "sat home with the babies" at night writing stories about naked girls while his wife "paraded the streets," as he put it. And why the Yellow Cab? Detective Tharp, astonished to hear that Rimrose did not drive a car, scolded him lightly, saying, "If you got out and drove a car yourself, this kind of a thing would never happen."

It had gradually become Rimrose's practice when reality defied him to confront the matter roundabout in fiction, take it by surprise and subdue it. He began to write a Kakapick story. He called it "The Tread of the Stalker."

Almost from the beginning of the story Rimrose suspected it would fail. He began. He moved along in it as if it stood a chance. Sure, why not? This story was being difficult. Yet it was fighting for its life. He cheered it on.

He had intended to write a high-minded story, but what he was getting was melodrama. Maybe he was following Lucy's actual experience too closely. Maybe he should set the story at a distance, locate it at a college far away, say northern North Dakota.

> Here one night in the library at Northern North Dakota State sat a young man familiar to the librarians of the place as one who could serve them, if they required his authority, as the perfect guide to a category of books of demented violent sexual fiction, for those were the books he read and no others. The jacket of the book he held before him illustrated in a symbolic manner an action familiar to readers of the genre: a man, a knife, a side of flesh, a crimson . . .

Lucy would find a home for this story in one of those high-paying brutality magazines on the supermarket stands. In a sketchy, disorganized way Rimrose completed a version of "The Tread of the Stalker." He was cautiously pleased with his scattered text. He said to Lucy, "Maybe I've got something going now."

"It's been sounding so," she said. She loved the smash and clatter of his busy machines. Out of his Underwoods came stories to sell.

"If the machine keeps going something's got to be happening," he said. Any moment this story might come alive. The moment of a story's birth was like the moment of human conception. One did not know right away how successful one had been.

To be truthful, however, he knew that this story was failing. "Maybe I shouldn't really be writing this story," he said. "It's your story," he said. It had begun with her experience, but her experience was not yet his. Maybe someday it would become his. Maybe he should allow the story to ripen further.

One morning he wrote only seven words: "He followed her. He had his knife." Oh, God, nothing could have been less convincing. That didn't sound like Rimrose. "That ain't me," said Rimrose to himself. The stalker's knife was getting in

Rimrose's way. Rimrose had never chosen in his stories to settle matters with weapons. The world had enough weapons.

Make him a harmless stalker, he thought, *maybe just a loud breather.* Rimrose was unable to understand what his stalker was up to. Well, the way to find out was to write forward, find out by surprise. If the writer was surprised the reader too would be surprised. "No tears in the writer, no tears in the reader," wrote Robert Frost.

But Rimrose was unable to ignite surprise in his stalker. He could not get his stalker moving. The fellow was stuck and nameless, a do-nothing stalker. He simply followed women, by his closeness frightened them, experienced some sort of thrill Rimrose had a hard time imagining. Rimrose himself had never enjoyed the thrill of scaring people—he never joined his brothers and sisters at jumping out from behind trees.

All right, back to the library scene. It is night. She is walking from the library. The stalker keeps a distance from her, but not so great a distance that she cannot hear his heels on the pavement. At the corner she stops. "The stalking man, too, stopped. She knew—"

What she knew we will never know. Rimrose did not know what she knew. He was stymied. He thought to send the frightened woman running into the street.

"She runs into the street."

No, thought Rimrose, *back where you were. Retreat.*

"She retreated to the sidewalk."

Rimrose changed his mind. "She changed her mind. She stepped off the sidewalk into the street . . ." but that was as far as she got, because that was as far as Rimrose ever wrote— one foot on the curb, one foot in the street, that was where she remained indecisive forever in the night.

In the end he had a title but no story. Kakapick had failed in the role. The Kakapick memorable to Rimrose was no stalker. Kakapick was only a futile suffering college boy, tormented but not violent, pitiful rather than sinister. Confronted with the difficulty of imagining Kakapick as he had never known him, Rimrose lost him. Kakapick was incapable of stalking Lucy, or so he seemed to Rimrose at this moment, a figure of Lucy's imagination, an illusion in a tunnel on a misty night.

3

WHEN Kakapick settled into a chair in his dentist's waiting-room, he recited to himself his prayer, his mantra, his litany of the years with which he had begun to liberate himself from the defect that was his life:

> *Practice smiling, practice speaking.*
> *Practice smiling and speaking at the same time.*
> *Smile and speak to the mirror—*

But here he was interrupted. His eye caught this *Sentinel* headline:

FORMER SENTINEL EDITOR CRASHES ESQUIRE
MAGAZINE WITH OLD-TIME CAMPUS TALE

Kakapick saw Rimrose's name. His heart froze and his eye sped down the page. "This story could just as well be entitled 'Westby Second East,'" the *Sentinel* reporter wrote. Kakapick flung down the newspaper, not in anger but in fear. He could not bring himself to read the article.

Instead of reading it, he imagined it. He also imagined Rimrose's story in Esquire. He imagined himself as the subject of the story, flailed, abused, and exposed in a "campus tale," humiliated before the world. He wished he were dead.

He had known this would happen, and he wished at this point that he could live his life over again in a better way. The time had come for reckoning. Kakapick was now about to pay for his evil thoughts and all the disaster he had wished upon the world. He knew he had been a contemptible person. The ghosts of Westby Hall were haunting him. Rimrose was calling him to account for every rotten deed. He knew he should have been kinder to people, should have permitted people to grow closer to him, should never have been so aloof and superior, should have shaken people's hands agreeably. Now a morbid revenge was coming down upon him, and he would deserve whatever he got.

Kakapick retrieved the newspaper he had thrown down. He learned from the article in *Sentinel* that the new "campus tale" focused upon one of the football players, apparently Herndon, Rimrose's roommate. When Kakapick thought of Herndon he remembered the immense force with which Herndon one night had hurled him through the doorway into the hall. Herndon was a stupid ass. They were all stupid asses. But Kakapick might have lived better with their stupidity. He should have been Rimrose's roommate. Kakapick had offered but Rimrose had declined. The athletes shunned him, excluded him, avoided him, called him *pig-fucker,* called him *jock-sniffer,* that was the kind of thing that came from Herndon. Now the world would know the names the athletes had reserved for Kakapick. It would all come out.

Long ago Rimrose's article in *Sentinel* had revealed him as a book thief. What would Rimrose reveal about him now in Esquire? The dentist's receptionist called his name. The torture of dentistry was to be compounded by the torture of exposure. Kakapick dashed from the dentist's office, his overcoat flying behind him. The day was cold.

He hurried to Polly Anne at the Office of Savings and Economy. She would admonish him for running in the cold in an unbuttoned coat. At the front desk he asked for her. He was told she was out. At the OSE everybody was always said to be out of the office. He knew she knew he was there, and in a moment she came forward and took his hand not in a handshake but in private affection, and they returned to her office.

They kissed. They were good friends. They embraced. Kakapick trembled in her embrace, and she said, "You're so excited. I excite you," and he said no, it wasn't she—she excited him, yes, of course she did, she knew she did—but his trembling of the moment arose from a certain agitation, from news about Rimrose in *Sentinel.* Had she read it?

Of course she'd read it. The first thing she read every morning of her life was *Sentinel*—No, had she read Rimrose's title in Esquire?—that was what he meant.

Not yet. "Pick me up a copy, I'll read it tonight," she said. She complained of her health. She was ill today. "I have a rash all over my body," she said.

But she often claimed a rash all over her body. Kakapick had never seen a trace of it. "You look perfectly well," he said. "You look marvelous."

"I don't know how well well is," she said, rereading the article in *Sentinel.* "This doesn't tell me much about the story. What in the world are you afraid of his telling? What's he going to tell about you?"

"He'll tell how the jocks made a fool of me in Westby. He'll murder me."

"Rimrose doesn't murder people," she said. "Murdering is in your head."

"I have a bad feeling about him. Do you remember he wrote an article about me in *Sentinel?* It got me in big trouble."

"The article didn't get you in trouble. The photograph got you in trouble. He didn't steal the fucking books, *you* stole the fucking books. I thought this was your dental day."

"That's where I read it."

"What's that?"

"The article."

"In *Sentinel?* You drive me wild. Go read the fucking *story,*" she said. "You're having a nervous breakdown over a story you haven't even read."

He echoed her. "Read the story," he said, as if that were the strangest sort of suggestion. Kakapick was unaccustomed to stories. It was a word he hardly used—what the world called stories he called "titles." He read *about* stories in reviews, articles, essays, commentaries, columns of opinion, theses and dissertations and excerpts and reductions, but reading a story on his own without coaching and clues was nothing he was up to. It was almost a new idea. His mind was not made for stories. He would not know what to think about a story if he read it.

"You may not enjoy my saying so," she said, "but I'd guess Rimrose very seldom gives you a thought."

"No, he thinks about me."

"What makes you think so?"

"Because I think a lot about him."

"That's your error," she said. "It's your trouble. It's going to be your undoing, you make a lot of mistakes thinking people are thinking about you when they're not."

"You think a lot about him, too," he said.

"He was a lovely boy," she said, "but I don't deceive myself that he's thinking about me."

"I doubt that very many people ever refer to me as a lovely boy," Kakapick said.

She kissed him again. "Button up your coat."

Kakapick hurried through the cold to the university bookstore. In this bookstore Rimrose and his father had bought the boy's textbooks on the day they had driven down from Zygmont. Now the boy's name was on the cover of Esquire. When Kakapick saw Rimrose's name he burst out aloud beside the magazine rack, "I know him, I know him." Then he thought, "This bastard, this fucking Rimrose."

He opened the magazine. Oh my God, read this. Unbearable. He had turned to the popular department, Backstage with Esquire. *Don't read it, turn the page,* but his eye caught Rimrose's name. It was more than he could endure.

If it still depresses you to think that nobody writes great short stories anymore, Rimrose lifts you up out of your depression.

He's nobody special, any more than Hemingway, Fitzgerald, Dos Passos were special. There's no difference between them and you except that they have all written stories for Esquire and the American canon. Be happy. If you can't write stories you can read them. Rimrose shares the taste of life with you. He lets you in on people in the midst of private struggle wherever he observes them. Here's Rimrose observing an old friend sleeping. It may have been someone he knew. In college he roomed with a football player whose name we all saw in the headlines a decade ago. The story is "Playing Sports While Soundly Sleeping." Turn to it on page 60.

Hemingway, Dos Passos, Fitzgerald, Rimrose, this could not be. Rimrose famous! The works of Rimrose taught in the universities with Hemingway, Fitzgerald, Dos Passos! But Rimrose was nobody. He was a fucking hick from Zygmont. He had lived down the hall in Westby Second East. Anybody could see him any day, coming and going, he had been to Kakapick's room and Kakapick to his, they had dined together with the woman they shared. *I personally know this fucking bastard,* Kakapick thought.

He began to read. He truly tried. "The marvelous athlete Hurlburt Drinnon steadfastly maintained that the first rule of success was—" But the language of fiction was not for Kakapick. Only the language of facts could serve him. Was this a good title? He was too distracted to read it. If only he had known how to rate it in the line-up of world literature, he would have read it through. But strange, new, untested, unevaluated writing enraged him.

He closed the magazine. He reconsidered the cover. It was a nearly nude woman holding in each hand a container of yogurt. Kakapick rubbed a finger hard across Rimrose's name. He could not erase it. It was there forever. Even so, as real as it was, he could not believe it. This could not be the Rimrose he had known. This was only Rimrose who had run down the halls of Westby Second East with a towel about his middle.

He was nobody. He edited the stinking *Sentinel.* He came from Zygmont, he married a cockteaser from White City. He was only an ordinary fellow.

To whom could Kakapick complain of these injustices? His heart was heavy with his powerlessness. If only he could write he could make the record clear. He could rescue truth from shambles. Would Rimrose become famous? Kakapick felt excluded. He thought again, *I know him. I knew him. For four years I lived down the hall from him. He was in my room. He knows my name. He once wrote an article about me. We shared the same woman.*

Again he opened the magazine, and again he began to read the story. It excited him, and he trembled, as he had trembled in Polly Anne's arms a little while ago—that is to say, the *appearance* of the story excited him. Not many people any-where could pick up a distinguished magazine and find in it a story by someone they knew, touched, talked with, sat with, dined with. Rimrose's distinction was Kakapick's distinction. For a moment this excited him. He would strive for pride and generosity. He knew that his resentment of Rimrose weakened him. He would try to conquer his own mean spirit even as he had triumphed over the tragedy of his teeth. And yet, think of it, Rimrose from Zygmont! The hick. How unspeakable it was. How Kakapick hated him!

He bought five copies of Esquire, saying to the clerk at the counter, "A friend of mine has a title in here." In the cold, hastening across the campus, he reread the opening para-graphs, but again he stopped. He believed he stopped because the stinging cold caused his eyes to tear—he would read the story later. In fact, however, he never again read a word of "Playing Sports While Soundly Sleeping," although in time he would present himself as the expert interpreter of the au-thor. The only Rimrose story he had ever read was "Getting to Class Regularly on Time"—the Marigold story.

A new idea came to him. He had a plan to present to Rim-rose. He would go to see him. Did Rimrose still live in University City? From time to time Kakapick had heard so, but now, with a story in Esquire, he might be living in ease and celebrity in New York, Paris. Rimrose must live somewhere, but Kakapick did not know where, nor in his frenzy or panic could he think how to find out. Kakapick with his copies of Esquire walked faster and faster across the campus. The faster he walked the better his idea. Polly Anne would know. There were many things she did not know but very few she could not find out. She loved to find things out, it was her trade, her specialty.

At OSE he gave her one copy of Esquire. She viewed the cover. "Boobs on that one," she said.

"I'm going to go see Rimrose," Kakapick said. "I have an idea. Where does he live, do you know? Isn't there some way you can track him down?"

"No problem," she said, copying Rimrose's address for Kakapick from the University City phone book.

That afternoon Kakapick stood before Rimrose with hand extended. When Rimrose took his hand Kakapick smiled the confident smile he had perfected after long hard work and practice. He had not been certain of being well received by Rimrose. Few people received him well.

> Practice smiling, practice speaking.
> Practice smiling and speaking at the same time.
> Smile and speak to the mirror,
> Smile and speak to your friends.
> Now boldly speak to strangers,
> Build confidence in your teeth daily.

Somewhere in the house behind him Rimrose heard the commotion of Lucy's gathering the children and fleeing out the back door. She did not intend to receive Kakapick well. She had last seen him in the pedestrian tunnel.

"It's amazing to see you," Rimrose said.

"I've wondered about you a lot," Kakapick said.

"I've wondered about myself," said Rimrose.

"I just read your title in Esquire," Kakapick said. "You're famous."

"I doubt it," Rimrose said, "but come in," and Kakapick stepped into the house. "Hey, listen, sit down, what can I get you—can I get you something?"

"That would be nice, yes, very nice," said Kakapick. "How is Marigold?"

"Lucy?" said Rimrose.

"Yes, Lucy I mean, your lovely wife from White City."

"She's very well, she's extraordinarily well, she had to run off somewhere." Lucy's flight from the house troubled him. From time to time he wandered over to the window. She had not taken the car. Therefore she had gone to a neighbor's. She had not taken the children's sweaters, either, and he worried about that. He guessed the neighbor as Millie Fishback.

Rimrose's cordiality exceeded his feeling. This was the man who had stalked Lucy in the tunnel. Yet Rimrose shared his luncheon sandwich with Kakapick, and half a leftover children's birthday cake. They drank coffee from silly university football mugs.

It appeared at first to Rimrose that Kakapick had come without purpose—"Just to say hello to my friend, the most famous student in the class." Whatever it was, Kakapick was taking ages getting to it. Rimrose felt a major headache coming on. In the tunnel too Kakapick had called her "Marigold." Rimrose never doubted under any circumstance that Lucy heard what she said she heard. He could hear it himself, "Marigold" reverberating against the walls of the underground tunnel. He restlessly said, "Well—" as if to ask, "Was there any reason in particular you dropped over?"

"Only to talk to you," Kakapick said. "You were the only person I could ever really talk to. You were the only person that ever really listened to me. You were a great listener. It was clear to me pretty early that people weren't going to listen to me. You were the only person at the university that was ever interested in my plan."

"Your plan for what? I'm not sure I remember."

"Why, the one you wrote the article about."

"I still don't remember. I remember your plan to unify the world with a booklist. That's the one I remember."

"That's the one."

"You were going to get everybody reading the same books all over the world. You were going to overturn centuries of tradition by passing around a list of required reading. You were drawing up the list—"

"I've abandoned that plan."

"I wasn't crazy about it myself," said Rimrose.

"Not everything succeeds."

"A lot of my stories don't succeed."

"I've had a number of plans, but now I've got a new one. This one's going to work."

"Let's hope so." Rimrose's head was splitting.

"I'm going to take the guesswork out of literary study," Kakapick continued.

"Oh, but the guessing's the fun," said Rimrose.

"I've got an evaluative procedure going," Kakapick said, "whereby we can find out statistically who's the best and who's the worst, whom people are reading and whom they're not reading, who really *matters* in literature and whom we can chuck out in the garbage."

"Chucking people into the garbage, are we?" Rimrose said.

"I've got a lot of new wrinkles. I'm still working on it. I'm instituting a point system for literary evaluation. A writer gets so many points for this and that, one thing and another. Consider yourself. I've made a number of test runs on you. You've been accumulating points for titles one place and another. You've got a lot of points already. But now comes a very big one, this is gigantic, this title this morning in Esquire. That's a big score, a famous longtime class-A magazine like that, they published Hemingway and Fitzgerald and Dos Passos, it shoots you up in the numbers like a rocket. I'm rating publications class-A, class-B and down the line. Magazines. Journals. You're reprinted in anthologies. You win a prize. Prizes are the best indicators going. I give points for a prize. Lots of them. Critical mention, an article about a writer by a critic. Critics score a lot of points for writers, a title about a writer, or a writer is the subject of a biography, or even a partial subject, depending on how many times a writer is indexed, even just a passing mention counts for something. Suppose, for example, you're mentioned in a television broadcast, or somebody mentions your name in a Broadway play, those are visibility points. But all these things took time. I'll tell you why."

"That's all right, don't bother, I don't want to know too much all at once," said Rimrose.

"I was years in the dentist's chair. But it was worth every minute of it," said Kakapick. "I got myself going at last by improving my appearance. Maybe you've noticed how different I look." He smiled to exhibit his teeth. Kakapick's teeth were no longer black but white. "My dentist is the most important person in my life."

"You're friendlier, you're more open, you've got more confidence. I congratulate you."

"See, that's just like you, that's what I could never do—I could never praise people. I can bring myself to praise somebody if I want something from him—that much I've got the hang of. People were always telling me I needed a psychiatrist, but it turned out what I needed was a dentist. Years of intensity calcification did the trick. Prior to that the world was laughing at my teeth. But you were one of the few people that never *mentioned* them. Everybody in Westby Hall noticed my teeth. They were *black.* They're white now. This is not just some artificial quickie polish job. This is my key to a whole new life. My teeth are white now and I'm going places."

The winter day had darkened. Rimrose yearned to light

lamps and turn up the heat, but he had come to the end of his hospitality.

"You had millions of friends in college," Kakapick continued. "I used to stand down at the end of the hall and saw them coming and going from your room, your door was always opening and closing. You were you, you were popular." Kakapick was speaking now from the dark. "People got very close to one another, but I never really got close to anybody, and naturally I'd never let anybody get close to me."

"The first time I ever laid eyes on you, you refused to shake my hand."

"That was the old me."

"It put a fellow on guard."

"That's exactly what I'm talking about. That's how I was in those days. Not any more. Shake hands," Kakapick said, "I owe you one," springing from his chair and shaking Rimrose's hand. Kakapick's hand was damp, moist, as it had always been. "I'm sure you wish I were out of here. You'd probably like me to go. It might be getting late and I know you write at night."

"I write night and day," Rimrose said.

"But let me tell you why I'm here."

Rimrose waited.

"It'll be quick."

It was not quick. It was slow and painful for him to tell.

Kakapick's goal beyond graduation had been to remain on the university Health Plan long enough to complete his dental work. Unfortunately, he was ineligible for the Health Plan unless he was employed by the university. To gain the employment for which he was qualified, he was required to become a graduate student. To become a graduate student he required tuition money. He borrowed a sum of money from Polly Anne Cathcart.

They were friends. "More than friends. Very good friends," he said. "We're a mutual aid society. She has the key to my apartment and I have hers. We exchanged apartment keys instead of vows. We phone each other to make sure neither of us died in the night. I used to ask myself, 'If I drop dead in my apartment I wonder how long it'll be until anyone notices I'm missing.' " He was about to say something more, but he hesitated. Then he decided to say it after all. "She's the lover you and I shared," he boldly said.

Rimrose was taken aback. "Polly Anne? We were never lovers. We were close working friends. We ran *Sentinel*. But just for the record, we were never lovers."

"She said you were."

"You and I went through this once before."

"I don't remember."

"I remember. Years ago."

"You never slept with her?"

"I don't know why she'd say so."

Kakapick proceeded, shrugging, as if it made no difference anyhow. Maybe it didn't, though it seemed to make a difference to Rimrose.

During the autumn term of each school year Kakapick was "on loan, like equipment," to Literature. He worked for professors for whom he performed a variety of research tasks for long hours in the close airless recesses of the library. His wage was desperately low.

For the same desperate wage he taught overcrowded spring classes of First Year Readings to undergraduate students who had hoped, prayed and petitioned for the abolition of this Literature requirement. The department of Literature, however, intended never to abolish it. The program in First Year Readings was the department bonanza. Tenured professors rose to distinction by producing scholarship for which Kakapick freed them by doing their research in the autumn and their teaching in the spring. Large classes taught by poverty-level teachers paid for it all. The department prosperity was made possible by Kakapick and forty abject peers, transient, without suffrage, barred from appointment as ranked professors, lecturing to hundreds of students, poring over thousands of student writing assignments.

Rimrose, responding to Kakapick, viewed this as an injustice, a wrong way to do things. That was what he thought Kakapick was talking about—the injustice of the system—but Kakapick harbored no objection. Not at all. He viewed the ranked professors as deserving of their privileges. He neither resented them nor ever lent his own name or signature to any of the campus protests against this form of injustice. The professors were powerful and comfortable, as he hoped to be himself someday. Power and privilege were the scheme of the system in which he foresaw his own fine future.

His trademark was his lists of world-unifying titles by dead authors on three-by-five index cards he had shuffled and reshuffled over the years. If only everyone would read these titles—these books—the world would be unified. With the beginning of every semester Kakapick's mission sounded good to students, for they favored world unity, but as the days progressed they detected that Kakapick himself could scarcely clarify his own theory, that he seemed to admire *titles,* not books, and that at many moments he appeared to be ignorant of the contents of the very books he intended to compel the world to read.

Kakapick's so-called office was a desk in a room hardly larger than a closet, in the basement of Literature. His students often laid siege to his little office to protest what *they* conceived to be his bullying them, his high-handed way of doing things. They confronted him in unpleasant ways, charging him to explain himself, but he rightly claimed authority, threatening at times to punish them with low grades. He dreamed of their deaths and his own. And worse than death! He dreamed of his students rising, rebelling, fleeing *en masse* from his classroom, destroying his career. In his nightmares as in his daily life, his students laid siege to his office. All this he confessed to Rimrose in the darkening afternoon at Listing House.

But then, he added, his moment of turning arrived. One day in the university bookstore, where only this morning he'd found Rimrose in Esquire, he came across a lightweight volume called *Stories for Our American Time.* Jacketed in stars and stripes, it offered "stories and poems by men and women alive and around the corner." Kakapick saw how he might disengage himself from the misery of resentful students by abandoning his quest for the eighty-nine indispensable books of creation in favor of this simplistic anthology.

He took up in his classes a vision of the world reduced to the United States, the centuries reduced to the present. The subjects of these stories appealed readily to students—stories about automobiles, baseball, bathtubs, intercollegiate sex and seduction, blood, murder, cannibalism, other worlds, birth control, Iowa farms, Sunday church, fast foods, car repair, rape and drive-in movies.

Kakapick had placed himself in a state of reduced ambition. This was not the lofty stuff of world unification. The sight of the unknown names of these American storywriters stirred his resentment. No body of critical opinion had formed to clarify them or stand them in order. If he had not heard of them, nor read about them, how could he approach them with a show of superior knowledge?

There lay his challenge. Imagining himself in the place of students, he asked himself what information he wished he possessed. Students would appreciate knowing in advance which authors were best. They wished to know how to make judgments of authors. Students preferred certainty above vague world-unifying theories. They would love a method of author-evaluation leaving nothing to chance. Kakapick devised methods to defend himself against students' demands and inquiries.

These living, modern authors confronted Kakapick with the chaos of their abundance. He had no idea what he could possibly make of them, no idea how he could present them to his classes, no way of knowing whether they or their stories were good or bad, worthy or unworthy. He could not understand them. What were they trying to say to him? He knew of no method or formula enabling him to know their true value. Who among these authors were good and who were bad? "People want to know how authors can be evaluated," said Kakapick to Rimrose.

"I don't," said Rimrose. "What people?"

"How can we rank authors and put them in order so everybody can know at a glance who's good and who's better, best, who's worth reading, who really matters in literature as opposed to who can be chucked out in the garbage?"

"Once more chucking people in the garbage," said Rimrose.

"Fortunately I found a solution," Kakapick said. "The answer is statistics. You can evaluate writing by a statistical system."

"Not I," said Rimrose. "I can't."

"Anybody can," said Kakapick, "as soon as we get it perfected. With computers coming along it's going to be easier than ever." He confessed that some people might think of his statistical evaluation as less altruistic than his world-unification project, but he saw how he could live with it, make a life of it, become famous with it. "I'd as soon be famous for one thing as another," he said. "People are going to listen to me. Nobody's listening to me now, but that's going to change. This thing is going to work. I regret your headache," Kakapick said, "so I won't keep you."

"I've had this headache for a couple of hours," said Rimrose.

"I want to have famous friends like you."

"I'll be your friend," said Rimrose, "on one condition—if you let me go right this minute so I can find my family."

But Kakapick was unwilling to release Rimrose. "There's something I still need from you."

"I can't give you anything more today," said Rimrose. "I'm done in. My family is off somewhere and it's getting damn cold and dark in here."

"The only thing I need is this—these days I need people to write me letters of recommendation. I've been having a hard time getting people to write for me. I don't know why. When I ask people to write me letters they say 'Oh, but shit, Kakapick, I don't really know you very well.' These are people who've known me for years. But you know me. Don't you think you know me?"

"I do. I know you very well. I can't believe this at all. Is this all you've been wanting to get at? Write you a letter of reference?"

"It might be more than one letter. Aren't we friends?" said Kakapick.

"Of course we're friends," Rimrose replied, and having so forthrightly and in so hearty a voice cast himself in that role, he felt free to add in a rush, in the permissive spirit of friendship, "Hey, listen, I've got to find my family," and he struggled from his chair and seized Kakapick and led him to the door, not with the force with which Delbert Herndon at three o'clock one morning had hurled Kakapick through space, but firmly nevertheless. He walked with Kakapick to his car. When he turned back to the house, Lucy and the children were arriving home from Millie Fishback's.

For many months Rimrose received inquiries about Kakapick, who was seeking a position as teacher and scholar wherever someone would have him. To the first few inquiries Rimrose replied with individual letters, but soon it was obvious he'd need to prepare some sort of form letter masquerading as personal, typed fresh for each occasion on letterhead stationery. He perfected his all-purpose Kakapick reply. He expected that Lucy would help him type them—

"Lucy will help you type them my butt," said the former Lucy Revere. "Lucy doesn't type letters for a man that stalked her in the street." Nothing could shake her conviction that it was Kakapick who had stalked her. In the worst moments of her nights she awakened, grinding her teeth—he stalked her still. He wore a mask. She struggled against his rotten breath, his clammy hands, forcing his mask from his face to reveal her stalker, and he was always Kakapick. "He's evil," she said, and perhaps he was. Lucy perceived many things in advance of the age, saw all sorts of crises of mankind where blander people saw only the cheery side of things. She was a beauty. She was excellence itself.

Her husband, on the other hand, favored forgiveness and reform, pity, rehabilitation. His impression on the day of Kakapick's visit to Listing House had been that the fellow was struggling free of his misanthropy. "My impression was," Rimrose said in his generous way, "that he's solving his problems. He was looking much better. I can't get over how healthy he was looking. What else have we got to go by? We can't really convict him on your dreams, can we? When I saw him I was wide awake right in this room."

"You couldn't see. You sat in the dark," Lucy said. "You had a terrible headache."

"I felt him getting hold of himself. His teeth were white. You weren't here. You ran out the door. You've got to give a person a chance to grow up. Here's a guy sat in his room for four years reading the classics of the world."

"Out of stolen books," she said. "I don't think he ever read them, either. I think he sat in his room with his door closed and jerked off. Professor Markell told us there were people like that."

"At least he closed the door," said Rimrose.

To the end, Lucy refused to type a single line of a Kakapick letter nor address nor seal an envelope nor lick a stamp nor carry a Kakapick letter down the street to the drop-box.

Inquiring institutions wished to know a variety of things about Kakapick. Would Rimrose tell them, they asked, the circumstances of his own acquaintance with Mr. Kakapick, offer his observations of Mr. Kakapick's character and achievement, and reveal any reason why Mr. Kakapick might be unsuitable for the position here described?

Rimrose replied by telling his interrogators of his earliest memory of Kakapick seen through his doorway, of being himself a bookish boy cast among athletes and therefore delighting to come upon another boy as bookish as himself. Here was the fixture of Rimrose's Kakapick letter:

Where most boys coming to college piled up their shelves with photographs of girls dressed for the prom and topical photos of athletic heroes and screen stars and more or less naked women and tri-cornered pennants and personal drinking records, Kakapick featured upon his shelves volumes of the literary wonders of the world; and while the rugged frivolous athletes consulted their souls all week to know in advance the Saturday football scores, Kakapick created, in the silence and solace of his private library, thoughts upon a system of universal assessment of the writings of the world from Homer to Mailer. Of this ingenious system and Kakapick's method I once wrote an article for our university daily, of which I was then editor-in-chief.

Kakapick was a book-lover indeed (Rimrose continued). His penchant for book-collecting had attracted widespread attention among the higher authorities of the university; and he was an *interesting* person, too, with noble plans for the world. He wished to unify the world through innovative bookish education and universal reading. And lately, in an even more recent plan, Mr. Kakapick had undertaken to stabilize the study of literature by establishing statistical bases for taste and judgment. "His is a marvel of imagination," Rimrose wrote. "In person he is affable and attractive, perhaps somewhat shy. He is no indiscriminate collector of friends—indeed, he has but few, of whom he tells me I am one. I recall him from college days as being by nature a generous fellow-student—"

Rimrose paused at his typewriter to recall the ways in

which Kakapick had been generous. He could not think of
any.

> I saw him here in town only recently. He came to my home to
> congratulate me on the appearance of a story of mine. He has
> become ever friendlier, his smile wider than before. At one time
> he and I discussed our becoming roommates, but other obliga-
> tions interceded. We shared friendships. He was not himself an
> athlete, but he was well known among the athletes of our dor-
> mitory, who joshed with him in the usual rowdy bawdy way.

Rimrose was surprised by the nature of the incoming letters
of inquiry. These letters lacked variety. They were stiff and
grudging, marked by self-contempt, empty of local pride—"Of
course we don't pay high salaries out here in the sticks . . .
Why Mr. Kakapick would want to leave University City to
come here I can't guess . . . the height of our culture in this
Bible Belt is the County Fair."

One letter, however, called itself to his special attention
with its opening sentence—"I am conferring honor on self," a
play on the title of Rimrose's story, "Conferring Honors on
Selves," in an obscure magazine called Hatchet. In all the
world, as far as Rimrose had known, only Lucy and the editor
of Hatchet had read that story. The author of the letter was
one Professor Marmonk, chair of English at Cactus Country
College, "soon to be University." Lucy knew the name. "You
don't know who Marmonk is," she said, "because you don't
sit in the library reading all the magazines."

Who was Marmonk? The illustrious Professor Marmonk
was the founder, publisher and animating spirit of a "hand-
held periodical," as he called it—MANNA, Marmonk's Notable Authors of North America. Its basic service was as a journal of record of the names, dates and significant works of all
the serious writers of North America, with brief objective
commentary about their new books, stories, poems and
drama.

Marmonk had given MANNA a character, setting it apart from all others. His sprightly, lively journal was positive and eclectic. In every issue it printed a leisurely essay on something or other connected to literature. It never exploited big names for their own sake nor sought sensation. Frequently it celebrated the writing of a neglected literary person whose particular distinction may have been only that a staff worker had fallen in love with his or her work. Professor Marmonk prided himself on being "a discoverer or a rediscoverer, never a knocker or a detractor." He was once quoted in an unsigned MANNA editorial (probably his own) to the effect that "critics should be fond of the work they discuss. A critic should never be premature about anybody. I never announce a writer dead. If I wanted to bury people, I'd have gone to mortician school. We had a very good one in my home town."

Annually Professor Marmonk collected his crop of MANNA in a single volume "providing a useful ongoing record of the births of many books, and giving employment and training to teachers and students here among the cacti."

Professor Marmonk went so far in his letter as to speak well of his own institution, not as a booster but as a worldly man who knew that a place was mainly as good as oneself. Cactus Country College is "perceived by some," Marmonk wrote in his letter to Rimrose, "as a sandy parched school far away in desert isolation. Actually we are not as provincial as our name may sound. We are an intelligently developing site of civilization."

Its English department, growing "decently bigger," Professor Marmonk said, was now advertising for a young professor devoted to good teaching and to sound research and scholarship. Kakapick was high on Cactus's "short list" of candidates. "This Kakapick intrigues me," Professor Marmonk wrote, "with his cutting-edge ideas about objectifying author achievements with ratings and rankings and statistical evaluations. Frankly, with so many writers in the running, it's a hard sorting-out."

Rimrose was delighted to receive such an informal letter among others so estranged from enthusiasm. In reply, he adapted his all-purpose Kakapick form letter to one that was more conversational. He concluded with a prophecy more deadly accurate than he imagined. "If I were a department chair hoping for distinction, I'd bet on Kakapick. He'll come in and take the whole thing over."

He mailed his letter to the cacti, wherever they were. He had meant to look up the place on the map, but he forgot.

4

DOWN from Zygmont came father and mother for the Fourth of July, along with Reveres from White City and brothers and sisters and cousins from everywhere for picnics and fireworks and a family softball game in Soapbox Park. (Today was the two hundredth birthday of the United States of America.) It was a spirited game but a short one. The field was damp from last night's rain. The rain had subsided to a drizzle, but the drizzle was wet enough and everyone sought the sheltered sidelines except for Rimrose and several enthusiastic athletic children. They were the young ones. They whacked the ball around. The turf was slippery. Lucy called to her husband, "You'd better quit before somebody gets hurt."

Rimrose had inexhaustible energy. He was the sparkplug. He galvanized the children. The families along the sidelines admired his youthfulness. He fungoed the ball too high for the children to judge and catch.

He relinquished the bat and took a place in the field. A sturdy child, his brother Alf's second wife's son, sent a fly ball into the damp heavens. Rimrose ran for it, his eyeballs jumping in his head. He crashed in a hole in the soft wet earth. The families gathered around him. Somebody snapped his photograph, prostrate on the shining grass.

It was his ankle. He had never felt such pain as this. Lucy and his mother and father took him to the emergency room of University Hospital, where his leg was x-rayed. "Nothing broke," the doctor said, "take it home and elevate it."

"I'm broke," Rimrose said. His mother paid the hospital charge.

At Listing House that idle weekend Rimrose reclined like a king at his levee. He kept his ankle iced and elevated, and Whites and Rimroses stopped by to say farewell and offer a joke. Sample: "What'll you have? I'll have an ankle on ice."

His father remained and sat with him and asked, "What did you mean when you said to the doctor—"

"What did I say?"

"You said you're broke. Are you really broke?"

"We're just about broke," said Rimrose. "We've got a couple of hundred dollars in the bank."

"You should have more than that at your age."

"Well, dad, we don't. What can I say?"

"I knew something bad was going to happen out there. I knew you were going to get hurt," his father said. "I really knew you would. You weren't moving like you used to move. You used to be able to watch where you were going and catch up to the fly ball at the same time."

Father was on the verge of inviting Rimrose once again to come home to the *Herald.* Father came at the matter obliquely. "It sounds to me like an awfully quiet shop in here. Is this how you like it? I don't hear your telephone ringing anymore."

"It's the Fourth of July weekend," Rimrose said. "Magazines don't work. It's ringing all the time."

"I haven't heard it ring much," his father said. "You know, at home, our phone rings twenty times a day, maybe more, maybe less, I don't know, I don't count them—I'm talking about in the house, not down at the shop—"

"We're in different businesses, dad. I'm not at a daily paper."

But his father pursued it. "It wasn't so many years ago we couldn't have sat here carrying on a consecutive conversation. The phone rang a lot. It was editors on the line, things they wanted you to do, you were a hot property. Now it's not ringing for you much anymore. Editors aren't calling you from all over the country anymore like they did. Now the patterns of your life are changing. You're not a part of things anymore like you were. That's all right, that's natural, I'm not worrying, it's all in the way of things. But what have you got to back you up?"

"I don't write as fast as I used to."

"Can you speed it up? Get a computer. They're the coming thing. The whole shop is going to be computerized one of these days. I never thought I'd see the day, but there I am like anybody else hearing myself saying 'I'll bring it up on my screen.' Can you imagine me saying a thing like that? The *Herald* never wants to be the first to take up a new thing—"

"But never the last either."

"That's right. That's what we say. But you were always a fast writer."

"My mind won't let me write as fast as I used to," Rimrose said. "These editors call, they're full of ideas, but their ideas aren't my ideas, we don't think the same way. A lot of their ideas used to be my ideas. A person changes."

"You change."

"That's what I mean."

"Change back. Take their ideas and run with them and make them your own. They won't notice. If you don't take what they offer, they call the next writer down the list. Soon they'll be skipping over your name altogether—hell, he turned us down three times, drop him off the list."

"Editors die," Rimrose said. "I had three stories on an editor's desk when he died."

"What's going to happen to them?"

"Oh, they all go to heaven."

"I mean the stories. Three stories are a lot of money, aren't they?"

"A lot of work. I don't know what's going to happen to them. I got a little note from the new editor saying they'll send my stories back to me if I send them return postage. The guy that died was a guy I never sent return postage to. He printed everything I sent him."

"Do you worry about it?"

"Of course I worry about it."

"What are you going to do about it?"

"Nothing. I don't know. I never wrote better. I'm in my golden age of creative poverty. Some days when things are going well I feel that I'm just now getting going."

"I don't like to hear you say *poverty.*"

"You hear *poverty* and I hear *golden age.*"

"One of these days you might have to take a job somewhere," his father said.

"On the Zygmont *Herald?*"

"Well, why not?"

"You don't want me. I don't think I'd really fit in. You never had a reporter that couldn't drive a car."

"Of course I want you. How can you say a thing like that? I want you more than I ever wanted anything else in my life. You know we can work around the driving. You won't be a reporter anymore. That's what I mean when I say you don't seem to be noticing the passage of time and the changing of the patterns. You're past that running around, that's kid stuff. I don't expect you to be chasing fire engines. We get kids to do that. You're an editor, you'll be the boss one day soon. Don't you understand that? You're not a kid anymore."

"It sounds good," Rimrose said. "If I thought it was for me I'd be up there in a minute."

"What's for you? I know you realize that in Zygmont you can buy a house four times as big as this house for the same money. Every kid will have a bedroom. Your back yard goes halfway up the mountain. Who can ask for anything more?"

"This house is big enough."

"This house is *small,*" his father said with a touch of impatience in his tone. "Why are you denying the obvious? I'd be so happy right now if I only saw you in a regular job somewhere, maybe not on the *Herald,* maybe right here in University City, catching up on your finances, working nine to five."

"Nine to five I write, dad."

"I don't see your writing around as much as I used to. Mother remarks on the same thing. Very, very often I used to see you on the magazine stand, there'd be a story of yours in some publication or another."

"Did you read it?" Rimrose asked his father.

"Mother read it. She reads them all," father said.

It was too true. His ankle had given him pause. For several days the pain prevented his writing. He was too old to learn to write with ankle elevated. For a week he was oppressed by the idea of his great advanced age.

He sat still. The idea of running dominated his thought. His mind relentlessly replayed the incident. Down he fell in the wet grass. His feet flew from under him. Time after time he ran for the ball dropping indistinctly from the dripping heavens. He was running out of stories to tell. He had run out of his past. One depressed day he thought, *I'm beginning to run out of life—what I mean is—*

He meant that he feared he was running out of stories to tell, running out of the energy to invent them, running out of the energy to reshape chaotic life into the satisfying order of a story. Running out of the desire. He had a hundred Zygmont memories he had once wanted to make into stories, but they were pale now. He had told of his college days, too, squeezed them dry with invention. He had exhausted his models, the characters he had drawn upon. Nothing was left of them. Westby Hall, *Sentinel,* Polly Anne, Herndon, gone from his life. He had told many Listing House stories, sports stories, children stories, animal stories. The house was full of children and animals. Listen to them now. Amidst more life than ever he had fewer stories to tell. His power of invention was faltering. He could feel it. He no longer saw stories around every corner, stories in every memory, as his father saw news stories every day around every corner in Zygmont.

Listing House grew smaller year by year. Lucy was pregnant again. This was the year Jupiter was born. Now everybody was aboard who was coming aboard. Rimrose wished they lived in a big house up against the mountains in Zygmont. His father said he could buy a house in Zygmont for the price of half a house in University City. And half a house in University City was what you got. Listing House was half a house, and no longer such a quaint funny little tipping-over house which once upon a time amused their friends. Their friends had all moved to sturdier places. Home sweet home in Zygmont.

Then, too, this writing business—this business side of the writing—required him to spend half his life reminding magazines of the money they owed him. The bastards, they knew it, they just hated to part with it. They were in a hurry for him to write fast, but they paid slow. He'd quit it all. He'd learn to drive a car. He'd drive a Yellow Cab all over University City. He once went so far as to phone the Yellow Cab company to ask about a job. The company man on the phone invited him to drop by. Of course the man assumed that Rimrose knew how to drive a car. Well, he'd learn, he'd drive a Yellow Cab and he'd never need to wait ninety days to be paid for his labor. A cabbie's customers never tell him the bookkeeper's on vacation, or lie to him, "Your check is in the mail." To be paid on the spot for service performed! To carry his day's pay home at evening! That was the bliss of a Yellow Cabbie.

He had told everything. He had poured out his soul and his spirit while the inspiration was upon him. The excitement of writing was growing thin. He hadn't beat the system at all. The system was beating him. If it was a contest, he was losing. Writing stories all day long had become less and less a pleasure, more and more an exhausting process of starting up the motor, getting up speed and suddenly coming to the end.

He needed a longer course. He should write novels instead of stories. What was a novel but ten or twenty stories all in a row?

Yes, but ten or twenty stories were ten or twenty paychecks.

He wished he were a nine-to-five fellow in an office. He'd be less lonely with people all around him all day. He'd socialize at the water cooler, that was the kind of life he had truly always dreamed of.

Not many years ago he could write several stories simultaneously. He'd felt himself to be the living imitation of the chessmaster in Soapbox Park playing many games at once. But nowadays Rimrose wrote stories one at a time.

He hadn't much confidence in his editors anymore. He had outgrown them. The infant editors straight from college began by asking, "Who am I to reject a genuine Rimrose story?" But they learned how. They guessed his age at ninety-nine. An infant editor said of characters in one of Rimrose's stories, "People don't think like that anymore," but Rimrose knew that people did, always had, and weren't about to stop. An infant editor said to Lucy, "Rimrose writes better stories than anybody else, but I don't understand them."

Editors were always changing jobs. Taking a new job. To an infant editor, two whole years on the same magazine was eternity. It took an infant editor three or four job jumps to discover that every new job was the old job all over again. Television was reshaping the magazines. Magazines were folding. Some of the old world was falling away, dissolving, vanishing. Rimrose had had four stories on his editor's desk at Antigua, bought but not yet paid for. Then Antigua folded. He had never been paid for them. Bankruptcy procedures offered Lucy a deal, nine cents on the dollar. She took the deal. A year later the money came. Antigua today—who next? What was the world coming to? The collapse of a venerable institution was a new thing to Rimrose, who was not really as old as he thought. He sat still with ankle elevated. He ran for the fly ball. He fell into a hole in the earth. His ankle throbbed. Much might be said for the old style of the little city in the shadow of the mountain. Only the Zygmont *Herald* was likely to last forever.

On the other hand, lucky things came along from time to time to ease the Rimrose money flow. Think of the royalties every year from a slender little accidental children's book begun as an adult story inspired by the revolving flip-flopping neon sign on the blue roof of Leslie's Blue Roof Hamburgers—

ALWAYS OPEN
NEVER CLOSED

Eartha and Marco as they grew had been fascinated by that remarkable neon sign. They studied it before and after hamburgers. The trickery of language was just the most marvelous thing. Two little phrases sounding opposites could say the same thing! One half of a neon phrase could dispute the other! It was just too fabulous.

Saying one thing by saying something else! Language had been invented to amuse children. The Rimrose children were wordsy people like their mother and father, language people, word-players, readers aloud, reciters of stories, tellers of tales, especially father, who told stories for a living or anyhow wrote them out for a living, or something close to a living with a little help from his folks in Zygmont.

One evening Marco eating applesauce remarked upon the resemblance between the word *applesauce* and the word *applause*. Everyone remained alert for some time thereafter for words that looked alike, like *father* and *fathead*, *brother* and *bother*, *heaven* and *heathen*, *worship* and *warship*, *peddler* and *pedaler*. Rimrose contributed to the table talk words with ironic resemblances. The word *faculty* often came to his eye as *faulty*, *gentle* as *gentile*.

He thought he might get into a story based on words that looked alike, just any old kind of amusing confusion, if only he could write it up. He wrote it up all right, but it came to very little. Still, it was done, which was to say he did not feel inclined to work on it anymore, and he threw it into the wastebasket. Lucy rescued it from the wastebasket and sent it away. You never could tell, could you? This was not the last time she'd rescue writing from Rimrose's wastebasket.

His story went round and round awhile, thousands of miles backing and forthing. Editors agreed it was a story that came to nothing, the author had forgotten what he might have had in mind.

One day Lucy received a letter of rejection from an old-friend editor who asked, "Isn't it sort of floating in space somewhere between something and nothing? Isn't it rather *childlike?*" That was the word Lucy needed—*childlike,* for children.

Yes. Why not? She should have thought of it sooner. Lucy had had some correspondence with a publisher at an outfit called Children Only Press. Now, when she sent him "Always Open Never Closed," he saw what she saw. He agreed with her that, seen in a certain way, edited and simplified, it could be made into an engaging book for children. He commissioned her for the task.

Rimrose was chagrined to think his story conceived for adults so clearly suggested something for children, but his chagrin lessened from year to year in proportion to the sale of the little book named *Always Open Never Closed.* It beautifully brought into Listing House two or three thousand dollars a year during a trying period in the lives of the Rimroses. In a dry authorial note up front he expressed "my affectionate appreciation to my children for their contribution to the making of this volume, which was supposed to have been something else, and to the mother of said children for having acted upon possibilities."

* * *

Ten thousand dollars' worth of good fortune blew in from yet a different direction. Rimrose received in the mail one of those funny halfway-dirty greeting cards, unsigned, addressed to him in Polly Anne Cathcart's bold, dark, angry, slashing proofreading *Sentinel* hand, postmark illegible, showing a photograph of a king-sized bed, rumpled and empty and warm with recent presence, and the legend "Wish You Were Here."

Lucy took unkindly to this card and to its author, "whoever she might be," she said, though she knew damn well who it was. She twirled the card across the room. It fell to the floor in front of the fireplace, and there it lay for days.

Rimrose tried to write a story about it, but the story failed and the card disappeared. His second attempt also failed. This time around he had arrived at the title "The Rumpled Bed." But false starts were expensive, two failures were more than he could afford, and he now knew enough about himself to know when to quit.

One morning at ten o'clock Polly Anne rang the telephone. She asked, "What time are you going for your afternoon walk?" He hesitated. "What's your hesitation?" she said. "It's not one of your awfully deep philosophical questions."

"I haven't made up my mind," he said. "I don't go any particular time."

"Let's name a particular time," she said.

She picked him up on Mile Wide Avenue. She was driving a university car equipped with two-way radio and a gun in the glove compartment. She smiled a sober smile. She showed him, as if it were a certificate of honor, her newly reinstated driver's license. "I've dried out," she said. "I haven't had a drink in a year and I'll never drink a drink again. Let's have a drink."

She drove him to a dark place called the Sauerhaus, where he drank two slow boilermakers and she drank fruit juice. She had just returned from a year's medical leave. "That's some Health Plan," she said. "What would *you* do with a year off?"

"I'd rest my typewriter fingers. I'd read a couple of hundred books I've been meaning to read. I'd hang around my children's schools. I'd store up stories in my head."

"You can do it," she said. "You can have a year off. You can have a lot of years off. Come to work for OSE if you want to store up stories."

"They haven't asked me," he said.

"I'm asking you now," she said.

"Are you officially asking me? Are you that high up in the outfit that you can go around propositioning me like that?"

"High up enough," she said. "My colleagues would love to have you. Journalists work out well for us."

"I wouldn't call myself a journalist. I'm long gone from journalism."

"You were. You'll get back in the habit easy enough. You're a good snooper. You know how to look things up and find things out. You're a question-asker. You're sly, you're foxy, you're basically a liar—isn't that what a storywriter is?—and you don't mind lying in a good cause."

"I don't think of OSE as a good cause. You're a spy outfit," he said. "You spy on people. You even spy on people who are supposed to be your friends. You tap telephones."

She looked him up and down. "I'm looking to touch you," she said. She touched him intimately. "Most of the people we spy on are creeps and crooks and worse. They use the university for agendas of their own. We're really the good guys, Rim, truly we are."

"Still a spy," he said. "I've never really understood how you could do it."

"For the Health Plan," she said. It had done wonders for the color of her cheeks, the brightness of her eyes, and her confidence in her future. Curing herself of alcohol, she had also cured herself of fingernail-biting "and other vices too numerous to mention. But not of men," she said. Men had come and gone in her life. Kakapick was gone. He'd been gone for a long time now. "Gone to where the cactus grows," she said.

"I knew he was looking for a job. He dropped by the house one time," said Rimrose. "That was the last I heard of him. He came to congratulate me on my Herndon story."

"No he didn't," she said. "He came to get you to write him letters of reference. Wasn't that it?"

"That's right, I wrote him a bunch."

"Kakapick never goes anywhere unless he's after something," she said.

"I thought you were fond of him."

"Love him," she said. "But I love to see him at his most hideous, sucking up for something he wants. One of the most fantastic mind-boggling things about him is his fantastic excess. He's got selfishness down pat."

"Then you've split," Rimrose said, somehow hoping so.

"Well, he's gone," she said. "When he comes to town we fuck around and then he goes away again. I never fall out of love with my lovers."

"It seems to me he could have dropped me a line and told me he got a job," said Rimrose. "I wrote a lot of letters of reference for him."

"He'll drop you a line when he needs you," said Polly Anne.

"I've always wondered," Rimrose said, "why you told him you and I were lovers."

"I never did," she said. "Did he say that? It was his own invention. He'll say anything. He has no moral genes. It made him important to himself."

"That's what he said about you."

"You and he—you know, well, fucking the same—you know, he thought the editor of *Sentinel* was the number-one man on campus, and that's where he wants to be, up close to number one. He's got the world's biggest hard-on for fame." She was between men now. "How about you?" she inquired. "Let's have a love affair and make Kakapick's lies come true."

"I live in a castle of love," Rimrose said.

"Shit, I can't beat that," she said. She knew it was true. She'd been listening to his phone for years. She played her fingers on his thigh. He kissed her on the mouth. "Come to work for the OSE," she said. "How I'd love it if you were my colleague again. Think of a regular university paycheck every two weeks."

"I've thought of it often," he said. "I'm thinking of money all the time." But he was thinking of Lucy now. Wasn't that odd? To work for the OSE would be more of a betrayal of Lucy than even a love betrayal. The whole point of OSE was to spy on one's fellows, to deceive, to steal their secrets and their good names. "It seems to me," he said, "you've joined up with everything you always thought you hated."

"Weren't we spies going around finding out where the money went for the Indian Fee?"

"No," he said. "We identified ourselves. People knew we were from *Sentinel.* I can't believe you're doing what you're doing. I never thought that's where you'd end up. Is it even exciting?"

"The Health Plan is exciting and the paycheck is exciting. Well, I had some excitement"—Rimrose was undecided whether this were real or invented—"a while ago when things came down to the moment in a certain risky business. There was a lot of money involved and a lot of desperation. We put the Program in International Management out of business, as you know."

"I never knew," he said. "I never heard of them. Is this something you're making up?"

"Right at the end it all became terribly exciting," she said. "They tried to kill me."

"You were exposing somebody?"

"Worse than exposing. They wouldn't mind being exposed. They have no shame. But we were driving them out of business. I knew everything they were doing. I'd worked for them awhile."

"You were a spy," he said.

"That's what I mean by work, Rim. One of their goons got me drunk in a bar just like this one. Then he tried to run my car off River Road. That didn't work. He unfortunately got himself drunker than he got me. I jumped out of my car and he tried to run me over with his. That didn't work, either."

"How not?"

"He drove off the bridge into the river, sailed through the air like the man on the flying trapeze."

"I wouldn't want a job doing things people want to kill me for," Rimrose said.

"That's why I make so much more money than you do," she said.

"I make good money," he said.

"Then you don't know what good money is," she said. "You barely feed your family. I don't know how you live. I know what you get for what you do."

"Have you got my phone tapped?" he said.

"I know everything, Rim."

"How can you go on doing things like that?"

"For the Health Plan." She paid the bill. "It's only company money," she said. He did not protest. "When we want money we ask for it. You'd love having one of our gorgeous expense accounts. I'm quite rich now with one thing and another. You should be rich. It's hard for me to believe you don't make more money than you do."

She drove him home. At the curb before Listing House they talked much longer than he wished. He quite lost track of time. At last he said, "I'd ask you in."

"But—" she said.

"But Lucy's looking at me right this minute out of the window and she's going to want to ask questions right away— gone all afternoon and I didn't even have the decency to phone her. We'll do it soon," he said. "We'll have you over." He turned to the house.

Readers fortunate enough to be well acquainted with Rimrose's stories written during his golden age of creative poverty have surely begun to recognize in the events of his afternoon with Polly Anne Cathcart a pronounced resemblance to his story "The Rumpled Bed," twice begun and twice abandoned.

But on his third attempt he triumphantly succeeded. Here is how he organized it. In "The Rumpled Bed" an admirable earnest family man named Guillermo Gardener, approaching middle life and its supposed crises, meets on the street a woman he had once known almost intimately. Her name is Angelique. (Perhaps Rimrose named her in tribute to Angelica Vanenglenhoven, well remembered by him from summer nights of his youth running the waves at Zygmont Lake.) Guillermo and Angelique step out of sight one afternoon into a darkened tavern. She had been away. Now she was back.

At suppertime (or a little later) Guillermo returns from the tavern to his house. His story is that his meeting with Angelique was accidental—she spied him from her car. The degree to which imagination and actuality merged on paper is also unclear, for Rimrose in writing "The Rumpled Bed" clearly confronted his need to conceal the perfect truth from Lucy. He does not mention, for example, Guillermo's kissing Angelique at the Sauerhaus tavern, nor does he mention Angelique's fingers stroking Guillermo's thigh.

In the tavern Guillermo tells Angelique of the difficulty she caused between his wife and him when she sent him a somewhat saucy greeting card. Angelique cannot remember having sent him such a card. She might have. "She had sent cards to anyone whose address she could remember during those drying-out months of her life when she wasn't remembering much." When Guillermo received the card he "hid the clever little thing with insufficient care." But his wife discovers it. Conflict ensues.

Here we leave "The Rumpled Bed" to return to real life. Rimrose, parting from Polly Anne at the curb after their rendezvous at the Sauerhaus, entered Listing House in a somewhat guilty mood. "Why was everybody staring at me out of the window?"

"Because we've been waiting a hellishly long time for dinner," Lucy said.

"We're hungry," Marco said.

"You should have gone on without me. We had a lot to talk about."

"Obviously you did. You were standing there half an hour," Lucy said.

"Never half an hour."

"Half an hour on the nose."

"Did you time me with a stopwatch? Is this the Boston marathon?"

"Are you drunk?" Eartha asked him.

"Do I look drunk?"

"No, you smell drunk."

"Well," said Rimrose, washing his hands at the kitchen sink, "we went to a bar and had a couple of drinks."

"Couldn't you have called?"

"I didn't know I was going to be there so long. I didn't know I was going to be there at *all*. I bumped into her on Mile Wide." This did not sound convincing even to him, and he added, "I was on my walk." This did not sound convincing either. "She spied me from her car." That sounded vaguely possible.

"Since when do you go walking on Mile Wide?" Lucy asked.

"You never go walking on Mile Wide," Marco said.

"She couldn't possibly have spied you," said Eartha. "It's too crowded to spy anybody on Mile Wide. Even if you spy anybody you can't *stop* on Mile Wide."

"She stops her car anywhere she pleases," Rimrose said. "She's the assistant director of the Office of Savings and Economy. She carries a gun in her glove compartment."

Lucy asked, "While you and she were whiling away the day

in the bar on Mile Wide, did you think to thank her for that funny photo card?"

"What funny photo card?"

" 'The Rumpled Bed.' "

"You have a photographic memory."

"It was a photograph."

"You mean that funny little card—that was a funny little card. No, I didn't ask her if she sent it," he said, smoking up the issue with collapsed logic, "I never knew *who* sent it."

"I thought she went away somewhere."

"She went for an alcohol cure."

"What's she doing back in town? Did she run out of people's husbands to steal? Did you really and truly enjoy lounging around all afternoon in a sleazy bar with your old school pal the drunken motorist?"

"Lounging around in sleazy bars is what writers do," Rimrose said. "She's on the wagon," he added.

"We'll see how long that'll last," said Lucy.

It was a small event soon cool. Its transforming effect was to restore Rimrose's interest in the abandoned pages of "The Rumpled Bed." Magically fusing and coagulating the premise of the funny dirty photo card with his rendezvous on Mile Wide Avenue, he formed his ironic, bitter, comic story.

Lucy sold it almost the day it was completed to the elegant periodical Various, which paid large sums for sophisticated fiction. For this tale it paid Rimrose $5,000. Not bad, it was a quick job—once he'd finally got the traction, he wrote it in a week. Six months later, before "The Rumpled Bed" was even in print at Various, it was announced as winner of the Picadilly Lettuce Leaf $5,000 Story Award.

Five thou twice. Pretty damn nice.

Thus the incident of Rimrose's wayward afternoon may be said to have been worth more than it cost. And yet, successful as the story was, Lucy could never truly take it fondly to her heart, for it revived her memory of an anxious afternoon and a tense family dinner not wholly forgotten by morning.

*   *   *

Yet another small bonanza a few days afterward. Once again Polly Anne rang the telephone. "Something awfully interesting I forgot to report to you," she said.

Her interesting report was this. Recently she'd been snooping about on business carrying her into *Sentinel* office where she saw a silly old object, an old-fashioned trunk containing old story manuscripts and ancient stinky athletic apparel which somebody said was Rimrose's. The old manuscripts indeed looked very much as if they might have been his. As for the jocks and socks she couldn't say, maybe they were his, too. "Could that be?" she asked him. "Do you by any chance remember leaving manuscripts behind in an old green—"

"Footlocker," he supplied. "The jocks I don't need but the manuscripts I'd be curious about."

"Wander over to *Sentinel*," she commanded, as in *Sentinel* days when he was her star reporter, "just ask them 'Oh by the way, did you notice an old beat-up green footlocker I left here fifteen years ago?' "

Many months passed before Rimrose and Lucy found the moment to retrieve his old green war-surplus footlocker from *Sentinel*. At the hour they arrived, a reporter was sitting on it. He rose and apologized. "Sorry about that," he said. "I never knew it was anybody's."

The *Sentinel* office had expanded. Technology had proliferated. Nobody had emptied the wastebaskets or cleared away the coffee cups in fifteen years. The footlocker contained articles of athletic apparel, tennis balls that had lost their bounce, a dead baseball bat, and unpublished abandoned manuscripts of stories Rimrose had written in the *Sentinel* office during the summer of his first devotion to his fiction-writing. He had not yet met Lucy.

Rimrose and Lucy seized the straphandles at either end of the footlocker and carried it out of the *Sentinel* office. In the same way he and his father had carried it on the day of his arrival into Westby Second East. Afterward, one oppressive summer day, Rimrose had tossed it out of his Westby window and jumped after it, intending to carry it home to Zygmont. He had carried it instead to *Sentinel.*

Lucy read his manuscripts attentively. Rimrose poked among them. Most of them he could not read through. He smiled at the whimsy of "The Airless Furnace, or Buckets of Melted Ice," and he was moved beyond his expectation by "His Father's Fingers Clawing at His Back," perhaps because he read it now as the father's story, not the son's. "I'm like an actor in a long-running play," Rimrose observed. "First I played the son, now I play the father." "Stories don't stand still," Lucy said.

In some of these unfinished stories his characters were frozen in postures Rimrose had got them into without ever having been able to get them out. The boy was leaping from his bed to intercede with his quarreling parents. The athlete's parents sat in the grandstand waving pennants before a game destined never to begin. And all these boys in these stories stripping all these girls!—"producing nakedness," Rimrose had written in an awkward moment of self-consciousness. Here was "Girls Will Be Girls," famous in its brief hour from one end to the other of Westby Second East. Here was a story called "Down in a Hole at the End of Their Rope and Hope." Rimrose could not remember having written it, nor what he might have intended, though Lucy admired certain of its passages polished so fine, speaking of love and loyalty. "How hard you worked at them," she said.

Such hard labor, Lucy felt, should be rewarded. These footlocker stories, she felt, would make a good and useful book. And why not along the way turn them to a bit of money? She negotiated with publishers. She argued: people would be fascinated to read stories by an accomplished writer before he had become so; the sight of these stories would encourage young writers by showing them how ambitiously inept even the best writer may be at the start; these stories would prove the encouraging theory that writers are not born but made; these stories would delight Rimrose's fans everywhere. Thus Lucy tried her persuasion on ten publishers and lost every time.

But after all, she needed to prevail not ten times but only once, and so she did at last, with the Pilgrim Readers Press, a fastidious little house in Manhattan which, after a series of delays, published *Footlocker Tales: Seventeen Early Stories by Rimrose,* paying him an advance against royalties of $2,500. Even in the golden age of creative poverty the sum was not much, you will agree, for six souls and many household beasts in a wintry clime. Still, it was something.

Wouldn't it be simply lovely, Lucy often thought, if Rim could whip up stories a ton a month as he had done in years gone by? He hadn't now the high rate of production he had had formerly, nor the high rate of *selling* success with the work he *did* produce. He wasn't as easy to sell as he used to be—as often as he complained of the scarceness of money, he never really aimed at it when he sat down to write.

Then, too, because of his perfectionism he declined to sell things he *could* sell if only he'd let them out of the house. Somehow between the moment he finished a story and the moment it was ready to leave for the market he ceased to believe in it. He encountered problems of credibility. Nothing in the action of his story struck him as ever likely to have happened to anyone.

Lucy wished her husband could write new and better stories with the same old *speed* in the same old *quantity.* Let *many* and *better* be the same thing. Would that that were possible! But his critical intellect restrained him, leaving him smarter but poorer. That wasn't the way things were supposed to go. One was supposed to grow smarter and richer along parallel lines. He saw too many sides to everything. His mind

outsped his hands, snatching away that lightness of spirit formerly holding his brooding at bay.

Lucy's account book revealed that the Rimroses were always in a financial hole and always miraculously pulling out.
They were never quite at the end of their rope and their hope,
but she also knew, projecting the shape of their future, that
unless something big happened they were headed for disaster.
The day would come when nothing would pull them out.
Then what? What did people do?

If only Rim had a better sense of economy, she felt, if only
he were easier on himself. He wasted too much of himself. To
put it quite literally, he threw too much away. For example,
one trouble with her husband was his mania for wastebaskets.
Sometimes he bashed away at his machine like an optimist all
morning, optimistically edited all afternoon, and threw all his
work into the wastebasket at night.

But if he had a mania, Lucy had a countervailing rule. Her
rule was, "No first-day trashing, no throwing pages away
while they're hot." Over the years she retrieved many pages
from his wastebasket and slipped them in among his files,
where he'd find them. Sometimes he'd get back to work on
them as if he'd forgotten that he'd thrown them out.

Of those of Rimrose's stories retrieved by Lucy from the
wastebasket, the best known, the most notorious, the most
controversial, the most morally condemned, the most frequently anthologized was "What They Were Doing Under the
Table"—truly a superior example of the long short story apart
from the public huzzah. Lucy sold it to Spectacle & Beacon
right after the merger for $4,000, pulling the Rimroses out of a
tough financial fix.

Luckily Rimrose had got off to a fine fast start on "What
They Were Doing Under the Table," plunging into it without a
lot of forethought. He just *began* it. The bell rang and he came
out of his corner swinging. Smash! Down went the foe. The
idea just jumped out of Lucy's mouth into Rimrose's mind all

of a rush at ten o'clock on a Saturday morning and by one o'clock that afternoon he had begun to write it.

What Lucy said was, "I should find myself a rich millionaire." She was sitting at that moment at her desk writing checks to pay their bills. Although she had paid only half their bills, the money was gone from their checkbook. She could have wept. Sometimes she did. She continued her thought: "If only I knew a very rich gentleman who wanted to pay me one million dollars per fuck I'd let him do it just once. What the hell. But I don't really know any gentleman of that description. Would you mind? Wouldn't it solve a lot of problems?" she asked.

"No. Think of the tax problems," Rimrose said.

"I don't anticipate a tax problem," she said. "He'd pay me under the table. People do that all the time, take their money in cash under the table. Cash only. Nothing in writing. No numbers, no Social Security, no withholding taxes, no IRS, no federal nothing."

"But would you really?" Rimrose asked his wife.

"Are we ready?" Lucy asked.

"I'm trying to think what I'd say if you did," Rimrose said. "I could probably handle it. I'm a big boy now."

"You wouldn't know," she said. "This would be my own personal project. I'd dash out of the house and you'd ask me where I was going and I'd mumble something. You'd never look up."

"Well, I'd know *something*. When you came home with a paper bag full of green money I'd know you'd been somewhere profitable."

"I might not bring the money home. I might squirrel it away right in the bank. I'm not really sure what I'd do, frankly, I'll have to give it some thought."

"I love your phrase," said Rimrose. " 'A rich millionaire.' "

"It'd make a good story," she said.

"It must have been done a hundred times. The Bible is full of it."

"There was a movie," she said.

"Did I see it?"

"No, you wouldn't have seen it. Millie Fishback saw it. Nothing's ever been done. Every writer does it for himself."

"Is that so?" he said. "I suppose it is, I just might try it out," and at one o'clock he began to write with impulsive speed, verve, craft and conviction the centuries-old story of the tempted wife, and at five o'clock he threw it into the wastebasket and went for a walk with Vanessa and the dog.

He had composed six pages. On a separate page he had jotted a title he almost liked: "What Were They Doing Under the Table?" Weeks afterward, leafing his way through abandoned pages in search of a fresh idea, he discovered the draft. Wasn't this odd? He thought he had thrown this junk away. Now that he reread it, it looked better to him than it had when he abandoned it. The shoemaker's elves had come in the night.

He did not quite like the title, "What Were They Doing Under the Table?" He saw no useful point in presenting the reader with a question. He thought he'd promise the reader an answer instead: "What They Were Doing Under the Table." He resumed work on his rechristened story. Soon he was moving along rather well. He liked the way it flowed. He enjoyed the challenge of creating the woman who, whatever her original intention, now suffered many second thoughts about presenting herself as a gift, even for a million dollars.

As always, Rimrose encountered unforeseen complications, problems of credibility. Who was this bloke with the money? Even to a rich millionaire a million dollars was a lot of money. An item. Well, of course it depended on how rich he really was and how much he desired the enterprising ambitious loyal family-centered daring young housewife. It was a great deal of money to spend for one-time lovemaking. A millionaire was a man of experience, he'd been around, he'd certainly know that the first time might not be the best; might not even be good. Therefore the millionaire required some sort of unusual obsession with the woman. How many back-up millions did he have? Truly, was he a *rich* millionaire or was he just one of your everyday run-of-the-millionaires? Ha ha.

Who was the woman? At first Rimrose saw her as not so special a person as the millionaire, not so rare. She had thought at first *Oh, for a million dollars I'll do most anything,* and he had believed her, but as time passed she began to draw a moral line, and after she had drawn one moral line she drew another, and as the action of the story proceeded she extended her lines to the point at which she began to view herself with a great deal of both admiration and alarm. She was wasting time. She was taking too long to make this thing happen. If only she had given herself to the millionaire in the beginning, without delay, the whole affair would have been history by now: she'd have gone her way and he'd have gone another. The longer she deliberated, the more inflexible her dilemma became. She became ashamed of herself, and guilty about the selfish way in which, by her delay, she was threatening the welfare of her family. How many goodies she could buy her husband and children with one million dollars! She utters, in one long agonizing monologue at the center of the story, her lament for her neglected family.

She made her decision. One must read the story to know it. Rimrose was unsatisfied with it. "The story never really does what I want it to do," he told Lucy when it was done, but she insisted that it nevertheless did enough, she'd like to have it, hand it over if he didn't mind, she knew right where to send it, the deadline was imminent. "Maybe they'll reject it anyhow," she said in a tone scorched by sarcasm, "but let's try, and if they don't take it we'll get it back and you can work on it the rest of your natural life until it does what you want it to do."

Lucy logically sent "What They Were Doing Under the Table" to Spectacle & Beacon for its annual Black Garter issue. An editor named Tucker took charge of it. "Love it," said Tucker on the phone. He mentioned having worked with Rimrose on a couple of Rimrose stories over at Atlantic. Rimrose did not remember, nor did he think it was even true. People claimed association. "Oh, yes, I remember," he said. It didn't matter. *Sell the tale,* he thought, *don't argue with the editor.* "Love it but what?" he asked.

"But nothing," Tucker said, laughing a little. "Everybody here just loves it all the way through from beginning to end. Only thing wrong is some of us found it slow going. Something is dragging its ass. She debates the whole thing too long."

"Overstocked with stories about moral dilemmas," Rimrose said. "One of the first stories I ever sent out, when I was a kid —that's what the magazine told me."

"We've got to speed this up," said Tucker. "I'm only referring to a little cutting. We wouldn't *add* anything. Nobody adds anything to Rimrose but Rimrose."

"A little cutting," Rimrose said.

"That's all."

"I thought you loved it from beginning to end," the author said.

"The middle's the problem," the editor replied.

Lucy sat close to the phone, slumping in her chair, signaling the victory sign to Rimrose—*Don't blow it.* Her tension smoldered in her eyes. Her future seemed to depend on Rimrose's working this out with Tucker of Spectacle & Beacon. Listing House and its occupants were too broke these days to stand on principle.

On the telephone Tucker said, "I've got to tell you as frankly as I can, we're taking a monumental chance on this. Mentally it's a literary piece—"

"I'm a literary man," said Rimrose.

"We don't always know how to gauge how much patience our on-the-run readers always *have* for this kind of piece. Especially in the Black Garter issue—we're not sure literature is what they're coming in the store for."

Rimrose had never allowed anyone to put a finger on his

work. He claimed the tail of every comma. Was he going to surrender his precious rights to a stranger named Tucker on the other end of the telephone?

Yes, in this case he was. "All right, speed it up," he said. "I know you're the guy that can do it, Tuck. That's how we did it when you were at Atlantic."

When copies of Spectacle & Beacon arrived with "What They Were Doing Under the Table" it was Lucy who lamented vintage passages lost to the speeding-up. To her eyes the printed story was a mournful sight, snaking its way in cramped columns through many slick pages of Spectacle & Beacon, suffocated among advertising claims and photographs of many young women dressed in black garters. "You were very mature," Lucy said, "you did it for the money."

5

ONCE on the day after Christmas Professor Marmonk of Cactus Country University (formerly College), one-time editor of MANNA, flew to University City for the annual conference of Literature, Language, and Linguistics. From his room at the University City Sheraton Holiday Ramada he telephoned Rimrose.

Marmonk's colleague Kakapick at Cactus having somehow given him the impression that Rimrose was unreachable (the implication was that only Kakapick could reach him), he was confused when Rimrose answered his own phone. It had also been the professor's impression that Rimrose lived in a mansion on country acres.

However, when he saw the modest reality of Listing House he adjusted himself to his surprise and sat himself in the very chair in which Kakapick had sat for a visit some years before.

He wore his conference name-badge like a medal on his breast; he had forgotten to remove it when he left the hotel. When Jupiter Rimrose saw it he wanted it—he *saved* name-badges, he said. That was the first his father had heard of it. Professor Marmonk unpinned his badge and presented it to Jupiter.

The professor on this day of his life might have given anything to anybody. His confidence had taken him over. He rejoiced that certain old truths, hopes, beliefs or virtuous convictions had come into their own. His lifetime of industry had been rewarded. "There were times," he admitted, "when I wanted to fire Kakapick while I could still do it, but when things came right down to the wire nobody was fighting harder for him than me. I was the leader of the Kakapick faction. We gave the job to the right fellow. It's a decision we're really proud of. He's a whiz, I can tell you that. He's putting us on the map and we thank you for it."

"Refresh me," Rimrose said. "What did I do?"

"For the letter you wrote. I know you must write a lot of letters for people." From his briefcase he extracted the letter Rimrose had written to Cactus Country in behalf of Kakapick. He did not read it, he did not pass it to Rimrose—he did not even *look* at it. It was sufficient, apparently, for him to hold it in his hand to recapture its force. "It's some letter, I'll tell the world," said Professor Marmonk. "It's a masterpiece. But I suppose we shouldn't have been surprised. It's only natural to get a masterpiece of a letter from the author of masterpieces—"

"Just one of my everyday masterpieces," Rimrose said.

The professor smiled, but he would not be detained. "One part of your letter really moved us all, we were all bowled over by it. You had a memory of him, you saw him through his doorway, just two freshman kids discovering each other up there in the dorm full of athletes. It was beautifully written, beautifully said. It's because you're a writer, I know. You made us see that lonely boy there with his noble plans for the world."

Professor Marmonk had attended many conferences. "I thought I'd seen them all," he said, "but there's never been one like this. As this year's Three-L conference proceeded Professor Marmonk had discovered that Cactus Country University had become a station of importance in the minds of many people. Why was this? "It's because for lots of people all over the country Cactus means MANNA," the professor explained.

"Refresh me again," Rimrose said. "What's MANNA?"

Marmonk thought Rimrose was joking. Then he saw it was

no joke. Rimrose was genuine. A whole universe beyond the hotel had never heard of MANNA. "You don't know MANNA," he said.

"I remember manna from the Bible," Rimrose said. "Free food for believers, wasn't that it? But I don't suppose it's the Bible you're talking about."

MANNA was the very brainchild of the professor— Marmonk's Notable Authors of North America, the sturdy venerable journal which he had so modestly edited for so long, which until recent years had been in decline until Kakapick revived it. "We're hearing it mentioned *everywhere,*" he said.

"All over the world?"

"All over the hotel," the professor replied, not without humor. "People notice my name tag in the elevators. They say to me, 'Oh, Cactus Country, that's where they do MANNA.' Do you see what I'm saying? Although the irony is that it's not really me anymore. I'm the *M* in MANNA, but Kakapick's taken it over."

People were beginning to think of it as the *new* MANNA, praising it for the confidence of its analysis, for its knowing who was who and who was best, who mattered and who was contemptible, what was worth reading and what was garbage, with statistical support for its opinions. MANNA kept score, MANNA gave points, MANNA ranked works of literature as they appeared, MANNA kept the standings of everyone competing in the grand universal literary contest, whether they knew they were competing or not.

"Kakapick has sort of driven me out," Professor Marmonk continued. "He took it over in a big way. He's certainly made the numbers jump. Your letter was so unusual," he said, "it had so much professional style to it. We'd have known you were a writer even if we hadn't known it was you who wrote it."

But here his mood veered from exuberance to the suggestion of doubt. Precisely because Rimrose was an artful writer his letter might be fiction. Rimrose's Kakapick may never have existed in mere life. "Frankly, here's what I've had on my mind off and on," said Professor Marmonk. "A lot of us down at Cactus Country can't help but wondering why your Kakapick is so different from the Kakapick we know. Of course you know him so much better—"

"Not so very much better, really. I haven't seen him for some years."

"Oh, I thought you saw him a lot. But you correspond. No? He said you did. You see, that's my problem right there. I don't always know if he's telling the truth. I don't think we can go on without truth. Well, Kakapick isn't exactly lovable, either, and I'm somewhat afraid of him. I hope you don't mind my speaking as frankly as I possibly can. He hasn't been entirely a blessing. After a while we began to wonder if he was worth it in the end. We've had our troubles with him. He terrorizes people. He's been rough on me, he's pretty much run me out of the editorship. It wasn't collegiality—it was more like the bum's rush. He took it over. He gave people to understand they were going to have to be either Kakapick people or Marmonk people, they couldn't be both, they had to be one or the other. MANNA was going places and people had better get on board before they got left at the station."

"I'm sorry if my letter misled you. I was trying to help him out. I was always able to go more than one way with him. I've always had a kind of sympathy for him, and I've wanted to help him out. My wife, though, she's never liked him at all, not in the least."

"You did what a friend's supposed to do. You cared about him. That's very funny, too, because he doesn't much care about himself. He doesn't care how he lives, he doesn't care about his health, he doesn't really *like* himself, but I'll tell you, he's really doing one whale of a job as editor."

"He ran you out of your own magazine," Rimrose marveled. "I can see it. I can see Kakapick doing that."

"Journal, not magazine," said Professor Marmonk. "People laugh at me. He gives me little chores to do around the office. He sends me on errands like I'm a student intern. I never would have made MANNA into what he's made it. I mean, he's tough. I mean, he flails around down there and barks out the orders and tells people what they're to do, and who's who. The whole thing is booming." He replaced Rimrose's letter in his briefcase. "It's so great to meet an author. I've been wondering all along what an actual author might think about MANNA."

"An actual author."

"You."

"To tell you the truth, I don't think about it at all," said Rimrose. "I don't know anything about it. It's criticism, right? A magazine of criticism—"

"A journal," the professor said.

"A journal of criticism. My wife mentions it."

"Bless her," the professor said. "I've been thinking that maybe as an author you had an opinion of him. People say MANNA murders authors now, *buries* authors. That's Kakapick. I didn't do it that way. I've always said, if you want to bury people, be a mortician." He laughed well at his own wit. "I could have been a mortician. We had a good mortician's school in my hometown. But I never knew people loved murder so much. Murder may be awful, but it works. People love to see the authors murdered."

"It saves people the trouble of reading."

"I never thought of it that way," said Professor Marmonk, "but you're right. Kakapick's a rascal. He's a kind of fanatic. He insists that you agree with him about everything—or else. That's what was so wonderful about your letter. You saw beyond the rascal to the genius. I admire the way you saw into him. Writers can see through people to their genuine character. You saw behind the superficial part of his character. You saw into the real man underneath."

Professor Marmonk had taken a strong liking to Rimrose. He was grateful to Rimrose for having been so accessible, for having given him his time, for having put him so wholly at his ease.

"I'd ask you to come down to the hotel tomorrow and have lunch with us, but I can't guarantee I can get Kakapick to join us. He's in demand all over the hotel," the professor said. "I was supposed to have lunch with him yesterday, but he didn't appear. I suppose there's no point having lunch at the conference anyhow, we can always have lunch down home. But can you believe this—I've never eaten a meal with him down home either."

"He lived down the hall from me for four years and I ate one meal with him. Plus one chocolate cake. I remember that."

"Writers and their memories," the professor said in the way of admiration. "Well, then, maybe you could fly down to Cactus Country sometime and give us a talk, conduct a couple of classes. We'd learn a great deal from you. We'll pay you an honorarium, of course. It can't be much, but we always have a little bit available for good causes. I'll find it."

"I'll take it," Rimrose said. His heart fluttered at the thought of making a speech. He did not want to do such a thing. "I always need the money."

"That surprises me," Marmonk said. "I'd have thought you —I mean, considering that you've been so widely printed, I'd have thought money wouldn't be a problem for you."

"It's a problem," Rimrose said. "We're short of it."

"I'll invite you down. I think we'll be able to get you a couple of hundred dollars, maybe three, four. That's not bad for an evening's work."

"And expenses."

"Oh, of course, everything. I'll talk to Kakapick about it. I'm sure it'll be okay with him. Anything relating to modern writers we pretty much clear with Kakapick."

* * *

One morning the mailperson arrived with the current copy of MANNA rubber-stamped *Complimentary* on its cover, featuring an article certainly complimentary entitled "Rimrose's First Fifty Stories" beginning, "Hail a new prince of the American story." The author of the article was Kakapick.

The pages of MANNA were lightly sealed with strips of tape already flapping loose. Rimrose recoiled from reading it. He'd rid himself of it by returning it to the mailperson even this moment retreating down the street—chase after him crying, "Refused . . . delivered to the wrong address . . . there's nobody here by my name." But he knew as he stood with the mail in his hand that he was destined to read it. He peeled the tape.

The occasion for "Rimrose's First Fifty Stories" was the announcement by the editorial board of MANNA that it had elected Rimrose to the "circle of highest excellence" among American writers of prose fiction. In this circle were forty-six persons, of whom thirty-seven were novelists and nine were storywriters; thirty-seven were men, nine were women. MANNA plucked numbers out of the sky.

Kakapick as a student had endeavored to reduce the indispensable "titles" of the world to ninety-six or eighty-nine. Not for him round numbers. He had been ambitious to choose the world's reading. Now he had scaled his ambition. He would stick to the United States, choosing its forty-six best writers of prose fiction with a measuring device he named in his own honor the Kakapick Universal Visibility Scale.

On the Kakapick scale authors were evaluated on the basis of the number of times their work appeared in "meritorious" journals or popular but meritorious magazines whose degrees of merit were in turn assessed according to the merit of the writers appearing in their pages; authors were evaluated according to the frequency with which their names were mentioned in journals or magazines and by the merit in turn of the people who had named them; Rimrose and other authors of stories won visibility points for stories anthologized—the greater the merit of the editor of the anthology, the greater the value of stories he or she anthologized; authors won points on the Visibility Scale according to the eminence of the universities with which they were in some way associated, if at all— if, for example, they had offered lectures attended by large numbers of people at meritorious universities, or participated *by invitation* in meritorious conferences, or had received an honorary degree or been awarded some other sort of institutionalized prize; authors were evaluated on the Kakapick scale by the numbers of times their names were mentioned or their works quoted or alluded to on meritorious television programs or during radio discussions; authors won visibility points if ever they were interviewed by meritorious persons reporting the news in the mass media, or if their names were mentioned in a public place by someone unconnected to literature but said to be distinguished nonetheless, as, for example, a meritorious senator, governor or the mayor of a large city.

Kakapick, having defined the circle of excellence and having elected Rimrose to it, assured the readers of MANNA that he could nevertheless write about him free of favoritism. True (Kakapick could not deny this), he and Rimrose were the "closest of friends." But Rimrose now was more than a friend —he was a statistical fact.

"As students," he wrote, "we lived in close confidence and dependence. I must confess that I am writing here about a friend of my youth—we were college roommates, I was best man at his wedding—" Here Rimrose was struck in the heart as if by a blow. His wedding had been one of the lovely occasions of his life. It had taken place in Lucy's family home in White City. Kakapick had never been within a hundred miles of White City.

Rimrose and Kakapick had been "chums," wrote Kakapick.

"More than chums . . . very close, inseparable, and we are still as close as any two buddies can be.

> We played ball on our college dormitory intramural teams, winning more often than losing, since we were a house of athletes. Rimrose and I were popular among the athletes of our hall. We were loud and rowdy, but social and amiable, too. We went out on the town, indulging together the lives of wild young college men. We shared women.

In a remarkable passage Kakapick wrote that he and Rimrose had "on one memorable occasion but in a fun spirit stolen articles of value later returned to their proper owners." He could recall, he said—pressing memory hard to bring these escapades out of the past—"once having stolen a book." He also recalled, "with memory ever fresh, my first proud sense of the fame that was awaiting Rimrose," coming upon the author all unannounced one day in Esquire. He quoted Esquire slipshod from his painful memory of that awful winter morning of his first reading it: "Rimrose is special, like Hemingway or Fitzgerald. Nobody writes great stories anymore. Rimrose lifts you up out of your depression. He's special. Rimrose tastes the thrill of life with you."

Rimrose tried to recall Kakapick as athlete. On what sort of team had they played together? None. Never. Rimrose had never seen Kakapick throw a ball. Kakapick watched from the grandstand. He crept as he could into the company of athletes. He'd have been their water boy if they hadn't chased him off. They laughed at him. They called him a jock-sniffer.

What women had Rimrose and Kakapick shared? Rimrose had never, in any version of this idea, shared a woman with anyone. What did Kakapick mean to say? Did Kakapick mean to give the impression that he had *had* Lucy, that he and Rimrose in their intimacy had possessed the same woman, that Rimrose married her and Kakapick slept with her? Why these lies? Perhaps by corrupting memories of Lucy—their wedding, this invented intimacy—Kakapick intended to hurt her, to stalk her in print as he had once stalked her on the street. Yes, in this moment, perhaps for the first time, Rimrose believed fully that it was Kakapick who had stalked Lucy in the library tunnel.

To whom did he mean to convey these impressions? Who would care? To whom was he telling this? Kakapick's invention of a past shared with Rimrose was intended to make a point about Kakapick himself, to show himself as the friend and companion of the writer bound for fame, to be seen as one who had engaged with the famous author in four years of deepest literary conversation; so close and confidential was Kakapick with the freewheeling author so high on the Kakapick Universal Scale that Kakapick, too, shone by reflected Visibility. In this way Kakapick supplied himself with credentials to prove his entitlement as literary critic. His intimacy qualified him.

But having understood the matter in these ways, turned it over in his mind, Rimrose soon saw it in yet another: why not see Kakapick at his best? Kakapick must have thought that his tribute to Rimrose was a great service which should have been pleasing to him and to Lucy. Kakapick could not have imagined Rimrose's caring the less for flattery simply because it was made of lies. Flattery inflated reputation. Enough to be written about and thereby made famous, to be discussed, mentioned, disseminated among the colleges! Most of the writers of the world would have rejoiced to see an article about themselves in MANNA. Whole pages! My God, poor wretched writers swoon for ten lines in print about themselves.

What was anyone to make of these first fifty stories? Kakapick presumed to know the chronology. But in fact he had no way of knowing the order of their making. Rimrose himself could hardly have figured it out. Only Lucy, working from records of her own according to a system of her own, could have guessed.

The thing was beyond belief. It fascinated Rimrose. He read along as fast as he could, missing as much as he could, as if the sight of it pained his eyes. But when he was done he was drawn back with unaccountable fascination to those passages he had skimmed. They had been college roommates, Kakapick said. But of course they had not. Nor had Rimrose ever gone out on the town with Kakapick. He could remember only the night they had gone with Polly Anne to dinner to celebrate her graduation, and from that night he recalled especially Kakapick's mournful confession, "Very few people invite me anywhere."

How was Rimrose to mention this to Lucy, whose spirit descended into hell at the sound of Kakapick's name? He would burn this thing, bury it, hide it from her. But he would do a better job than Guillermo Gardener in "The Rumpled Bed," who had never successfully hidden the saucy greeting card. How easily Guillermo's wife had discovered it! Rimrose would hide this issue of MANNA in a perfect place where Lucy never looked.

Where could that be? He strolled about Listing House, looking for the perfect place, but the house refused to yield such a place. He saw what a small house it was. How poor they were! And when Lucy returned he was unable to keep this news to himself. "I've got something to mention to you you're going to find depressing," he said. His wife lifted her chin for whatever distress her husband was about to share with her. "Kakapick wrote this detestable lying article about me in that magazine of his—totally insane, making up a whole past we never had or anything near it."

Lucy, hearing this, spoke in the way she had prepared. "Oh, that," she said, "I saw it in the library. I knew it would only make you angry. Don't be angry. It's worth money to us."

Rimrose wrote a story called "Exclusion," renamed it "First Month's Rent in Advance," then returned to "Exclusion." He was confident it was the best story he'd written in a long time. "I really feel it's the state of my art," he said.

"It's Jamesian," Lucy said. It was going to be a hard sell.

Only after his story was done did he recognize it as having sprung from Lucy's memory of something that had passed across her mind at Thanksgiving dinner. Simply told, it was this: once, when she was a girl, a certain man still vivid to her memory had been present as a Thanksgiving guest in the house of the Reveres in White City. Something happened to make her uneasy. She had come upon the man in a shadowed corner of the house, in conversation with her mother. The man was speaking hastily, quickly, in a guarded and unnatural way, glancing down at Lucy as he spoke, as if he wished she'd go away. Long afterward the idea dawned on Lucy that the man, whoever he was, had been her mother's lover.

A quarter of an hour after completing the story Rimrose received a phone call coming as if to reward him for his dedicated labor. One Professor Perch, chair of English at Randolph B. Kendall University, was asking if Rimrose would consent to be a candidate for a position teaching writing. The position paid "in the neighborhood of forty-five thousand dollars to start."

"I'd love to live in that neighborhood," said Rimrose. "I accept."

Not that easy. Professor Perch invited him to come to Randolph B. Kendall University "for a few days and let us look you over, and you look us over too, you know," and Rimrose said he would if Kendall paid his fare. "I hate to sound like a cheapskate, but we Rimroses live on a close budget." Professor Perch said golly, sure.

And would Kendall University pay Lucy's fare, too, Rimrose asked, admiring himself for his businesslike foresight, because in the end the decision must be Lucy's who was mother, wife, cook, chauffeur, bookkeeper, accountant and literary agent. "Well, golly," said Perch, "it hasn't been Ran-

dolph B. Kendall University policy to pay fare for one's wife."
He said it couldn't be changed—policy was policy.

"Then I just couldn't come," Rimrose said, remembering
from his *Sentinel* days how people improvised "university
policy" from moment to moment.

Professor Perch promised "I'll be back to you," and so he
was in twenty-four hours to say golly, sure, Randolph B.
Kendall University could pay Lucy's fare after all.

The children pleaded to be left home unattended except by
one another—"no sitter," they demanded, they would not
murder each other, they would not set the house afire, they
would feed and water the animals, they would lock the doors
at night. "You'll be surprised when you come home, we'll all
be here just like you left us," Eartha said.

The problem was not the children but the Cingalese watch
bird, who had been ill and whose care Lucy would entrust to
nobody. Thus Lucy and Rimrose and the bird in his cage flew
to Chicago, and from Chicago in a small airplane of the Randolph B. Kendall University Airline to the Randolph B.
Kendall University Airfield, where they were greeted by the
assistant chair of English, representing the *actual* chair, Professor Perch, who had been unavoidably detained at a meeting with the dean. The assistant chair spoke the word *dean*
with mock respect. "I consider it an insult that Perch didn't
come to meet you."

"Let's think nothing of it," Rimrose said.

"It's not doing his job. A man of your literary stature takes
precedence over a dean," the assistant chair replied. He
added, willy-nilly, "I read your article in MANNA." That was
to say, *Kakapick's* article. It was Kakapick's article that had
fired enthusiasm for Rimrose at Kendall.

Rimrose was determined to enjoy this January vacation. Enjoy everything, he thought; dine out, observe people, think
long thoughts, be one of the people on whom nothing is lost,
sleep well on vacation from children pounding upstairs and
down in their boots.

Lucy and Rimrose were housed with their Cingalese watch bird in a spacious bright suite in the Randolph B. Kendall University Visitors' Center. The bird thrived and screeched a noisy watch when they were gone from their suite. They were passed from person to person, they dined in good restaurants and enjoyed several home-cooked meals besides. They dined out more in five days at Kendall than they had dined out in months at home, and none of it cost them a penny. Rimrose never touched the green money in his wallet.

His presence was advertised on bulletin boards. Lucy carried home posters to impress the children—

A WRITER IN THE HIGHEST CIRCLE OF EXCELLENCE
HAIL A NEW PRINCE OF THE AMERICAN STORY
—MANNA

Three of his story collections were stacked in the bookstore among pyramids of toothpaste and coffee mugs painted with funny thoughts, bringing back to him that long-gone moment in the university bookstore on the day he and his father had come down from Zygmont. And here was that memory in print before his eyes, "His Father's Fingers Clawing at His Back," in *Footlocker Tales: Seventeen Early Stories by Rimrose.*

He saw in the *Student Voice* that he was to offer a reading one evening in the Randolph B. Kendall University Holden Caulfield Auditorium. Holden would have observed with richest irony the frequency of the sight of the phrase "Randolph B. Kendall University." The late Mr. Kendall had stipulated that the name of Randolph B. Kendall University never be abbreviated. His face appeared on every bank check issued in the name of the university. When Randolph B. Kendall gave $150 million to the former Bissell College, he expected a little something in return.

Yet even this week, however, the student newspaper, the *Student Voice,* had entered upon a campaign to revoke his edict. In a lively editorial it computed the cost in labor and newsprint of writing out "Randolph B. Kendall University" where "Kendall" would do. Rimrose, pressed in an interview by a student reporter, praised the editorial.

He might in that moment have cost himself the job. Rimrose the dissenter had revealed himself. This was a job he hoped to win. He should keep his mouth shut. His income had never approached forty-five thousand dollars a year. The job offered a fabulous family medical plan and educational benefits for the children if they didn't set the house on fire. The mightiest advantage of all, as he could feel it, slicing forty-five thousand dollars in his head, was the way in which the job would ease his brain, rest his emotions and all his muscles of contrivance and invention, for it would permit him to write two or three good hard, solid, durable stories a year instead of a dozen under forced draft. It would make life possible for him again in ways it had not been for a decade. He was dry, he was weary, he was writing too fast, too much. Now he could rest, recover and in significant ways begin again. The money, the money—he envisioned himself free of necessity, free to keep every story at home until it was absolutely done.

From the stage of the splendid Randolph B. Kendall University Holden Caulfield Auditorium the nervous professor introducing Rimrose to his audience referred to him repeatedly as "famous . . . well known," read the names of eight or ten Rimrose stories in no particular pattern from a piece of paper in his hand, and spoke Kakapick's sugar-filled passages from MANNA as if they were his own.

Rimrose read two stories. One was very old and the other was his newest. He read "His Father's Fingers Clawing at His Back," which he had not for years read all the way through. He took pride in the stalwart enduring sound of it.

The second story he read was "First Month's Rent in Advance." This was the work he had completed just before Professor Perch's phone call, adapting to a fresh premise Lucy's memory of her mother and the Thanksgiving visitor. In the present version a young woman leaving home for the first time introduces her father to her landlady. Father and the landlady are instantly mutually attracted. They pursue a romantic conversation. The presence of his daughter sharpens the father's subtlety. Seeming to speak of the dangers of a young woman's living alone in a college town, the father and the landlady, by revealing their own passionate youth, are in fact engaged in a flirtation so discreet as to be inaudible to the daughter.

Now, hearing the story in his own voice, Rimrose knew how very good it was, a masterpiece, surely, of broad temptation uttered in a language of utmost indirection, quite Jamesian indeed, as Lucy had said. The students of Kendall, who had mightily applauded "His Father's Fingers Clawing at His Back," sat silent through the new story. Only the rarest college student could have received it. The students were excluded from the story even as the daughter in the story was excluded from her father's conversation with the landlady. Exclusion *was* the story. Rimrose thought, *Of course I should have known,* and of course he should have, but it had always been his illusion, renewed with each round of creation, that everything he wrote was already too clear.

Lucy and Rimrose slept poorly at Kendall. They lay awake late talking through this whole possibility. Would they come if they were asked? "Are we ready?" Lucy said. Did Rimrose really want to teach? How would teaching affect his writing? When at last they had talked themselves to sleep the Cingalese watch bird for some unexplained reason awakened them.

At receptions and dinner parties at the homes of professors they met many people. The houses of the professors were grander than Listing House. Rimrose came away with sweet sensations of the comfort in which the faculty lived. Comfort, security, the future. The education of the professors' children was assured. Professors traveled about the world. They were awarded sabbaticals and paid leaves almost for the asking.

The Randolph B. Kendall University Endowment earned more money than the university found ways to spend.

The professors promised Rimrose and Lucy that the weather was not really this bad year-round. They guaranteed that housing was affordable. Banks loved to lend money to Randolph B. Kendall University professors. The cost of living was lower than you'd expect. The academic calendar was favorable to anyone who loved long vacations (as who didn't, eh?). In exchange for these blessings one spoke as instructed the mouthful "Randolph B. Kendall University," one didn't call it Old Kenny or Old Randy or RBK in the manner of the sportswriters. It was a small price. "You get used to saying his name," one professor said, "just as you get used to his face on your paycheck."

Professor Perch's plan for Rimrose was to present him first to meetings of faculty and students. If the masses found him acceptable, Professor Perch would pass him along to the finer sensibilities of the men and women of the upper bureaucracy. On the fourth day of his visit Rimrose met alone with Professor Perch and Dean Astralzy in the dean's private inner humming office: the lights, the phone lines, the dean's private personal humidifier—everything hummed. Dean Astralzy said he had read Rimrose's novels, and Rimrose said he had not written any novels, he'd written only stories. He should not have said this. He never told Lucy.

Dean Astralzy proceeded as if he had not heard. He assured Rimrose that Randolph B. Kendall University was "competitive with all the big ones, and while we're talking size," he said, rising from his chair and inviting Rimrose to join him at the wall map, "look here how Randolph B. Kendall University spreads itself across acres after acres of unlimited future. I was about to say virgin territory," he said, "but I won't," laughing man to man. Rimrose tried to laugh but failed.

Dean Astralzy expected his faculty to be writing and publishing books and getting their names in the literary journals. He was "extremely grateful" to Professor Perch, he said, for having shown him the write-up of Rimrose in MANNA. He challenged Rimrose in the following way: "When you think of such a thing as MANNA coming out of a little old backwater place over there like Cactus Country University, doesn't it make you begin to think what a whale of a little publication you might print right here? Think how it would start to make a name for us."

Rimrose thought that with $150 million Kendall U. could make a name on its own. He did not say this. He said as earnestly as he could, "Yes, that's the way we've got to go, we've got to make a name for ourselves."

Two English department faculty members were assigned to escort Lucy and Rimrose one rainswept morning to the Randolph B. Kendall University Antiquarian Collection, where they saw or hurried past some very old books, and to the Randolph B. Kendall University Rare Manuscript Section, where Rimrose examined with natural interest manuscripts of stories by Melville, Tolstoy and Flaubert, from whose scratchings and painful revisions he received even through glass the vibrations of the writers' struggle for alternatives in every line, their return to first choices, their changing their minds again, their indecision, their falling back, their recovering, their advancing.

From the Randolph B. Kendall University Rare Manuscript Section Lucy and Rimrose were escorted beneath umbrellas to the football stadium and the baseball field, out of the rain into the basketball arena, and from the basketball arena through a half-mile underground passage to the Randolph B. Kendall University Physical Fitness Complex, where they were taken by surprise to see a naked young man running screaming down a public hallway. Weeks afterward, from the Randolph B. Kendall University Director of Physical Education, Lucy received a dainty letter apologizing "for any inconvenience you might have experienced during the time frame when you as a distinguished visitor were being conducted through our ultramodern Randolph B. Kendall University Physical Fitness Complex."

Lucy, Rimrose and their Cingalese watch bird were to have been driven back to the Randolph B. Kendall Airfield by the assistant chair, but today it was *he* who had a meeting with the dean. They were driven instead by two graduate students whose plan it was to drive on to a town beyond the airfield and marry. They invited Lucy and Rimrose to their wedding, but the Rimroses declined on the grounds they'd been gone too long from their children.

The bride said she hoped he'd get the job. "If there's anybody we need," she said, "it's you." Rimrose said he hoped so too. The bride said she heard the decision would be made by Easter, and Rimrose said yes, that's what he was told. The bride and groom asked Rimrose if he'd mind reading the manuscript of a novel they had written, and he said okay, send it on to University City, but luckily they had it right there with them in the front seat. They passed it back.

On the airplane Rimrose sketched a sentence many readers will recognize as belonging to the clean line of his sardonic story "The Dean of Virgin Territory": "The dean from his humming two-speed swivel chair said, 'I've read all your books,' by which was meant 'My secretary only this morning placed some of your books on the corner of my desk.' "

All Rimrose children home alone in Listing House had managed almost perfectly well without their parents. Jupiter, in the interest of science, had drained the hot water from the tank "just timing how long it would take to heat up again." His inquiry shut down the system. Millie Fishback came across the street, got it started again, became alarmed at the sound of little explosions within, and recommended the plumber, who with a twist of his wrench revived the system for fifty-five dollars.

The trip to Kendall had restored the Cingalese watch bird to his former health, refreshed Rimrose, and done good things for Lucy, too. The prospect of change in their lives delighted them. They had lived a long time in one small listing house. Rimrose imagined a more spacious life with his forty-five-thousand-dollar job in a house he and Lucy would be able to purchase with the help of the free-spending bankers of Kendall. He sketched the arrangement of a new workroom for himself. He drew a list of useful writing implements he had never had space to own. He wrote several stories, among them "The Dean of Virgin Territory," which in his optimism in the days after Kendall he expected to sell readily.

He had a fine feeling about Kendall, as if everything had gone right every minute. But Easter came and went without news; no word, no message from Professor Perch or Dean Astralzy. From whom was he to hear anyhow? He had no idea. Really, in fact, he recognized that he had no idea how things worked at this level of a university. Who told whom what? Who made these decisions? He had heard that the "committee" would decide.

How would the news be conveyed to him? By mail? By telephone? The mail from Kendall had consisted thus far of letters from two professors he had met, and from the wife of another, each of whom possessed a treasured literary manuscript he or she knew Rimrose, inundated as he was by the obligations of his profession, could not possibly take the time to read—and yet, and yet, might he not just "take a look at" what they had done. He was at pains to agree, not to take a look at but to read; looking wasn't reading.

He also received from Kendall the good surprise of a $500 honorarium, as it was called, for "Reading and Lecture Vendor Service," much reduced by deductions for city and state taxes in a city and state in which he did not reside and in which he gradually began to assume he would never vend again. He also received reimbursement for Lucy's and his airfare, this too with city and state taxes deducted as if it were earned income. Should he protest this? Should he antagonize the Kendall checkwriters precisely at the moment he was hoping to be appointed to a job at that place? The checks bore the photograph of Randolph B. Kendall. Even so, he returned them uncashed and eventually received adjusted compensation at a welcome moment. For money, every moment was a welcome moment at Listing House.

He read the novel submitted by the wedding couple in the car and the works by the two professors and the professor's wife. He responded to the writers with letters of genuine admiration for aspects of their works mingled with discussion of their flaws. He never heard in return from any of the writers—not the briefest thank-you note for his time, his hard work or his arduous diplomatic criticism.

The Rimrose children tired of dinner-table speculation on the question of whether they ever *would* hear from that mythical institution called Randolph B. Kendall University. "Let's either go or not go," said Vanessa, "tell them to make up their minds so we can make our plans." "Don't be so shy," said Marco, "get them on the phone, you went all the way down there, the least they can do is give you an answer. Get on their ass."

When Rimrose and Lucy wondered one day whom they knew at Kendall who might possibly explain the delay they became aware that the people most likely to speak confidentially with them were the people least likely to know anything. The people for whom they had instinctively felt affection were powerless faculty of lower rank, older professors above the battle or cringing polarized artists frozen out of the line of bureaucratic power. "Our crowd," Lucy said. Had they been done in by their Cingalese watch bird crying midnight alarms in their suite in the Randolph B. Kendall University Visitors' Center? To some people it had seemed odd that Lucy had brought the bird. Was Lucy Rimrose quite right in her head?

Maybe Rimrose should have spent less time with the powerless faculty, more time with Perch and the dean. This may have been his big mistake, he thought, he should have gone harder for the company of the decision-makers. As days passed he began to imagine ways in which he had offended Professor Perch or Dean Astralzy. Had he bargained too hard with Perch during that first telephone call? Perhaps Perch or the dean had read into his interview in the *Student Voice* things he had not intended. During one long fretful weekend Rimrose suspected he would be rejected on the grounds of his not having earned an advanced degree. Among the professors at Kendall a mere bachelor's degree was no degree at all— everybody in the world had a bachelor's degree.

Perhaps Perch and Astralzy had not liked his story, "First Month's Rent in Advance," which Rimrose had read that night in the Holden Caulfield Auditorium. Perhaps it had offended them—though come to think of it, Dean Astralzy had not even been there for that occasion. Perch and Astralzy were always excusing themselves to go off to fulfill unbreakable prior commitments. The thing was, Rimrose thought, he should have shown more *enthusiasm* for everything—for example, more enthusiasm for the idea of making Kendall famous with a new MANNA. Not that he'd have edited it himself, but he'd have supported it, encouraged it, written for it, that sort of thing; he should have come right out and said so, exhibited *enthusiasm*. Damn it, he should have been more of a good fellow, should have gone tagging around everywhere with Perch and Astralzy and shown them the qualities they were looking for in him, shown them a stable fellow, a party-going sort of fellow, a mixer, not the sort of person that hung around with the department yarn-spinners and low-ranking ragged bearded artist types.

Here's what the problem was, Rimrose thought: he had not sufficiently concealed his dislike for the dean. No, said Lucy, the dean to begin with never looked at anybody steadily enough to perceive such a thing. She thought Rimrose had behaved very well, very tactfully, he'd seemed to be in a happy mood the whole time, no lurking animosity, he'd been honest and yet "not too awfully truthful," she said, he'd been a good job applicant, she thought, he'd played his part well, he'd acted as if he had become immediately fond of everyone they met. With gusto he had shaken every hand in sight, smiling insanely like a politician.

"We were *too* agreeable," Rimrose said.

"Agreeable is what they're after," Lucy said. "They want everybody to get along."

"I got along with everybody for five whole days."

"What more could they have asked?"

At some moments, reviewing those Kendall days, Rimrose suspected that the students had not liked him. They liked his early stories better than his later stories, the early man better than the present man. For all its wealth, the university was loath to displease students. The students thought he was peculiar. The word went round that he did not drive a car. Possibly his age was wrong. He was too old. Unless he was too young. They wanted a pal or a grandfather type. Next time he'd tint his hair gray. But there was no next time—this was the time that mattered. If Kendall didn't take him he was in a lifetime jam. Nothing as good as this could ever come again.

Whenever the telephone rang he thought it might be Perch or the dean, and he invented extremely brief speeches for them to deliver. "Congratulations, you're hired."

Polly Anne Cathcart, lately appointed director of the Office of Savings and Economy, phoned at mid-morning asking him to lunch. Rimrose accepted happily, yes, he'd love to, love to go to lunch with her anywhere nonalcoholic because he'd heard a while ago she'd been in big drinking trouble, not for the first time. "Drunk and reckless," she said. Her license had again been suspended. For eighteen months she'd been "on foot and taxicab," but that was over, she was so happy now to be driving again she couldn't wait to go to lunch with him. "I pleaded guilty to the reckless but not the drunk," she said.

The university had appointed her director of the OSE in spite of her sins. "My talents exceed my liability."

"They always did," Rimrose observed.

She was no longer a mere sleuth but a master sleuth, director of sleuths, buried among her telephones tapped in to other people's conversations, sending her staff sleuthing as she had once sent *Sentinel* reporters on their altruistic missions, getting the evidence on bad guys and turning it over to the good guys. "And as soon as the good guys start turning bad, I get the goods on them," she said. It was exciting work, lots of variety, and above all the perquisite of the Health Plan. "I haven't been sick in weeks," she said.

She picked him up on Mile Wide Avenue, at the intersection where she had picked him up once in the past. She did not remember that occasion, but he did. "We went for a drink at the Sauerhaus. The afternoon went by so fast I was late for dinner and Lucy got mad. But I got a good story out of it. 'The Rumpled Bed.' "

"I don't think I ever read it," she said. "Was there a girl in the rumpled bed?"

"A woman," he said.

"Was it I?"

"It really was and wasn't."

"That's how you do in all your stories."

"Sort of. A woman sends a man one of those funny cards his wife doesn't find so funny."

"Oh, that sort of woman. Where can I read it? I'll see if it was me in the rumpled bed."

"Does this worry you? You look worried."

"Not a bit," she said, but she was. She feared his making stories of fragments of her past. "There's nothing you can write about me that worries me. Everybody knows I used to be a virgin. I hope you made a lot of money revealing these facts of my private life."

"Actually I think I made more money from that story than

any story I ever wrote. It was in *Various,* and then it won a big prize."

"How much?" she bluntly asked. "How much did it make? Give me the sum total. Round figures."

"Ten thousand dollars," he said.

"I make ten thousand a month," she said. "Around the calendar. How'd you like to make ten thousand a month?"

In the university district they walked familiar streets, choosing finally a modest place called the New Delhi, formerly the Old Delhi; formerly alcoholic, now dry. Each of them had the vague impression at the same moment, as they entered, that they had been here before, a long time ago, years ago, perhaps together, perhaps not.

They had been here with Kakapick. Neither remembered now. "Did you ever write a story about Kakapick?" she asked.

"I started one. Then I wrote a piece about him once for *Sentinel*—"

"I remember that. It got him arrested for book-stealing."

"The article didn't get him arrested. The photograph did."

"Did you see his article about you in that bloody boring scholarly rag he runs? What did you think of it?"

"It made me angry and uncomfortable. I walked around the house furious for half a day and then I began to put it out of my mind. It was full of terrible lies—big lies."

"Kaka wouldn't be caught dead telling the truth," said Polly Anne. "It's awful stuff, just so awfully badly done. We did *Sentinel* a million times better, and we were the merest children."

"I'm told it's influential," Rimrose said.

"Of course. That's why he does it. What he wants is influence. He wants to rule the world."

"Do you ever see him?"

"He comes to town," she said. "He's a big wheel in the college racket. He's going to the top of things if he isn't there already. He's in demand. He's juggling job offers all over the place."

"Is he still down there at—"

"Cactus Country," she said. "But not for long. What was the story about him you never finished?"

"Oh, it wasn't really about him."

"No, I know, none of your stories are ever about anybody—"

"It didn't come to anything. It was about a man stalking a woman down dark streets—"

This alarmed Polly Anne. "Kaka doesn't stalk women down dark streets."

"I'm sure not," Rimrose said, though he was not sure at all. "It was just that I took him into my mind's eye, that's all, he was my image while I wrote."

Polly Anne was not appeased. "Why him? Why did you take him in your mind instead of somebody else? Where did you print it?"

"I never printed it. It never got printed. I guess it never got finished."

This relieved her somewhat. "Are you still working on it?"

"Oh no, God, no, it's buried under tons of stuff if it's anywhere at all," he said. "You look so worried. I don't imagine it even exists anymore, we must have thrown it out long ago, burned it up—"

"He'd die if he thought you were putting him in a story."

"He puts people in his articles in his damn little MANNA."

"That's his business. He's a critic."

"Critics hurt people. Critics kill people. Critics run artists out of business."

She was astonished to hear this. "I thought artists didn't care," she said. She imagined that writers of fiction were indifferent to critics, that though their hard labors and precious works were trashed in public places they felt no pain. She startled him by asking, "Are you writing any stories about your experiences down at Kendall?"

"How did you know I was down at Kendall?"

"Oh, we know everything," she said. "That's the fun of it."

"Do you mean to tell me you're still tapping my telephone?"

"I don't mean to tell you anything."

What else did she want him to know she knew? He was determined not to ask her. "Do I want to be eating lunch with somebody that taps my phone?"

"Sure you do," she said. "Because you'll find things out you didn't know. It's a service I run for old friends. I've got something to offer you. I wouldn't have known how badly you needed it if I hadn't found out things on your telephone. I've got a job for you with very good money."

"And a Health Plan," he said.

"Oh, the best," she said, "for everybody in the family and the cats and dogs and mice and birds and horny toad. I wouldn't be caught dead without my Health Plan. Suppose you don't get the job at Kendall?"

"I'll feel extremely downcast all day and into the night," he said. "Then Lucy and I will make love."

"Will you consider coming to work for OSE?"

"I don't know what I'll consider. Probably I'll just go on pumping out stories harder and harder with less and less pleasure."

"I need you so badly. A man like you, you're the steadiest most brilliant most moral man I know, and you're money honest—you wouldn't pinch a penny not your own—and you're sober and you're motivated. That's a rare combination of things. You're the only man in the world I can trust."

"Hire a woman," he said.

"Can't trust them, either. You're not making any dough," she said. "You need this job—"

"Would I really make ten thousand a month?"

"No, not right away, maybe never. How about we start you at five? How about five thousand a month? It's three times what you make now. That's not bad as a starter. Consider it's a noble cause. It's a rescue operation—you're rescuing the university. Consider the university—just the wonderful idea of the university. The university is terribly big money, you wouldn't believe it, money's not supposed to be what a university is all about. Then scandal follows money, and you and I at OSE put down the scandal. We catch the crooks, we put them in jail. You and I keep people honest like we did on *Sentinel*. Is writing a noble cause?"

"Not as noble as it used to be," Rimrose confessed. "It's harder going than it used to be. I make some big compromises."

"Big compromises for little money," she said, not with contempt but with pity.

"I wish I could write less."

"You had a chance once to come to OSE. I asked you in, you remember? Now I'm giving you a second chance. Most people only get one chance. Come to OSE." Her patience was gone.

So was his. "I'm going to Kendall," he said.

"Rim," she suddenly said, "you're not going to Kendall. You're not getting that job there. They're turning you down at Kendall."

So that was what she knew. He felt her gaze upon his face to see how he was taking it, and he said what she'd known he would say. "Lucy is going to be disappointed." He hated Polly Anne for telling him the news. She took some sort of pleasure in being a witness to his defeat. "You're enjoying yourself," he said.

"I don't mean to."

"Why did they turn me down?"

"They had bad stuff on you."

"Like what?"

"Oh, a whole great big stack of stuff, especially from your student days. The Indian Fee campaign, lots of your editorials, your down-with-football, up-with-female-archery campaign. People were ready to lynch you about that. That archery cost the university a lot of friends. By friends we mean money. You knew football was sacred."

"You told them the bad stuff about me."

"I didn't tell them anything about you. Nobody asked me. The university told them."

"The university got it from you."

"OSE's got a file on everybody. We've got one on me, too. I was as much of a troublemaker as you were. But when they need somebody really really good and brilliant, they're bound to end up with a troublemaker. You were a bad boy, you know, you gave the university lots of trouble, lots of grief."

Polly Anne had shocked Rimrose with her news. Now he shocked himself with his own. "I'll go home and edit my father's paper," he said. "He'll pay me the forty-five thousand dollars Kendall was going to pay me. Forty-five thousand in Zygmont is like ninety in University City."

Not until this moment had the idea become real to him. Not until this moment had Zygmont become an alternative to Kendall. It sounded right and good to him now.

Polly Anne's eyes narrowed with envy at the thought of the idyllic life she imagined him living in Zygmont, turning out the town daily in the bosom of a loving family. It was a life she could now happily accept.

Rimrose saw Zygmont in his mind. He saw at last a place of safety, a haven. Home to Zygmont, he thought, like the poet said. "Home is the place where, when you have to go there, they have to take you in." Home he would go with his wife and his children and their numerous zoo.

6

ONCE again in glorious autumn his loving, affectionate father drove him one hundred miles between University City and Zygmont. Twenty-one years ago he had driven his boy in the other direction, from home to school.

His father today was discreetly joyful, for his son's coming home was the father's victory. Father tried hard not to say "I told you so," although he had told him so, having followed over the years all the forecasts of failure. He had heard the silence of the telephone at Listing House. The moneyed editors had stopped calling. The boy had ceased to produce the stories they wanted. The boy was stubborn, difficult to work with, somewhat too keen to see the moral angle everywhere. In this he was like his mother. Only the moneyless quarterlies called.

"I remember the first time we took this trip," his father said.

"Yes, I remember it very well," said his son. "We had that old beat-up green footlocker with us."

"I don't remember that," his father said.

"We still have it around the house. We keep old manuscripts in it. It's got a book named in its honor—*Footlocker Tales.*"

"That's right. We've got the book. I've read all your stories and I love them."

"I doubt that you've read *all* my stories, dad."

"I read every story mother ever gave me to read."

"The first time we took this trip I was inspired to write a certain story," Rimrose said.

"I read that story," his father said. "I know the one you mean. I didn't like it. I raised the roof about it with your mother. Well, it embarrassed me. It wouldn't embarrass me so much anymore, but it embarrassed me then."

In the story the boy was departing from home for the university. The father had wanted the boy to remain at home in the family business. The father feared the subversive influence of the university. In the story, the boy condemned his father's narrowness. He accused his father of reaction. They strolled about the campus. They visited his room, where his roommate lay sleeping.

What was it that had embarrassed Rimrose's father as he saw himself in the story? It was the moment of parting. The boy attempted to kiss his father farewell, but his father's head turned from the kiss. Yet, a moment afterward, "the boy could feel his father's fingers clawing his back," and the boy knew or understood and could certainly feel through his father's fingertips his father's deepest and most genuine love and urgency.

Rimrose's father had read the story as a tale of his own defeat. He denied that such a parting had occurred. When at last he understood the story as a tribute to his own struggle to reveal his love, he chose to believe the incident had occurred as his son had written it. But having denied it, he could not then confess it. The editor of the Zygmont *Herald* seldom retracted anything.

In Zygmont his father introduced him everywhere as "my boy." "This is my boy, he's taking it over."

Rimrose was the father of four children. How then could he be a boy? If Rimrose was a boy in his father's tongue, Valerie Eischberg was a "girl" who would find him a house. Father introduced her as his favorite real-estate agent, and so she might have been. Rimrose remembered her. She had worked awhile at the paper. Once he had seen his father kiss her beside the teletype machines. Had she been his father's lover, or had it been just a passing affectionate kiss in the office? Rimrose had been too young to differentiate one kind of kiss from another. He thought now he might write a story about a son's encounter with his father's lover. But he was not here to write stories. He was here to preserve his family's business.

The Eischbergs were an immense force in Zygmont. There were more Eischbergs in the Zygmont book than anybody else. Valerie's grandfather had been one of ten brothers. Rimrose recalled many Eischbergs he had gone to school with. Lining them up in his head, he amazed Valerie with his memory for detail.

She was half a generation older than he. She talked freely about everybody who had ever set foot in Zygmont. She was amusing and restful. He was with her for almost two weeks, in and out of her automobile a hundred times, and afterward he found her style of conversation useful in stories: long monologues with truth at the center. She drove him everywhere looking at houses for rent, houses for sale, and houses-for-sale-or-rent-with-an-option-to-this-and-that. "It's a wonder you never took up car driving," she said. "I'd have thought a grown man would have mastered the idea by now."

"I get everywhere," Rimrose said.

"Sure, you get everywhere," she said, "because people take you."

"You don't have to take me," he said. "I'll try to get somebody else."

"I love taking you," she said. "You're handsome and interesting—why shouldn't I want to drive you around? You remind me of your father."

She escorted Rimrose to many houses potentially suitable for rent for his family and its numerous animals. But landlords declined to accept so many animals. Valerie was unreconciled to the idea that Rimrose and his family and their animals were united and inseparable. She urged him to part with his animals. But that was impossible. Well, then, she urged him at least not to mention the animals to the landlords. But that also was impossible. "I could forget to mention a medium-sized dog or one or two small cats," he said, "but that's only the beginning."

"You'll have to buy. Nobody will ever rent to you," said Valerie.

One afternoon during his days of house-hunting Rimrose dropped in at the First Town Bank and Trust of Zygmont to see how its president, Angelica Vanenglenhoven, might appear to him and he to her so many years after their summer of love on the beach at Zygmont Lake. She knew it was he when he walked in. He looked like his father, she said.

He had not recognized her, but he did not tell her that. Her body was bones. Perhaps she was ill. Her appearance so shocked him he blandly said she hadn't changed. She knew better. "You'd need to be blind to think so."

He could not believe that her body had so grossly withered. He remembered her as beautifully robust and glowing, the portrait of athletic energy. He saw again in his mind's eye the flowing strength of the girl she had been. He saw her running nude by moonlight, tireless across the beach. He could not help himself. The vision had drifted for years in his head. Could this woman really have been that girl? There must be some mistake. Suppose he had married her.

Whether Angelica visualized *his* body he did not know and did not ask. In her office behind the vaults they drank tea. She prophesied that he'd do a good job on the *Herald*—he'd done such a good job of the university paper. And what had he been doing all these twenty years between? She knew he'd been "some sort of a writer," she said—she had once begun to read a story of his in a magazine on an airplane. "I couldn't understand the words," she said.

He winced. "That'll stop you," he said.

She too had returned from another life to work for her father. That had always been the plan, but when the time came to return to Zygmont her husband demurred, and she came alone. She did not know where her husband was now. From time to time he telephoned, left his number, but she forgot to call him back. "I never had the knack of returning calls," she said.

"I remember," he said. "I waited one whole autumn for you to phone me."

"God punished me for not answering calls," she said. "He gave me bums for husbands." Her children were scattered, out of touch with her and each other. She blew on her tea although it was already cold. Her father's bank had sapped her health. First Town Bank and Trust had prospered even as she declined. She recited numbers to Rimrose to prove the strength of her bank, but he was as little capable of understanding her numbers as she had been of understanding his story on the airplane. "Your dad's reporters wrote me up a couple of times in the paper," she said. "I'm the only female bank president for miles around."

But that was not the story Rimrose saw. Her story lay in her withered body, which Rimrose imagined as the outward sign of her dead or despairing soul or interior, not at all the angle his father would have featured in the *Herald*.

After a week Rimrose and Valerie Eischberg carried their search from the city to the countryside featuring here and there the loveliest graceful old farmhouses, cheap to buy and impossible to maintain.

The prospect of the countryside introduced the question of distance. Rimrose had committed himself to a different kind of life from any he had led. He was no longer to spend his days writing in a little room in his little listing house. He was to live the days his father had lived through Rimrose's boyhood—breakfast meetings, dinner meetings, civic meetings, fraternal meetings, early mornings and late night crises. It was a mighty distance between country and city for a man who did not drive. He might buy a second car and a chauffeur to come with it. After all, he was to earn forty-five thousand Zygmont dollars. "Make your wife drive you," Valerie said.

"That's not how it works in our family," he replied.

"Make one of your children," she said, "or you'll have to learn to drive."

The first house he looked at one morning in the middle of his second week of his search was neither in city nor country. It was neither large nor small. That is to say, it was by every measure larger than Listing House, and yet it appeared from every angle of vision smaller. It was brown. It was a box. Rimrose laughed when he saw it—yes, a brown box set down neither on the flats nor on the slopes. Directly seen, straight on from any of the corners of the compass, it appeared to have no depth, to be but a wall, not a house but four independent unattached freestanding walls. At such a sight one could only laugh. Of every house except this Valerie Eischberg had said, "It has character." Of this she said, "It has no character." She was surprised that he had even the slightest interest in it. She had begun to believe that he had no interest in any house anywhere in Zygmont; that he did not really want to find a house; that he wanted to go back to University City and write those endless vague stories nobody but his mother read.

He paid on deposit five hundred unrefundable dollars borrowed from his father—one month's rent. He said, "Lucy will make a house out of it," but Valerie Eischberg said nobody could make a house of it, it hadn't the makings of a house, she had showed it to him only out of perversity: he had not liked anything good, perhaps he would like something grotesque. And yet, if he wanted it she'd help him get it as long as he promised never to invite her into it. Her job was not to condemn his taste but to find him the house he thought he wanted.

Lucy and Vanessa came to Zygmont to see the square brown house Rimrose had found. When Lucy saw it she laughed.

"After all," she said, "we won't be able to see it from the inside." To console herself she added, "It's not as if we own it."

Rimrose immediately regretted having paid the deposit. He supposed he had made a decision only to end the search, rest his feet. "All right," his mother said, "you'll have fun in it awhile until you find something to buy." When his father saw the brown house he laughed and said, "They should have painted it brown."

In the car, on the hundred-mile drive from Zygmont back to University City, Eartha burst into tears of anguish and rage. She declared that she would never invite her friends from University City to visit her in her family's ugly brown house in Zygmont; or, if she invited friends she would blindfold them and rush them inside. She was angry that her father had found this house amusing. No true normal father had a right to be amused at his children's expense. He had become a senile money-mad barbarian desperate for salaried work.

Lucy at the wheel imagined herself one day soon conveying her husband, her children, her goods and animals from Listing House to the quaint brown house in Zygmont. Her mind dwelled first upon the animals. The project called for a certain segregation of the species. She would rent a small van. She would move the animals by van in two or three well-organized journeys. Her scientific son Jupiter could figure it out. The fish would travel in sealed tanks. The bird cages would swing by wire suspension from the ceiling of the van. Lucy imagined for herself an orgy of housecleaning. She would fulfill her long-time ambition to abandon to the trash accumulated objects which had burdened her sight for years, ten thousand things nobody cared for and nobody could part with. She would jettison tons of junk in the night. Now she was ready to start her life fresh. She could name every item of possession her family had ever brought into Listing House and guess the year if not the month of its acquisition. She had a memory for pots and pans and fishbowls and for every story her husband had written. She knew every book in her house.

But the more she contemplated their future, the less likely it appeared. She could not honestly imagine her husband a single day in the editor's chair at the Zygmont *Herald*. Who would drive him to work? She saw herself become the mother of a family of chauffeurs. Each child in turn would tire of the task. She could not begin to imagine her husband's lunching with Rotary, dining with Kiwanis, twisting the Lions' tail. She said to him as they drove, "I'm trying to see it."

Rimrose tried in his mind to move his family out of Listing House into the brown house in Zygmont, but his imagination failed him. He ceased to be able to imagine anyone's living in the brown house. He could not envision the house furnished. He saw it remaining empty forever, as he had seen it on the day he rented it. As the miles dissolved between Zygmont and University City he ceased to be able even to imagine himself imagining it. His defeat was utter. He came to believe he would never live one day or one night of his life in the brown house. Where then would he live and how?

In his stories Rimrose had written everything he had known or felt about the boy's life he had lived in Zygmont and left behind. He told himself now that by living there again he would see it all anew. Zygmont had formerly been a place in a boy's mind. It was another place now—all to do over. When he was a boy the mysteries of Zygmont had lain beyond him. His years of absence had been his means of seeing it again with a mind enlarged by experience.

Thus consoled, he was cheered for some miles by the prospect of his new life in the service of his family's provincial newspaper. Once a certain passage in Willa Cather had deeply impressed him, and now he understood its consolation. Someone had said to her, "Of course, one day you will write about your own country. In the meantime, get all you can. One must know the world *so well* before one can know the parish." He resigned himself to the idea that for a while he would write nothing at all, but then!—then he would spring forth into the clearing with stories of his parish. These would be the stories of his maturest life, his art in fullest form.

To be practical, however—exactly what hours of the day would he devote to writing these parish stories for which his knowledge of the world had prepared him? At the Zygmont *Herald* the editor's work was never done. To be truthful, the thing Rimrose faced was a death, a silencing of himself. He was to be not a writer but a manager of scribblers and space salesmen. The business of the Zygmont *Herald* was to tell a kind of story, not fiction, not invention, but only the utter truthfulness of absolute factual verifiable occurrences like fires, police chases, political races, varieties of violence, drownings in Zygmont Lake, and news from afar—reports from a distance about Zygmonters gone away and become successful elsewhere.

In the world's opinion Rimrose's father was right about life, and Rimrose was wrong. Stories were things seen, not hearts or minds imagined. Not father alone but the whole hard pragmatic world preferred the daily *Herald* to Rimrose's stories. He had had his chance. He had made a run for it. He had never really earned much of a living. Father had won. The boy was coming home to edit the paper to the taste of the world, to be a consenting partner to the idea that a dog fight on Mountain Avenue was bigger news than revolution in China. In Zygmont only Zygmont mattered, advertising space, the opinions of merchants and the scores of ball games. Readers of the Zygmont *Herald* cared to know which roads were closed by snow. Father's readers liked to be able to phone the paper to verify the year of the Zygmont flood, the Zygmont rockslide, the year of the fire, and the scores of those games during that miracle season when Zygmont High triumphed undefeated, untied and unscored upon.

And what of his father's five hundred dollars paid down as deposit? At first he could think only of that money, dwelling in his mind upon it as if he could persuade himself that it represented the whole sum of his father's disappointment. "We've got to live in that house," he said. "My father put five hundred dollars down on deposit."

"Undeposit it," she said.

"Can't be done," he said.

"Can't be helped," she said.

"We'll lose it."

"Lose it."

Lucy had driven one hundred miles in two hours. The journey had seemed to her longer. Her husband's face, as they drew to the curb at Listing House, was ghostly pale. No moment of their lives had ever been more discouraging.

And yet, in the few seconds which followed, all existence transformed him, turned him about. At the corner of the porch he took from the mailbox a letter in a familiar university envelope on familiar university stationery, from Kakapick, newly appointed chair of Literature, inviting Rimrose to accept a position as professor in University City. In his mind Rimrose accepted the position before he finished reading the letter. It stipulated a salary he would have seized had it been only half. He was saved from Zygmont. Lucy saw his pale face regain its color, his life and health resume.

The text of Kakapick's letter was this:

> *Accept herewith my formal invitation on behalf of the University to accept a position as professor in the department of Literature of which I am to become Chair beginning Fall term. I hope you will notify me immediately accepting this position. Within one week thereafter you will receive formal notice of your appointment from the President of the University.*
>
> *I hope you will appreciate the fact that I fought hard night and day amidst many complexities to make your appointment a reality. During long ongoing negotiations with the University I have made your appointment one of the chief conditions of my accepting this Chair.*
>
> *Your basic salary will begin at $60,000.00 for the academic*

year. Your appointment is as a tenured professor, permanent and irrevocable. In addition to this basic salary you will receive annual increases of pay as state law provides and many family and personal health and welfare benefits, travel perquisites and professional aid and assistance to you in your work as Fiction Writer.

You will teach two courses, called Writing the Story, serving a maximum of fifteen undergraduate or graduate students in each. Students will be selected by you as you see fit from a pool of well-prepared applicants.

I hope it will be an inducement to you to know that I am also bringing to the Department, in addition to other professors of extreme distinction, the publication MANNA, which I am sure you have had occasion to examine. I hope that from time to time you will write critical and imaginative articles for MANNA. I have edited MANNA for several years at Cactus Country University, but I am happy to come to this city and this university now with ever greater freedom to pursue especially the working out of the Kakapick Universal Visibility Scale which you and I discussed together so often so many years in the past.

We too, as a department, are going to become great and visible. That is my ambition. In that venture I am hoping you will play a vital role, for we have before us every advantage of a mighty and well-respected institution in a favorable location poised on the cusp of the future. We are to become the greatest and most formidable, best-known department of Literature in the world. You and I, Rim, will sweep everything before us.

Kakapick

ל

IT was a new life.

On the morning of his first day of his new life one half of his mind computed the number of days to payday and the other half struggled to discover what to say to his students and how to say it. Lucy drove him to the campus. She turned off her motor and alighted and ran round to his side of the car and kissed him and embraced him for reassurance. With her kiss she also gave him the best advice on teaching he'd ever get. "Just be yourself," she said.

Sounded good. He thought he'd try it. Payday came once a month. God knows that was what he was here for. It was the money they needed.

He met his first class in a small room in the one-time Chapel of God, whose name had been altered to Chapel Arts under the combined pressure of *Sentinel,* the changing age and Polly Anne Cathcart. In an auditorium across the hall he had first set eyes by the luck of the alphabet on his fellow-student, the former Lucy Revere of White City. There they had studied Marriage and the Family 424. In the doorway one morning in exuberance he had kissed her.

Today in the vicinity of Chapel Arts he lost his way. Where had that pile gone? In the university scheme Chapel Arts had once been a big building on campus, but it was almost invisible now, dwarfed by sleek haughty high-rise right-angled functional steel and glass. Rimrose asked a passerby—a young man, a boy, a mere red-haired student—"Do you happen to know what they ever did with Chapel Arts?" The young man was charmed by Rimrose's irregular way of asking the question. He replied, "I'm going there myself," and they walked together.

The young man had been scouting for a course to take. A friend suggested a course in writing to be taught by the writer Rimrose, but Howard Malone (for that was the young man's name) had never heard of Rimrose. "So I thought I'd come down and take a look and see what he looks like," Howard said.

"How will it help to see what he looks like?" Rimrose asked.

"I'll see if he looks like a writer."

"I really seriously wonder," Rimrose said, "if anybody can tell who's a writer just by looking at him."

Howard replied, "Oh sure you can."

"I'm Rimrose," Rimrose said.

"You don't look like a writer—not that you don't *look* like a writer," Howard continued, quite as if he had not said what he had said, "it's only that you look like something else. That's all I was saying. If I was asked if you were a writer I'd say maybe."

They paused at the doorway to the classroom. "I hope I look like a teacher," Rimrose said.

Twenty students awaited him. Counting Howard, twenty-one. Kakapick's letter had said fifteen. No matter. Here he was obliged to remain three hours, though as far as he knew he hadn't three minutes' worth to say. The first words he spoke as teacher were, "I was a student in this building twenty years ago or thereabouts."

What did they make of that history? Nothing. They weren't about to make anything of it. He was the teacher and *he* was supposed to make something of something. "In this building I met my wife. We took a course called Marriage and the Family, and after the class was done we went away and gave birth

176

to four children. I wrote many stories I disseminated to the world and now here I am again back in this old red building. That's the whole story of my life."

His students by their silence challenged him to make it lead somewhere. "Well," he said, "maybe that's all it's worth—silence. You didn't come here to hear about my life. Maybe I shouldn't say anything more. But think of the wonder of this —even if I say nothing at all I get paid for it. Thinking of payday strengthens me." He thought of the money he owed. One way or another he'd get the hang of this class. It was a problem to be solved, like a story. He'd arrive there. How to begin?

He said, "The way I teach a class—" as if he had taught many classes. "I understand you want to be writers," he said, but that was not the case, really; some of his students did and some did not, and on the whole they had no idea how to measure their lives against the thought of writing. Rimrose confessed that he himself had not intended to write stories. From his father he had inherited journalism. He could remember no moment of decision. The idea of stories had just come to him all on a summer day when, between spring and autumn, he'd caught the summer bug, he'd become infected, addicted; his fever persisted to the end of summer into the rest of his life, and here he was now, standing before them, fool that he was, as deep in debt as a man could be who hadn't credit enough to go deeper. "We lived our best years on seventeen thousand dollars and help from home."

The beauty of the women dazzled him. The women were readier than the men to smile at him. Their naked bodies were covered by mere clothes. *Just be yourself,* Lucy had said. One very young woman with black hair in bangs put him in mind of his daughter Eartha. What would Eartha demand of the teacher? "First off, no bullshit, dad." Well, he'd try.

Rimrose suddenly said, "If you won't talk I've got to lecture. Here's a lecture. A person starts to make a story the way

I'm talking now. You have a sort of idea in your head and you want to get to it, you want to spill it out and educate the world, but you don't want to write it like an essay, you want to write it like a story. You want to tell it through incidents and actions. You start with an incident. It was Thanksgiving Day and you went to your grandmother's house. Or maybe you start with a person. You take somebody into your mind. Your grandmother again. The boy next door. Your mother, your father, your fellow-student, your boss. I've got somebody in my head I'd like to write a story about someday. Maybe I'll start it tonight, maybe I'll never start, I don't know, I've got to sit down and see what happens."

"Who was she?" one of the women asked.

"She wasn't a she. He was a schoolmate of mine. He roomed down the hall in my dorm. He was a strange fellow, he had strange habits, he was fairly misanthropic and he made an awful appearance because of his—well, he had a conspicuous defect that made him not want to smile. It occurs to me just this minute, the way things occur to you once you get a story in motion, that his whole feeling about life was shaped by his defect. If he couldn't smile he wouldn't even try. He'd take the position that the world didn't deserve to be smiled at. People stink. Let them die. He was an ambitious fellow. After college he dropped out of sight and I didn't see him for years and didn't expect to see him again, but now and then he popped back into my life in surprising ways. In my heart I never knew whether to laugh at him or pity him or fear him or take him very seriously, and I don't know even now, how to feel about him. Is he just a nut or is he a very danger-ous nut? He frightened my wife. She couldn't stand the sight of him. Once when he came to the house she ran out the back door with the children. Then one day after all those years apart he ended by doing me a great favor. He suddenly came into my life again. He made me an enormous gift, coming at me with enormous largesse out of the blue, so it's hard for me to write about him or tell the truth about him, or think straight about him.''

"What was this enormous gift?" Howard Malone asked. "Was it a car?"

"What's going to be the point of your story?" another student asked.

"I don't really want to make a point of anything. I don't want to use a story to pay off debts, and I don't want to grind an axe, I just want to write about him and see what I discover. I'll just make him a character, I'll put him in one fix or another, I'll present him with a predicament and I'll imagine how he'd get out of it. In his terms, not mine. That way I'll know him better than I've ever known him in life. Maybe by writing him out I'll understand him, I'll become acquainted with him as I never could in life. Now," said Rimrose, "I feel right this minute that the more I talk the more I confuse myself, and the more I confuse myself the more I want to find a story to write about this man, hoping that by writing about him I can finally understand him or know him. Beginning a story is like beginning a class called Writing the Story number-such-and-such in the catalogue''—here several students supplied him with the correct number.

The worst was over. Rimrose saw how this might be the most beautiful job in the world: three hours of conversation with twenty-one intelligent innocent striving people, and payday down the line. His body was released from its tension, as after the first pitch of a ball game. Now he knew everything he needed to know to begin.

Howard Malone drove him home. Rimrose could have reached home quicker by some other means. Howard made everything more difficult than it ought to have been. He was unable to remember where he had parked his car. "Describe it to me, I'll help you look for it," Rimrose said, but Howard declined. "It's indescribable," he said. Rimrose waited at the tollbooth while Howard found his car, which appeared to Rimrose as describable as any other—a dented red Datsun several years old "donated to the cause" by Howard's parents, and at present low on gas. They stopped for gas. Rimrose's legs were too long for the Datsun front seat. Howard said he'd "snap the seat back," but he instantly forgot.

After a distance on Mile Wide Avenue Rimrose urged Howard to try for the left lane for the turn at Bismarck, but Howard missed it. "I'll know better next time," he said, counting already on a next time and a next time. In Rimrose he divined a man whose heroic soul invited his allegiance. Three hours earlier Howard's conviction had been that Rimrose did not look like a writer, but his conviction now was that Rimrose looked *exactly* like a writer.

He lived in a state of amazement. Dozens of things amazed him every day. Pausing at Listing House, he said, "Do you realize something amazing? Your house lists." Moments later when he met Lucy he shook her hand and said, "I'm just dropping by, I can't stay, but I'm telling you, your husband, Professor Rimrose, is the most amazing teacher I ever had."

Rimrose could hardly believe the luxury of his university job. He was certain this bliss would end at any moment, that he would wake from tranquility to the reality of four stories on his desk in wretched stages of incompletion, and Lucy's table covered with unpaid bills. At that edge they had always lived.

His teaching week was over before it began—began on Thursday and ended on Friday. On the first payday of this new life Rimrose endorsed his check and passed it to Lucy, who made a sizzling sound between her teeth and said, "For what? For two afternoons a week?" For many years he had worked long days of a seven-day week with no certainty at week's end of selling the work he had written. His father still worked seven days a week at the Zygmont *Herald.*

*   *   *

His students charmed him every day. Their virtues of mind and spirit soon became apparent even in those from whom Rimrose began by expecting least. On the whole they admired him, too. He recognized that the qualities they perceived as the wisdom of the master was only his paternal inclination to strengthen young writers (as he encouragingly called them), to give them the benefit he had had of his mother's art and his father's discipline. As he would never discourage a child of his own from any venture, he would never discourage anyone else's.

His university office was a splendid domain. From its wide windows he enjoyed an excellent view of a shady walkway where romantic students gathered. Rimrose came to know who was whose. In his mind he developed stories for them. On the walls of his office hung photographs of several professors of a former era. Rimrose had no idea who they were. His students concocted lives for them.

His office was furnished with a subtly glistening cherry-wood desk and a rolling swivel chair, straight chairs for visitors, a filing cabinet, bookshelves, a word processor, a printer, a telephone. When he opened his filing cabinet the odor of chocolate improved the air. Someone fond of chocolate had kept a supply. In his cabinet with the chocolate odor Rimrose also retained copies of student stories. During his first year of teaching he read one hundred stories. During his second year, as he grew ever more skillful at the art of encouragement, his students would produce twice that number.

Over time he acquired a reputation for steady habits and reliable availability. He was always at his office when he said he would be, faithful to the hours posted on his door. He gave his telephone number to anyone who cared to have it. He never missed a class.

*   *   *

At the year's first department faculty meeting Rimrose sat in the last row of an assembly room charged with the heat of ninety-seven bodies beside a man named Jackson who introduced himself as a professor of medieval literature and said, "You probably don't know many people yet. Of course you know Kakapick. You went to school with him."

"I'll know everybody soon," said Rimrose.

"Now you know me." They shook hands. "I've been waiting all summer to see how Kakapick runs it," Professor Jackson said. "Everybody's got his style, you know."

The meeting was late beginning. It was Kakapick's style to be late. Jackson said, "He's the star. You'll never see so many people at a meeting again." He fanned himself with a manila folder.

When the door opened a hush fell upon the room, but the newcomer was not Kakapick. She was a young professor not without wit. When she saw the disappointment in the faces of her colleagues, she said, "Sorry about that," and found a seat.

Kakapick entered with a touch of theatrical surprise, not from the front of the room but from the back. He was accompanied by an assistant carrying only a clipboard and appearing underemployed. Kakapick strode to the front of the room. Somebody down Rimrose's row asked, "Is that Kakapick?" and someone replied, "You better believe." Kakapick stepped up to the lecture platform. His assistant handed him his clipboard, which Kakapick tossed to the table with a kind of disdain. He did not introduce himself. He was no longer an anonymous boy with a calling card. He was a man who was visible.

He was waiting for something. It dawned upon Rimrose, perhaps sooner than upon anyone else in the room—perhaps because half his life he had been meditating on the character of Kakapick—that Kakapick was waiting to be applauded, that he had been awaiting this moment longer than anyone here could imagine. But the only sound was silence, and Kakapick in confusion began to speak in a halting, hesitant manner, as if he expected the lost moment to return, which, in his imagination, it did, for actually he raised his hand to subdue the sound of the absent applause nobody heard but him. Into Rimrose's mind flew an odd bit of doggerel from a source he could not name nor even try to place—"He stilled the rising tumult, he bade the game go on."

With the deepest interest Rimrose observed Kakapick. The least likely boy in Westby Second East seemed to have taken command of his profession. There stood the boy at the door to his dormitory room—half-open to invite a visitor, half-closed to reject a visitor, the boy who declined to shake hands or lend a book. As Kakapick spoke he walked. Long ago the athletes at Westby Second East had satirized his slinking gait. "It was like he just picked your pocket," someone once said. But he had come a distance up from insult to authority. He was the boss here. And where were the athletes now?

Kakapick welcomed the members of the faculty back from their summers of study, travel and all good serious things, prepared now "to confront the challenge of the year ahead." How could Kakapick welcome the faculty back? He was new here himself. "Literature is becoming more and more visible," Kakapick said. By "literature" Kakapick did not mean literature, he meant the *department* of Literature of which he was Chair and whose greater glory was his plan, his dream, his intention; to make the *department* visible, to put the name of the department on everyone's tongue, to double and treble its enrollment, to be known all over the academic world and beyond.

Consulting his clipboard, he offered several announcements, among them the news he had told Rimrose in his letter, that he was bringing MANNA to the department. Its name would soon be changed (he did not mention this today) to KINANA—Kakapick's Index to Notable Authors of North America. It was his dearest hope and expectation that members of the department would, by writing for MANNA, improve their own visibility in the profession. The department, too, on the Kakapick Universal Visibility Scale, was certainly to become great, visible, vital, the greatest, most formidable, best-known of all departments of Literature anywhere, "poised on the cusp of the future."

Now the department *did* applaud. Kakapick would make things happen. He was a dreamer out ahead of things. No doubt the increase in the visibility of literature would assist humane purposes of every sort, although it was also true, and for most members more to the point, that the larger and more visible and more renowned and more influential the department became the more money it would command and the greater the happiness of all the men and women of its faculty. Their wages would rise. Their schedule of benefits would expand.

Kakapick extended his congratulations to those members of the department who had made "productive use" of the summer by completing essays, studies, monographs, books, who had delivered talks, lectures, readings, who had attended conferences and workshops, traveled to literary sites, or been mentioned in print or over the airwaves as having in some way distinguished themselves. Their advancement within the department depended upon their being noticed somewhere by somebody. "The thing we value is recognition."

The hour was at hand, said Kakapick, to introduce to the members of the department its illustrious newcomers. For each of these newcomers the summer also had been its own triumph—was it not a triumph to have been hired *here?* And the department, too, by engaging these people, added distinction to distinction—nay, *multiplied* distinction. "These are people who have *done* something," Kakapick said.

He presented the newcomers one by one: their names, their fields of study, the colleges and universities they had attended. Consulting the papers on his clipboard, he cited the academic achievements of each of the newcomers, the prizes they had won, the notices their work had received and the words of admiration with which they had been described by notable persons in their respective fields. This room burst with distinction.

As each person was identified by name and credentials he or she stood at a signal from Kakapick awkwardly and uncomfortably to be applauded, to wave one's hand a little, to speak a few words, usually platitudinously, always nervously, sometimes cleverly, turning first in one direction and then in another to be seen from every side. Soon the applause wearied and sounded mechanical.

Kakapick came in time to "the last and the best," he said, "the famous writer we've been waiting for." He tossed his clipboard to the table again—this was a man he *knew*. "The last and the best," he said, "is our outstanding newcomer, our master storyteller who has made a very great reputation in the world, a man I have known a very long time, he's an old pal of mine, my old classmate, we were roommates down the line in Westby Hall, house of athletes. Professor Rimrose, please stand."

Rimrose could not stand. The weight of his body oppressed him. To stand was to lend the idea of truth to all that Kakapick had said. He sank low into his chair. Afterward he thought that the word *best* had arrested him. If only Kakapick had not said *best*. Nobody was best. The room was filled with people who were good at what they did. One was one's own best. He also remembered afterward his numb perception of many members of the department turning this way and that in their chairs, stretching their necks—*to stretch one's neck; how had he never noticed before how perfect that phrase was?*—stretching their necks for a glimpse of this best person whoever he was, this famous fellow, this athlete, this outstanding master of whatever it was.

Kakapick waited for Rimrose to stand. But something had gone wrong. There sat Rimrose with bowed head as if he had not heard himself introduced. He should have been standing.

Kakapick had asked him to stand and Rimrose had for some reason defied him. Kakapick's teeth turned black again, as they had been before, in his past life. So it felt. He found his voice. He spoke. But his voice, too, had failed him, rising in his throat as it had risen on that terrible day when he had run to Rimrose to plead with him to expunge his name from the police report in *Sentinel.*

So he began again, as if he had only this moment entered the room. "I'm Kakapick," he oddly said. He thought that if only he named himself Rimrose would stand. Kakapick felt himself obliged now to tell the world once again who he was. He spelled out once more his youthful intimacy with the Rimrose he now celebrated, he told of the athletes among whom they had lived. He invented lives past, bringing Rimrose and himself forward together as two wild boys grown now to distinguished manhood. "We were as wicked as we could be," said Kakapick. "We were rakes, I suppose, and then, too, there was Marigold; we boys had a name for her, we called her Marigold the Naked."

But who then was Marigold? Rimrose sought her in his mind. She was the girl in his story "Getting to Class Regularly on Time," read and savored by all the young men in Westby. But she was only a creation in a story. She was not a figure of life as one knew life. Kakapick had never learned to separate story from life. He believed that Marigold was real and that Rimrose had married her. He had come once to Rimrose's room in the middle of the night to discuss this very question. Herndon had thrown him out.

Once again Kakapick asked Rimrose to stand. Rimrose understood himself to be proof or evidence of Kakapick's claim to license as a literary man. Rimrose was to be his proof of identity, his verification, his entitlement, his certification of himself as rightful deserving chair of a body so rare as a department of literature. But Rimrose could not stand. He spoke from his chair, and when at last he spoke he could speak only in the direction of the truth as he remembered it. He addressed Kakapick in a clear, calm voice, as if they were alone. "I need to tell you before we go any farther that you've lost the facts over the years. We really never shared anything, not rooms, not books, not girls, not campus mischief, nothing, nothing; we never stole anything together, we never stole books together, and there was no woman named Marigold."

Kakapick burst forth. "Marigold the Naked."

"She was an invention in a story."

"She was real."

"She was not real."

"She was your wife."

"She was not my wife. My wife is Lucy, not Marigold."

"Marigold the Naked," Kakapick said again. "We shared everything."

"We did not share my wife."

Kakapick tried to smile. He said again, "Professor Rimrose, please rise," but he could not persuade Rimrose to rise from his chair, and he spoke once more in the thickening silence. "People are waiting for you to stand," but Rimrose had no more to say.

Professor Jackson, sitting beside Rimrose, was mortified. He spoke urgently to Rimrose. "We should do what the Chair asks us to do. You must stand up. He's the Chair. He's *introducing* you."

"That isn't me he introduced," Rimrose said.

Someone applauded—striking hands together three times, three angry claps. Then throughout the meeting room many people applauded, perhaps to shield Kakapick from his humiliation, perhaps secretly to praise Rimrose for his resistance to ritual. The applause sounded the end of the meeting. The members adjourned themselves. Later the minutes of the meeting, official memory of the department, named the newcomers whom the chair had introduced, Rimrose among them, as if he had stood with the rest.

* * *

In the first hours after his humiliation Kakapick's mind failed him. His necessity overwhelmed reason. As he had once imagined that books became his property by his stamping his name in them, now he imagined he had the power to place Rimrose on trial and punish him. Was he not an administrative officer of the university? He was the department Chair. As Chair he was surely empowered to hold hearings, call witnesses, charge Rimrose with malicious arrogance, with assuming an attitude of superiority. All the newcomers but Rimrose had stood when they were asked. Why not Rimrose? Kakapick in his thinking suddenly became a democrat. "Nobody is better than anyone else," Kakapick declared to himself. "Does Rimrose think he's better than everyone else? Does he believe the conventions of the department apply to everyone but him? The department is a democracy. One person, one vote. Mere distinction counts for nothing here."

When Rimrose declined to stand, Kakapick felt doomed. In that moment he lost all appetite for life. His body conspired to starve him. At the dinner hour he walked from his apartment to the Faculty Club, but the odors of food repelled him. He saw at a distant table a member of the department whose name he did not know. The face of the member seemed to say to him with satisfaction, "Kakapick has lost his lion. So! You captured him but you couldn't keep him a week."

Kakapick had not only lost Rimrose but lost him at a meeting conducted before that world which was his public life, his constituency, the base of his power. One hundred members of Literature would carry forever their memories of the spectacle of Kakapick's abasement and rejection. Kakapick had been toppled in a moment.

At the Faculty Club he glanced at the menu, put it down and returned to his apartment. His body trembled and faltered. He believed he must have done very wicked things in life to be made to suffer in this way. That night, during his sleepless hours, the idea occurred to him to reconvene the meeting, assemble all the department members once again to a meeting which had not even been properly adjourned. There he would have it out with Rimrose.

He went to his telephone, intending to sound out his most reliable associates on the idea of reconvening the meeting. He would recommend that the department censure Rimrose. He would fire Rimrose. If only he could! He had not asked much of Rimrose. He had asked Rimrose only to stand and make his face and presence known. That was a little thing to ask, it was only a formality, a courtesy. Every department of literature should have one famous member, someone visible, national, widely reviewed, a prize-winner who nevertheless participated in the daily life of the department, serving on committees, obeying the Chair, being a team member. At the reconvened meeting Kakapick would once again ask Rimrose to stand, to show his cooperativeness, to show that all members were equal in obedience to the Chair.

By what right did Rimrose make claims upon the rules? Nothing distinguished Rimrose from anyone else. This Kakapick had discovered during his weeks as Chair. Half the people in the department had never heard of Rimrose. Few members had read anything he had written but his best-known stories, the stories "everybody knew." Many members knew him if at all through Kakapick's widely known heralding article in MANNA. "Hail a new prince of the American story."

Rimrose had been made by Kakapick. If Kakapick had made him, Kakapick could unmake him.

On the other hand, Kakapick had become aware of the powerlessness of the Chair. The department of Literature had been governed for years by elected committees and old established bonds of friendships, cliques, prejudices, antagonisms grounded in custom and time. He had begun to discover the inconvenient degree to which the department was governed by regulations. He had thought the office more powerful than it now appeared.

He sat at his telephone table. But he perceived his good idea to be a bad one. Sensible people would tell him he was making too much of this matter. Yes, right, much too much. He hoped so. Let it blow over. Therefore it occurred to him to make nothing of it at all, never to mention it to anyone, never to think about it again, to be sensible. And yet, if he had been simply sensible through life he would not now be Chair. It had not been sensible professors who had saved him, but his dentist. Fatigue overcame him at his telephone table.

When Polly Anne awakened him his body was stiff, his muscles were sore, he was frozen to the shape of his chair. The morning sun shone fiercely bright on the stark walls of his apartment. She sat in the chair beside him. She had come because she was frightened. Now she was only angry. "You look fucking dead," she said.

"I am," he said.

"Who killed you?" she said.

"Didn't you hear?" he asked.

"I didn't hear anything," she said. She had heard several versions of things. "What should I have heard?"

"Rimrose broke up my meeting. He sabotaged me."

"Sabotage is what the university does best," she said.

He told her his misfortune. Partially she listened. Not his misfortune but his dead white face distressed her. "Are you sick?" she asked. "If you're sick why didn't you go to bed? It was your chance to read a book. You look dreadful. Have you eaten anything?" She toured his kitchen but she found no food. "Not even a can of coffee," she said. Spiders had spun webs in his kitchen sink. "I heard you made a mess of introducing him. You told them how you and Rimrose were old buddies from way back in college days, how you screwed the same girls. He never went for that. Don't you learn anything?

Why did you expect him to like it now when he never liked it before? I'm dying for breakfast. Let's go somewhere."

"He was lying in wait for me."

"Don't flatter yourself. I thought you had his cock in your pocket."

"I thought so, too."

"You told them you and Rimrose not only screwed the same girls but one of them was Lucy. He wouldn't have liked that. I could have told you he wouldn't have gone for that."

"I never mentioned her name."

"Whose name did you mention?"

"I mentioned Marigold."

"Who the fuck is Marigold?"

"She was the girl in the story."

"Who you always mixed up in your head with Lucy."

"They're going to talk about this forever," said Kakapick.

"Nobody's going to talk about it. Nobody cares about it but you."

"He'll write about it," said Kakapick. That was his worst fear, to be written up, to exist forever as a joke. "He's going to ruin me."

"He hasn't the least interest in ruining you," she said. "He didn't like what you said so he didn't stand up. It's over. He's a writer, they're always taking moral positions on things. All you do with a writer is twist the language around the way they want it and they think the problem is solved. Don't you have at least some kind of old used beat-up instant coffee somewhere around?" She went again to the kitchen and slammed the cabinet doors so hard they bounced open when she shut them. She was angry. She wanted her breakfast. "Forget it," she said. "When you lose pretend you won." She sat beside him again.

"He's a famous man," Kakapick said.

"Fame's not worth shit," she said.

"A famous man made me look like a moron in front of my department," he said. "He'll make me into a story."

191

"You're not on his mind that much. He put me in a story once. I was a girl in a rumpled bed. So what? It didn't make any difference in my life."

"He knows a lot of confidential things about me. Do you ever hear him talk about me?"

"I don't see him much."

"You listen to his phone."

"I don't listen to his phone."

"Sure you do."

"I never heard him talk about you."

"I wish I could listen to phones. It would make running a department much easier."

"It sure makes running a university easier," she said.

When Kakapick arrived at his office one of his assistants said, "We missed you." Since none of his assistants, nor anyone dropping into the office, nor anyone on the telephone mentioned the terrible event of the faculty meeting, Kakapick began to form the impression that it had never happened. And yet since the thing so obviously *had* happened, the universal silence was the more sinister.

As the day progressed his life returned. He realized how wise he had been not to have telephoned people in the night. Up and down the department corridors he saw that nobody seemed to have taken this matter seriously. On the battlefield of this war nobody had been wounded but him.

When you lose pretend you won. His appetite stirred. He could smell his own hungry breath. He thought he could help his cause with nourishment. A bowl of cafeteria soup might sit just right.

But at that moment the sight of Rimrose destroyed him again. Here came Rimrose up the quadrangle stairs into Literature in the company of a student, a red-haired boy. There the man walked guiltlessly, whole and healthy, as if nothing had gone wrong, as if the faculty meeting had never occurred. The student walking with him appeared to be listening to him with awe beyond attention, as if Rimrose knew more than anyone else. So too had Kakapick once believed of Rimrose the writer, and so he believed to this day. Rimrose saw Kakapick's inner mind. Rimrose saw Kakapick's fantasies of the night. Kakapick in the night had destroyed Rimrose in violent ways, flattened him, stomped him, punched him to death. He thought he had done with Rimrose. Yet here Rimrose was, climbing the quadrangle stairs. Then Rimrose disappeared into the labyrinthine Literature building.

Kakapick returned to his apartment. He slept hard all afternoon. When he awoke he experienced the helpless sensation that his sleep had been neither sleep nor rest. He attempted to dine at the Faculty Club, beginning with the soup he had thought to enjoy for lunch, but before he had eaten half his cup his exhaustion overcame him. He walked halfway home. The fresh air restored his appetite, and he returned to the Faculty Club to finish his meal. His waiter, who had cleared his place, was confused to see him.

At home his weariness returned with such force he had not the strength to sleep. He dreaded the hours ahead. He did not believe he could endure another sleepless night. It occurred to him to swallow a quantity of sedatives, but he feared oversleeping and then missing his morning appointments. Again and again he drifted toward sleep, but each time he was almost asleep the memory of yesterday's meeting returned.

He envisioned a wonderful, blissful reconciliation with Rimrose. If only he and Rimrose could have a good heart-to-heart talk they could settle all things. He would telephone Rimrose this minute. But the harm had been done. No matter what action was taken, the horrifying event itself could never be canceled. It was lodged forever in the memories of a hundred people, carried abroad in the world. Members of the department had already written letters to their friends, telling how Rimrose had defied the Chair, how the author had declared his contempt for the critic, how the artist had declared his contempt for the man of mere authority.

Defiance and contempt had been followed by applause. That moment of applause came back to Kakapick. What had been the meaning of that applause? Someone had begun to applaud and everyone took it up. Were they applauding Rimrose? Did everyone rejoice in Kakapick's defeat?

He walked long distances through the bare rooms of his apartment. His heels echoed. He thought again to call Rimrose. Rimrose should have stood when Kakapick asked. What could have been simpler? Rimrose had embarrassed Kakapick before the department. Kakapick had hired Rimrose, given him everything he could have asked, but in return Rimrose had assaulted him. Why was that?

At half-past two in the morning he left his apartment. His destination was Listing House. Mile Wide Avenue was deserted all the way. Kakapick had visited Rimrose at home some years ago. Lucy had absented herself. She had always fled from him. He would awaken Rimrose now and have it out with him at half past two in the morning. He had no clear idea what he was going to say to Rimrose once he found the house. He would begin, "We're old friends and we can speak frankly. Isn't that true? I have things to give and things to take away. I want you to apologize to the department for the thing you did to me. I can do terrible things to you. I can make your life misery here. I can make you suffer."

But what could he actually do to make Rimrose suffer? He was uncertain about that.

He would destroy Rimrose's animals. Often he thought of such a thing. He could not imagine Rimrose and Lucy and their children loving animals as they did—not dogs and cats alone but all sorts of fish and beasts and birds and creeping crawling things, lizards and snakes and rats—and yet he supposed it was so, disgusting as it was. He did not himself love animals, and he felt the Rimroses' love of animals as a rebuke to him. He would set their animals afire.

194

He almost sped past Listing House. Then he recognized it. It was an odd little tilted house. He braked his car hard with a terrible noise on the quiet street in the quiet night. The house was dark. He ran from his car up the walk and up the steps of the porch to the very door of the house and stood with his finger inches from the doorbell. Then he caught hold of himself. Only days ago, a week ago, ever since Kakapick had first dreamed of being Rimrose's benefactor, offering him a fine job, Kakapick had seen himself working with Rimrose. Rimrose was to have been the shining star of Kakapick's department . . . old friends from long ago . . . athletes . . . rakes . . . "You and I, Rim, will sweep everything before us."

Now things had turned about. He had been divested of all power. Rimrose's life was beyond Kakapick's control. Against Rimrose, Kakapick was defenseless. Rimrose would make Kakapick the doomed subject of his writing. Rimrose would destroy him with his writing. And why not? Kakapick would have destroyed Rimrose if he could.

He ran to his car. But he turned and ran again from his car to the house and jumped to the porch. The house trembled. Somewhere inside the trembling house the Cingalese watch bird awoke and began to sing his morning song, but when the bird saw that morning lay still in the distance beyond darkness he ceased to sing and began to screech in alarm, to cry in the most distressed and ominous way, forlorn and afraid, raising his warning. He awakened the dogs. The cats raised their heads. Lucy lit her bedside light. Kakapick at the sound of the bird turned from the house and ran again to his car. He was so weary he dreamed of sleep.

8

ONE day, one month after the unfortunate faculty meeting, Rimrose arrived at his lovely office to discover that he was unable to turn his key in the lock. This was extremely uncomfortable, placing his senses in question. It was a mistake, obviously, for the number on the door was his, and his name was on the door. But no, his name had been stripped away.

He hurried to the department office to complain to Kakapick that something wicked had occurred, unless it was only the simplest sort of silly mistake, which he doubted. "Right you are," he was crisply informed by one of the young women of Kakapick's staff, "it was no mistake, it was Professor Kakapick's decision, he's moving offices around like mad."

Rimrose asked to see Kakapick. But Kakapick at the moment was neither being seen nor seeing, he was out of the office, said the young woman of his staff, he had gone to "a crucial meeting" either over at his KINANA office or at the president's office; and when he was done wherever he was he'd be "scooting on down to his shrink," she said, whereupon Rimrose said he would wait.

"Why don't you wait in your office, we'll give you a call when he comes back?" the young woman asked.

"Because I don't have any office to wait in," he said, and he sat.

"Why don't you drop down and see your *new* office?" She was sure it would please him, and she gave him his key.

Drop down indeed! It was a fact. Rimrose descended to the basement to see his new office. It was tiny. It was dark and airless, its walls scarred and punctured over the years by its occupants, who were young short-term temporary untenured teachers, often graduate students, often feeling that they hated this place. The office had no window, no shelves, not even a hook on the wall for Rimrose to hang his hat. It contained a beaten desk but no chair. In this office Kakapick had shuffled three-by-five cards, indexing dead authors until the day came when he substituted for theories of world unification dreams of statistical evaluation.

Rimrose remained half a minute. He returned to the department office to wait for Kakapick, who, it turned out, had not actually gone to his KINANA office or to see the university president, or to his shrink, but to his dentist. Kakapick's dental problem so far preoccupied his mind that he presented it instantly to Rimrose without even a word of greeting, as if Rimrose had come to talk dentistry.

Kakapick was convinced, in spite of anything his dentist or his mirror told him, and in spite of Rimrose's reassurance (for Kakapick opened his mouth wide to show Rimrose inside), that his teeth had begun to grow black again. Years ago they had been black. "Then years of intensity calcification pulled me out of the muck and slime. Don't think I didn't know the world was laughing at my teeth."

In recent years his teeth had been white, as a man's teeth should be. But now he saw or felt that they were turning black again—"invert calcification," he said, "that's what they call it"—in spite of anything anyone else might say.

"They look perfectly white to me," said Rimrose.

"They look perfectly white to my fucking dentist, too," Kakapick said. "I used to think he was the greatest man who ever lived because he rescued me from hell, but I don't know now, he may have lost his touch," once again opening his mouth wide for Rimrose.

"I didn't come to examine your teeth," said Rimrose. "I'm

not a dentist, you know." His sympathetic tone turned to anger. He had not meant to sound so angry. "Why have I been moved out of my office?"

"Because I moved you out," said Kakapick.

"I want to be moved back."

"You're not to be moved back."

"Why is that?"

"Because you double-crossed me," Kakapick said. Now he, too, passed beyond the question of his teeth.

"I can't work in that office," Rimrose said. "I need a better office than that. I'm not a kid anymore."

"I thought you were going to be a team player. I was counting on you. It was ungrateful of you to fight me like you did in the meeting."

"This is crazy."

"It really is," said Kakapick.

"What shall we do about it? I can't write in that office."

"Nobody cares whether you write or not." Kakapick enjoyed a feeling of power or authority arising from Rimrose's having come, after all, to see *him* at *his* convenience at *his* office. Kakapick no longer thought of Rimrose as someone higher than he on the scale of distinction. Rimrose the prince of the American story had ceased to exist. Rimrose, however skillful his art, however sound his reputation, was only one more department professor living in a little house crowded with children and animals and crazy birds in the night.

It had all been an illusion. As Kakapick had discovered the reality of the department, so had he discovered the truth of Rimrose too, whose fame and celebrity, Kakapick now understood, had never really amounted to much in the first place. Kakapick could not deny, even to himself, that in the act of hiring Rimrose he had made a fatal error. For the rest of his life he must live with Rimrose.

Really, actually, Rimrose was nobody. Fame and celebrity were nothing. Rimrose had no sort of power, no influence upon anything or anybody. To Kakapick's surprise even Rimrose's colleagues in the department scarcely knew who he was. His was a name vaguely heard. Was he a poet? Some sort of critic, wasn't he? Colleagues had heard of one or another of his stories, especially "Playing Sports While Soundly Sleeping" because Herndon the famous football star had played right here, but if people knew the story they could not name the author. Ah yes, hadn't Kakapick heralded Rimrose in MANNA, now KINANA? Rimrose had been *made* by Kakapick. If Kakapick had made him, Kakapick could unmake him.

Only now, too late, Kakapick saw how by exaggerating Rimrose's power he had actually endowed him with it. He had bestowed upon him the gift of a lifetime job. This need not have been. Kakapick could neither forgive himself for having allowed it to happen, nor endure it. His anger at himself was limitless. He said to Rimrose now, "You wouldn't have defied me if you'd been a lowly nontenured teacher. You'd have helped me out. Why didn't you help me out? You disputed me in front of everybody. You'd have stood up with the others when I asked you to stand, just like everybody else. You'd have known which side your bread was buttered on. You would have rendered unto Caesar—"

"You were lying about me. You were inventing my life."

"It was only fiction. You write fiction."

"If Caesar wants his money's worth from me, he ought to want me to tell the truth about things. I thought that was what a university was supposed to be all about."

"Nobody needed the truth right that minute."

"It was a small dispute. I didn't raise my voice."

"You didn't stand up."

"I tried. My legs wouldn't hold me. I was nervous. I apologize to you for what I did."

"I'm sorry I hired you."

"I'm sorry you feel that way. You couldn't have found a better fellow."

"My teeth," said Kakapick.

"Your teeth look fine to me," said Rimrose. "I don't care about your teeth."

"What do you do in your office? Do you write in your office? There's nothing wrong with being down in the basement. I was down there myself for years. Why should I give you an office for you to sit in writing stories about me? You're writing about me," Kakapick said. This he knew, or thought he had reason to know. He was convinced that Rimrose was making him the villain or the fool of a story. This he feared beyond almost everything, this distressed him most, the idea that Rimrose was making him a character in a story. Against such an assault he had no defense. "You can appeal it. We have appeals committees all over the place. There's a whole long list of them in the manual. Every place you look there's somebody who'll take up your case. We've got ombudsmen by the ton all over campus. There's a department ombudsman and a college ombudsman and a university ombudsman. They're all listed in your faculty manual. Do you have your faculty manual? I didn't think so"—here Kakapick became enraged, as if Rimrose could have committed no crime worse than this, to have lost or misplaced or abandoned his faculty manual— "you're not the kind of faculty that would save his manual. I should have known all this from the beginning. Polly Anne told me you'd be trouble. You can pick up a manual from the girl on your way out."

As Kakapick had banished Rimrose to the basement of Literature, he banished him as well from the records and memoranda of the department. He savored the illusion that by depriving Rimrose of notice he deprived him of life itself, that even to deny his existence on paper drew breath from his body. Kakapick's department roster of All Tenured and Tenure-Stream Faculty of the Department of Literature listed the names of all the members from Acton to Yang, excepting only Rimrose.

201

On several occasions when Kakapick was asked by the dean or president to suggest the names of "distinguished faculty" for important professional or social occasions, he omitted Rimrose.

Everything that might have been industrious in Kakapick he poured into his fantasies of Rimrose. Kakapick would have hastened Rimrose's death if only he knew how. Polly Anne knew about such things. She knew about people who hired people to kill people. Someone had once been hired to kill her —got her drunk in a bar and tried to drive her off River Road. Somebody could be hired for anything. Kakapick imagined Rimrose disabled, the athlete immobilized. He held in his mind a constant vague plan to hire strong university athletes to break Rimrose's legs with heavy boards.

Kakapick wished he knew secrets of Rimrose's private life sufficiently scandalous to rout him by exposure. Writers were perverted. He attempted on several occasions to persuade Polly Anne Cathcart to enable him to listen discreetly to Rimrose's telephone conversations. "Connect me up," he said, but in this venture Polly Anne thwarted him, denying, as she always did, that the Office of Savings and Economy monitored people's telephone conversations.

When Kakapick passed the department mail table he sometimes stole a piece of Rimrose's mail, swiftly and furtively plucking an envelope from Rimrose's box, letting it fall among his own papers, and carrying it away. He opened it hoping to learn the dirtiest secrets of Rimrose's life, imagining himself confronting Rimrose with disgusting revelations. But the contents of the stolen envelopes never revealed anything useful.

In the corridors of Literature Kakapick ignored his once-famous writer Rimrose as if he were transparent, a ghost or an unknown thing, a stranger to this earth, a creature from whom a sound man withdrew his gaze. He did not speak to Rimrose, nor did he respond to any sort of word or greeting Rimrose addressed to him. He who had yearned so long to be seen as a part of Rimrose's literary life now turned Rimrose out of his own.

After several weeks, however, Kakapick adopted some sort of new corridor policy. He began to greet Rimrose in the friendliest manner. "Hello, Rim," "Good morning, Rim," "How's it going, Rim?" It sounded to Rimrose as if Kakapick were searching for a policy or stance to govern their relationship. First he had ignored him. Now he attempted to greet him. Soon he ignored him again, but then he greeted him briefly, curtly, and yet again, at other times, in bursts of effusion. Upon one occasion he admired Rimrose's bright sweater, and on another he praised his handsome tote bag. Sometimes he spoke to Rimrose as if on the point of conversation, taking a certain delight in bringing Rimrose to a pause. But when Rimrose paused, Kakapick continued swiftly on his way.

In conversation with his colleagues, Kakapick frequently made the peculiar claim that from the beginning he had been opposed to Rimrose's appointment, that he had tried to prevent it, but that his efforts had been thwarted by an edict from a higher office. Hearing this, some of his colleagues lost confidence in Kakapick, for they easily recalled his having boasted of Rimrose's appointment even before it was final. He had campaigned to bring Rimrose to the university, trading commitments with members of the committee on hire. Why should he insist now that he had not done what his colleagues had so clearly heard him do?

Kakapick proposed to his department curriculum committee that it abolish Rimrose's courses called Writing the Story, but the committee in its inquiry had heard good things about the course and declined to abolish it.

Kakapick subsequently proposed to the admissions committee a reduction of the number of students engaged in writing. Students inclined toward writing were unruly and hyper-critical, always petitioning the department for something or other. He had known too many of them. Rimrose himself had been that sort of rebellious, unreasonable student. As editor of *Sentinel* he had caused all kinds of expensive trouble for the university. The committee felt itself reluctant to entertain this proposal, characterizing it as "not useful."

The death of Rimrose the storywriter was announced in KINANA, formerly MANNA, in a brief unsigned note which Lucy read in the library and copied by machine for fifteen cents but decided not to take home with her. As far as she knew, Rimrose never heard of it. If he had he never told her.

"We writhe in pain," KINANA wrote, "to see our friend go down, to see the once-vigorous storywriter powerless, silent and dried up. He has published no new story anywhere for two years, nor has any been announced. He shot up like a rocket in the sky, blew apart and expired and fell to earth."

Fell from the sky. Worse, fell from the Kakapick Universal Visibility Scale! Rimrose's work had not lately appeared in "meritorious journals," his name was seldom mentioned in magazines by illustrious people. He had not lately delivered public lectures attended by large numbers of people at merito-rious universities nor participated *by invitation* in meritori-ous conferences or roundtables and critical debates. He had not lately been interviewed on notable or meritorious televi-sion programs or radio discussions or been featured by per-sons reporting the news in the mass media.

But although Kakapick had declared for all the world to know that Rimrose had ceased to be a writer, he had not set his own mind at rest. He was desperate to know what might be known about the progress of the stories he believed Rimrose was writing about him.

During the Christmas season he found himself in his dreams standing before the University Book Store gazing through the glass at Rimrose's new book, *Kakapick the Pig-Fucker,* in its colorful jacket. Mobile graphs in the bookstore window bedecked with flashing dancing lights of every color showed the book rising to the number-one place at the top of the Kakapick Universal Visibility Scale. Everybody in University City was receiving Rimrose's book for Christmas. Kakapick attempted to read the price on the flap of the book, but he could never quite make it out. When upon entering the store he was told the book did not yet exist, he awakened to the sound of his voice crying out, "Reprieved, reprieved."

For Rimrose in his dim, airless, cramped, battered, defaced office in the basement of Literature, Lucy purchased a red-white-and-blue clothes-tree. In time, though not promptly, Maintenance delivered a computer and printer to Rimrose, but when he plugged those contraptions into the outlet flames flew out of the wall. His telephone was one of eight extensions of a line he shared with enthusiastic graduate students and their friends. For the repair of the wall he summoned Electrical, but Electrical assumed that Rimrose, too, was a graduate student and delayed almost a month before coming.

His writing collapsed or stalled or died. His student Howard Malone taught him how to make his computer and his printer do all sorts of tricks. But computer tricks were not writing. Rimrose began to live through a hard time. He was unable to write easily or well either on his computer at his office or in his old-fashioned way at home.

He began one story based on his elaboration of a view he had had (from his former office window) of two lovers alternately caressing and quarreling; another based on one of the men (that is to say, on a *portrait* of one of the men) who had hung on his former office wall; and yet another based on the health problems of a man who had fallen in love with his physician's wife.

Now and again he began a story based on his long-term memories and brief present glimpses of Kakapick, but these Kakapick stories displeased him and he dropped them into the wastebasket. He began to worry darkly, as he had never before worried about himself. He seriously feared that he was done with writing forever. The confidence he instilled in his students far exceeded his confidence in himself.

It was a new life but disheartening. Now, for a year, he had written hardly half a page worth saving. His early sense of university luxury declined to nothing. His relief from the tension of free-lance stories amuck and bills unpaid had been succeeded by frustration more formidable than any he had known.

Rimrose had always believed his motivation to write arose from the finest intentions, never from money alone. Perhaps he had been mistaken. He considered the probability that he could slip easily back into his former happier misery by resigning his university job, letting the money run out, bringing down upon himself once again the pressure of the free-lance life. Were the Rimroses ready to return to the place they once had been?

Lucy would listen to none of that. One day, passing his paycheck to Lucy, Rimrose mentioned his recent opinion that his mind truly required the incentive of struggle as he had known it in their golden age of creative poverty—the litter of debts and threats. *"My* mind doesn't," she replied, and snatched the paycheck out of his hand.

All right, once *again* he tried to write about Kakapick. He had never written about him—well, correction, he thought, yes, he *had* written that ironic little article for *Sentinel* years and years ago. The accompanying photo touched off the whole book-stealing scandal. Kakapick was arrested.

That was all the writing Rimrose had ever done about Kakapick—well, no, another correction, that wasn't all, he had tried several times to write that damned ill-fated story about Kakapick's stalking Lucy down the streets at night. They'd called it "The Tread of the Stalker" and sent it out and never sold it.

Was that it? Lucy had never been able to sell it. No, not that Lucy had never sold it but that he had never finished it. She'd urged him to finish it but he never did, or if he did she didn't sell it. Hard to remember things so long ago. Enough to remember that it was a jinxed story. Rimrose kept going back to it but he could never bring it to life. God damn the stories he'd spent his life's blood on that never came alive. Think how much life he'd dropped into the wastebasket.

He could not write about Kakapick and should not even try. He owed him a debt of gratitude. This glorious regular paycheck he owed to Kakapick.

At one point Rimrose thought he'd found an idea for a story he could cast Kakapick in. He'd make him a failed athlete. In what sport? He could not find the really right sport for Kakapick to play, and he therefore altered the course of his story, casting Kakapick not as a failed athlete but as a hanger-on among athletes, the kind of person the athletes called— they had had a name for it in Westby Hall—a jock-sniffer, a man who loved to hang around the athletes but had no sport of his own, couldn't play a thing, had no instinct for any kind of sport, no talent, no strength, no stamina.

Rimrose's working title was "Kaka the Jock-Sniffer." Of course he'd change the name before he sent it out, but meanwhile it was helpful to his writing to call the fellow Kakapick, and away flew Rimrose on his magical writing machine. He sped ahead for twenty or thirty pages of chaotic draft over the course of an encouraging week. Some of the old touch was coming back into his fingers. He was confident he had a viable beginning, a tentative draft. "Print it," he cried to himself in his office, and he ran it off on the marvelous printer his student Howard Malone had taught him to use.

Alas! No printer had been invented that could make a story

better than it was. The printer did a splendid job but the story was poor. Rimrose read it several times and tore it up. Lucy would have urgently appealed to him, "No, don't! Save it, don't tear it up, never tear anything up the day you write it, give the poor little thing overnight in the incubator, there might be more to it than you know."

But Lucy was not here to prevent him from tearing it into halves and dropping it into the wastebasket, and after he'd done that he got to thinking he'd rather not have the university janitors reading his halved pages with Kakapick's name all over them. Years ago Polly Anne encouraged *Sentinel* reporters to look for interesting revealing things in people's wastebaskets. After he'd dumped the halved remains of "Kaka the Jock-Sniffer" into his wastebasket, he fished them all out again and dumped them into his tote bag to carry home.

Ridiculous carrying his trash home! Most people left their trash for the janitors.

Therefore he dumped the pages from his tote bag back into the wastebasket.

All spring Rimrose felt himself in the grip of an illusion. He could have sworn that here or there in the vastness of the Literature building Kakapick lurked nearby, observing him from a place of hiding, following him, stalking him as he had stalked Lucy once upon a time—if indeed it had been Kakapick. Lucy always thought it was, she said it was, she claimed the footsteps were his.

Rimrose had never truly known whether she had been in the grip of some sort of illusion. In "The Tread of the Stalker," based on Lucy's account, Rimrose had never been able to make the thing happen her way. Therefore he had become somewhat impatient of Lucy—if he could not make a thing happen in a story, it could not have happened in nature. Lucy "just knew" Kakapick was stalking her. Now Rimrose knew what Lucy had known. Now he too "just knew."

He could smell Kakapick—that was to say, smell himself, a sickly odor of himself, the odor of a dry cold sweat which came to appear to him to be the odor of his fear. He saw with the passage of time and the repetition of brief occasions an undeniable connection between his imagination of Kakapick's presence and the outbreak of the odor of his own body.

His odor was a warning, arousing in him the most uncomfortable emotion, calling upon him to exert particular care, restraint, caution, to be prepared to fight back. His fear distracted him. When Rimrose sat late at his office, attempting to write, he grew fearful of Kakapick's lurking nearby. He could not write. Yet he refused to fly from a danger as little real as his own odor. He had no reason to believe the thing he believed. He had no evidence that Kakapick was near. He could not even believe he believed it might be so. Yet it seemed so to him.

He suspected that he was indulging himself in the thrill of fear like a boy invoking ghosts in the night. Now and then toward midnight, when he left his little office, he departed Literature by alternate routes, never the same corridors two nights in a row, avoiding above all the short route carrying him upstairs past Kakapick's office to the logical exit. He walked far out of his way, crossing from one end of the building to the other, through the Foreign Languages corridor and down the fire stairway, or through the basement as fast as he could go. Once, thinking he heard Kakapick's tread behind him, he positively *ran* from the building, feeling foolish indeed.

Rimrose ceased to use the elevators in the Literature building. He used the stairways at all times, dashing down, racing up, lickety-split, cautious by day, breathless at night. He feared Kakapick's waiting for him in enclosed places, if not in an elevator then in an alcove, in the shadowed corners and turnings of this labyrinthine building.

*   *   *

Rimrose avoided the Literature men's room. He climbed the stairs to the Foreign Languages men's room. One day a professor of a foreign language—of *what* language Rimrose did not know—said to him in plain perplexed English, "I wonder why you always come up to this floor," to which Rimrose replied in a casual way, "There's somebody I want to avoid killing." He was shocked to hear himself speak in such a way. He had not known that that was the truth in him. The professor turned away.

On a night in May when Rimrose left for home down the long Literature corridor Kakapick appeared suddenly ahead. He had been waiting. It could not have been otherwise. Rimrose imagined Kakapick's striking out at him. Rimrose's fear was not of being struck by Kakapick but of his returning Kakapick's blow and killing him. Rimrose thought to turn and walk in the direction from which he had come. Instead, he continued toward Kakapick, who stood in his path, presenting himself in a challenging way, as boys do, for argument, for dispute, for a fight, or, as it seemed to Rimrose, for death itself. *There* would be fame for you, Kakapick struck down and delivered to history by a famous author in some mysterious confidential dispute settled one night in a deserted corridor. For who among all the doubters of the world would be capable of doubting then, when Rimrose had killed Kakapick, the passionate confidential secrecy of their association?

Rimrose attempted afterward to recover in his mind the course of those seconds as they occurred. He said or should have said or meant to say, "Kakapick, I don't know what you're doing but it's awfully dangerous, you're getting my juices going, if I hit you I'll kill you."

"I'm afraid of no man," Kakapick replied, as he had replied years before to the director of student housing. But he was afraid of Rimrose, who knew his character well and was writing it up. "I hear that you're writing me up," he said.

"You've heard it wrong," Rimrose said.

"You're exposing me for the whole world to see," said Kakapick.

"I'm not sure the whole world's got its eye on us," Rimrose replied, stepping around Kakapick.

But Kakapick blocked his way. "You're in there all the time. What do you do in there if not writing?"

"I watch the little flashing light blinking on the screen," Rimrose said.

"You're trying to write."

"Always, yes, of course, I'm always trying to write. I'm hoping. I'm counting on it."

"You look so very happy," Kakapick said.

"I am so very happy."

"You're happy because you're writing."

"I'm happy in spite of not writing. I'm happy because the world goes well with me. My family is well. I've got a very good job. Our pockets are full of money. We feel very rich now—" and saying this he broke into a run, darting past Kakapick, who pursued him and ran to overtake Rimrose and wrest from him the promise not to write about him, not to tell the world he was an outcast held in contempt by his fellows— whose very name meant pig-fucker when translated from the original Barbarian by the distinguished linguist Herndon the football player. Kakapick had run only a few breathless steps when he saw he could never overtake Rimrose, and he stopped and called after him, "Hello to Marigold," in the jovial way of good fellowship, as if they were friends parting for the evening. "Rimrose," he called, "stop writing about me."

As it happened, on the following Friday afternoon Rimrose phoned home from his little office and said, "You can come and get me now," and Lucy asked, as she usually did, "How did it go?'' Of course it was the writing she meant. He said he wasn't sure, maybe it was happening and maybe it wasn't.

Lucy could feel that it was going to get started very soon, the biggest era of his writing life was just around the corner— of course she always said that—and that she felt it in her bones and heart and mind, wait and see, she said, you'll see it will, when Rimrose heard Kakapick's step in the corridor. "Here he comes," he said.

"Who comes?" she asked.

"I hear the tread of the stalker," he said.

He thought to kick his door closed, but he did not. He became utterly silent, and Lucy at the other end of the telephone seemed to be talking to someone, perhaps to an animal, perhaps to her God. It occurred to Rimrose, as he heard the footsteps draw close, that he was about to be shot to death. Kakapick was going to fire a gun through the doorway and Rimrose was going to fall off his chair dead.

This did not occur. Kakapick paused at Rimrose's door. "So," he said, "this is where they keep you. If I'm not mistaken this used to be my office." He did indeed carry something in his hand, but it was not a gun. It was an envelope. He appeared to Rimrose to be in good spirits and good health, rested, refreshed and above all serene. He had made up his mind to something. He held up the envelope for Rimrose to see, as if by the sight of it Rimrose would know what it was. "I've resigned," he said, and he continued on his way.

Lucy on the telephone said, "What did he say?"

"He said he's resigned."

"To what?" she said.

Rimrose never knew whether Kakapick had intended him to be the first to know his news, or why, or whether perhaps it was only in the extremity of his distress that he had somehow found himself wandering the Literature basement. The envelope bore his letter of resignation from the university, which he carried beyond Rimrose's office and out of Literature and across the thronged mall to the office of the president, who, when he read it, was as dismayed as any conscientious president of any university would have been to lose a loyal fellow.

Monday morning Polly Anne Cathcart ran up the walk at Listing House and rang the bell and greeted Lucy at the door with nothing like Good morning or How are you or even May I come in, but said "Something terrible has happened."

"Rim's writing," Lucy said.

"I'm glad he's writing. I heard he was stuck," said Polly Anne.

"Being stuck is part of writing," Lucy replied, which was to say she wouldn't disturb her husband even for a visit from Polly Anne, rare as it was, when down the stairs came Rimrose with his coffee cup in his hand. He was as surprised as anybody to see Polly Anne in Listing House, where she had not set foot for years.

"Well, it's important," she said.

"It must be," Rimrose said.

She was dressed for work at the Office of Savings and Economy, but she had never reached her office. She coughed and sneezed. "It's the season," she said, though she coughed and sneezed in every season. "I ought to be home in bed."

"What about a cup of coffee?" Rimrose said.

"I'm on my way to the morgue." She gained their attention. "I wanted to see your face when I told you." She meant she wanted to see Rimrose's face, but to be courteous she looked at Lucy, too.

"Who died?" Rimrose asked.

Lucy knew who had died. Polly Anne saw by Lucy's face that she had guessed the news. "Kakapick is dead," Lucy said.

Rimrose set his coffee cup on the dining-room table and picked it up again and said, "I'm going to have another cup. Would you like a cup of coffee?" and Polly Anne said she might as well, too, and they sat with Lucy at the dining-room table. "I'm trying not to say I can't believe it," Rimrose said. "I'm awfully sorry. That's a place to begin. I'm wondering, when did—this happen? I saw him Friday afternoon. He came past my office."

"He probably died that night," she said.

"He said he was resigning. He had his letter with him."

"Resigning wasn't enough for him," said Polly Anne.

"Died of what?"

"Of a University Book Store plastic bag," Polly Anne said. She had found him this morning. He'd lain there all weekend with his head in the bag. "I don't think he really expected to lie there so long. He thought I'd be dropping by sooner than I did, but I didn't, I was in bed myself with this damn respiratory shit."

Rimrose said, "I remember his saying once, 'If I drop dead in my room I wonder how long it'll be until anybody notices me missing.'"

"I heard him say it more than once," said Polly Anne. "You'll have somebody saying it in a story any minute now. It was a hell of an inconsiderate thing to do. It was an awful thing to walk in on."

"All those index cards with all the names of all the great literary figures," Rimrose said, "and up in the corner on each card he'd write the word *dead.* He liked his literary people dead. Did he leave any word? Any kind of note or anything?"

"He left me a list of the ninety-one best books in the world," she said. "He left a lot of books to go back to the library. Hundreds of books all over the place."

"Years overdue," Lucy said.

"Lucy is unforgiving," Rimrose said. "The man had his problems, right?"

"He was never lovable," Polly Anne said. "But he was still hoping everybody was going to have a good opinion of him. He was living in deathly fear of the stories you were writing about him."

"I wasn't writing any stories about him."

"One story anyhow. One story? Weren't you writing a story about him? It was our information—"

"No, not even one story."

"Oh, but you were. You had a wastebasket full of papers with his name all over them."

"Do you dig stories out of the wastepaper basket?" Lucy asked.

"You dig stories out of the wastebasket," said Rimrose to his wife.

"We dig for different reasons," Lucy said.

"It's how we find things out," said Polly Anne.

Lucy protested that. "How was it any part of your job to find out what Rim was writing?"

"It wasn't. I did it as a favor to Kakapick. He was so awfully worried. He was sure Rimrose was sending him down into history as the prick of the universe. Rimrose telling the world how black his teeth used to be. The poor boy couldn't face one more sleepless night. But he wouldn't take sleeping pills. He was afraid of missing his morning appointments."

"I hope we'll have a good service for him," Rimrose said to Polly Anne.

"Will you make a little speech?"

"Sic semper critics," Lucy said.